BOLT

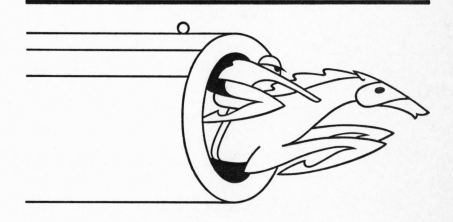

DICK FRANCIS

G. P. PUTNAM'S SONS
NEW YORK

G. P. Putnam's Sons
Publishers Since 1838
200 Madison Avenue
New York, NY 10016

Typeset by Fisher Composition, Inc.

Library of Congress Cataloging-in-Publication Data

Francis, Dick.
Bolt.

I. Title.
PR6056.R27B55   1987   823'.914   86-25167
ISBN 0-399-13226-0

Printed in the United States of America
3   4   5   6   7   8   9   10

for
Danielle and Holly
both born since
Break In

BOLT

Bitter February, within and without. Mood to match the weather; raw and overcast, near to freezing. I walked from the weighing room to the parade ring at Newbury races trying not to search for the face that wouldn't be there, the intimately known face of Danielle de Brescou, to whom I was formally engaged, diamond ring and all.

Winning the lady, back in November, had been unexpected, an awakening, deeply exciting . . . happy. Keeping her, in the frosts before spring, was proving the merry devil. My much-loved dark-haired young woman seemed frighteningly to be switching her gaze from a steeplechase jockey (myself) to an older richer sophisticate of superior lineage (he was a prince) who hadn't even the decency to be bad-looking.

Unmoved as I might try to appear on the surface, I was finding the frustration erupting instead in the races themselves, sending me hurtling over the fences without prudence, recklessly embracing peril like a drug to blot out rejection. It might not be sensible to do a risky job with a mind two hundred miles from one's fingertips, but tranquilizers could come in many forms.

Princess Casilia, unaccompanied by Danielle, her husband's niece, was waiting as usual in the parade ring, watching her runner, Cascade, walk round. I went across to her, shook the offered hand, made the small bow, acknowledging her rank.

"A cold day," she said in greeting, the consonants faintly thick, vowels pure and clear, the accent only distantly reminiscent of her European homeland.

"Yes. Cold," I said.

Danielle hadn't come. Of course she hadn't. Stupid of me to hope. She'd said cheerfully on the telephone that she wouldn't be coming to stay this weekend, she would be going to a fabulous Florentine gathering in a hotel in the Lake District with the prince and some of his friends, where they would listen to lectures on the Italian Renaissance given by the Keeper of the Italian paintings in the Louvre, and various other things of that sort. It was such a great and unique opportunity, she was sure I'd understand.

It would be the third weekend in a row she'd been sure I would understand.

The princess looked distinguished as always, middle-aged, slender, intensely feminine, warm inside a supple sable coat swinging from narrow shoulders. Normally bareheaded, dark smooth hair piled high, she wore on that day a tall Russian-type fur hat with a huge up-turning fur brim, and I thought fleetingly that few could have carried it with more style. I had ridden her string of twenty or so horses for more than ten years and I tended to know her racegoing clothes well. The hat was new.

She noted the direction of my glance and the admiration that went with it, but said merely, "Too cold for Cascade, do you think?"

"He won't mind it," I said. "He'll loosen up going down to the start."

She wouldn't mention Danielle's absence, if I didn't. Always reticent, sheltering her thoughts behind long eyelashes, the princess clung to civilized manners as if to a shield against the world's worst onslaughts, and I'd been in her company enough not to undervalue her chosen social façades. She could calm tempests with politeness, defuse lightning with steadfast chit-chat and disarm the most pugnacious adversaries by expecting them to behave well. I knew she would prefer me to keep my woes to myself, and would feel awkward if I didn't.

She did, on the other hand, understand my present predicament perfectly well. Not only was Danielle her husband's niece, but Litsi, the prince currently diverting Danielle to a fifteenth-century junket, was her own nephew. They were both currently guests under her Eaton Square roof, meeting from breakfast to dinner . . . and from dinner to breakfast, for all I really knew.

"What are our chances?" the princess asked neutrally.

"Pretty good," I said.

She nodded in agreement, full of pleasant hope, the prospect of winning real enough.

Cascade, despite an absence of brains, was a prolific winner of two-mile 'chases who had shown his heels in the past to every opponent in that day's field. Given luck he would do it again; but nothing's certain, ever, in racing . . . or in life.

Prince Litsi, whose whole name was about a yard long and to my mind unpronounceable, was cosmopolitan, cultured, impressive and friendly. He spoke perfect idiomatic English with none of his aunt's thickened consonants, which was hardly surprising as he'd been born after his royal grandparents had been chased off their throne, and had spent much of his childhood in England.

He lived now in France, but I'd met him a few times over the years when he'd visited his aunt and escorted her to the races, and I'd liked him in a vague way, never knowing him well. When I'd heard he was coming again for a visit I hadn't given a thought to the impact he might make on a bright American female who worked for a television news agency and thirsted for Leonardo da Vinci.

"Kit," the princess said.

I retrieved my attention from the Lake District and focused on the calmness in her face.

"Well," I said, "some races are easier than others."

"Do your best."

"Yes."

Our prerace meetings over the years had developed into short comfortable interludes in which little was said but much understood. Most owners went into parade rings accompanied by their trainers, but Wykeham Harlow, trainer of the princess's horses, had altogether stopped going to the races. Wykeham, growing old, couldn't stand the incessant winter journeys. Wykeham, shaky in the memory and jerky in the knees, nevertheless still generated the empathy with horses that had put him straight into the top rank from the beginning. He continued to send out streams of winners from his eighty-strong stable, and I, most thankfully, rode them.

The princess went indomitably to the races in all weathers, delighting in the prowess of her surrogate children, planning their futures, recalling their pasts, filling her days with an unflagging interest. Over many years she and I had arrived at a relationship that was both formal and deep, sharing intensities of success and moments of grief, understanding each other in easy accord at race meetings, parting to unconnected lives at the gate.

Unconnected, that is to say, until the previous November when Danielle had arrived from America to take up her London posting and ended in my bed. Since then, although the princess had undoubtedly accepted me as a future member of her family and had invited me often to her house, her manner to me, as mine to her, had remained virtually unchanged, especially on racecourses. The pattern had been too long set, and felt right, it seemed, to us both.

"Good luck," she said lightly, when the time came for mounting, and Cascade and I went down to the start with him presumably warming up from the canter but as usual sending no telepathic messages about his feelings. With some horses a two-way mental traffic could be almost as explicit as speech, but dark, thin, nippy Cascade was habitually and unhelpfully silent.

The race turned out to be much harder than expected, as one of the other runners seemed to have found an extra gear since I'd beaten him last. He jumped stride for stride with Cascade down the far side and clung like glue round the bend into the straight. Shaping up to the last four fences and the run-in he was still close by Cascade's side, his jockey keeping him there aggressively although there was the whole wide track to accommodate him. It was a demoralizing tactic that that jockey often used against horses he thought frightenable, but I was in no mood to be overcrowded by him or by anybody, and I was conscious, as too often recently, of ruthlessness and rage inside and of repressed desperation bursting out.

I kicked Cascade hard into the final jumps and drove him unmercifully along the run-in, and if he hated it, at least he wasn't telling me. He stretched out his neck and his dark head toward the winning post and under relentless pressure persevered to the end.

We won by a matter of inches and Cascade slowed to a walk in a few uneven strides, absolutely exhausted. I felt faintly ashamed of myself and took little joy in the victory, and on the long path back to the unsaddling enclosure felt not a cathartic release from tension but an increasing fear that my mount would drop dead from an overstrained heart.

He walked with trembling legs into the winner's place to applause he certainly deserved, and the princess came to greet him with slightly anxious eyes. The result of the photo-finish had already been announced, confirming Cascade's win, and it appeared that the princess wasn't worried about whether she had won, but how.

"Weren't you hard on him?" she asked doubtfully, as I slid to the ground. "Too hard, perhaps, Kit?"

I patted Cascade's steaming neck, feeling the sweat under my fingers. A lot of horses would have crumbled under so much pressure, but he hadn't.

"He's brave," I said. "He gives all he's got."

She watched me unbuckle the girths and slide my saddle

off onto my arm. Her horse stood without moving, droop-
ing with fatigue, while Dusty, the traveling head-lad, covered the brown dripping body with a sweat-sheet to keep
him warm.

"You have nothing to prove, Kit," the princess said
clearly. "Not to me. Not to anyone."

I paused in looping the girths round the saddle and
looked at her in surprise. She almost never said anything of
so personal a nature, nor with her meaning so plain. I
suppose I looked as disconcerted as I felt.

I more slowly finished looping the girths.

"I'd better go and weigh in," I said, hesitating.

She nodded.

"Thank you," I said.

She nodded again and patted my arm, a small familiar
gesture that always managed to convey both understanding
and dismissal. I turned away to go into the weighing room
and saw one of the Stewards hurrying purposefully toward
Cascade, peering at him intently. Stewards always tended
to look like that when inspecting hard-driven horses for ill-
treatment, but in this particular Steward's case there was
far more to his present zeal than a simple love of animals.

I paused in midstride in dismay, and the princess turned
her head to follow my gaze, looking back at once to my
face. I met her blue eyes and saw there her flash of comprehension.

"Go on," she said. "Weigh in."

I went on gratefully, and left her to face the man who
wanted, possibly more than anything else on earth, to see
me lose my jockey's license.

Or, better still, my life.

* * *

Maynard Allardeck, acting as a Steward for the Newbury meeting (a fact I had temporarily forgotten), had both bad and good reasons to detest me, Kit Fielding.

The bad reasons were inherited and irrational and therefore the hardest to deal with. They stemmed from a feud between families that had endured for more than three centuries and had sown a violent mutual history thick with malevolent deeds. In the past, Fieldings had murdered Allardecks, and Allardecks, Fieldings. I had myself, along with my twin sister, Holly, been taught from birth by our grandfather that all Allardecks were dishonest, cowardly, spiteful and treacherous, and so we would probably have gone on believing all our lives had Holly not, in a Capulet–Montague gesture, fallen in love with and married an Allardeck.

Bobby Allardeck, her husband, was demonstrably not dishonest, cowardly, spiteful or treacherous, but on the contrary a pleasant well-meaning fellow training horses in Newmarket. Bobby and I, through his marriage, had finally in our own generation, in our own selves, laid the ancient feud to rest, but Bobby's father, Maynard Allardeck, was still locked in the past.

Maynard had never forgiven Bobby for what he saw as treason, and far from trying for reconciliation had intensified his indoctrinated belief that all Fieldings, Holly and I above all included, were thieving, conniving, perfidious and cruel. My serene sister, Holly, was demonstrably none of these things, but Maynard saw all Fieldings through distorted mental pathways.

Holly had told me that when Bobby informed his father (all of them standing in Bobby and Holly's kitchen) that Holly was pregnant, and that like it or not his grandchild would bear both Allardeck and Fielding blood and genes, she'd thought for an instant that Maynard was actually going to try to strangle her. Instead, with his hands literally stretching toward her throat, he'd whirled suddenly away and vomited into the sink. She'd been very shaken, telling me, and Bobby had sworn never to let his father into the house again.

Maynard Allardeck was a member of the Jockey Club, racing's ruling body, where he was busy climbing with his monumental public charm into every position of power he could reach. Maynard Allardeck, acting as Steward already at several big meetings, was aiming for the triumvirate, the three Stewards of the Jockey Club, from among whom the Senior Steward was triannually elected.

For a Fielding who was a jockey, the prospect of an Allardeck in a position of almost total power over him should have been devastating: and that was where Maynard's good and comprehensible reasons for detesting me began, because I had a hold over him of such strength that he couldn't destroy my career, life or reputation without doing the same to his own. He and I and a few others knew of it, just enough to ensure that in all matters of racing he had to be seen to treat me fairly.

If however he could prove I had truly ill-treated Cascade, he would get me a fine and a suspension with alacrity and joy. In the heat of the race, in the upsurge of my own uncontrollable feelings, I hadn't given a thought to him watching on the stands.

I went into the weighing room and sat on the scales, and then returned to just inside the door to see what was going on outside. From the shadows, I watched Maynard talking to the princess, who was wearing her blandest and most pleasant expression, both of them circling the quivering Cascade, who was steaming all over in the freezing air as

Maynard had commanded Dusty to remove the netlike sweat-sheet.

Maynard as always looked uncreased, opulent and trustworthy, an outer image that served him very well both in business deals, where he had made fortunes at others' expense, and in social circles, where he gave largely to charity and patted himself on the back for good works. Only the comparative few who had seen the mean, rough, ruthless reality inside remained cynically unimpressed.

He had removed his hat in deference to the princess and held it clasped to his chest, his graying fair hair brushed tidily into uncontroversial shape. He was almost squirming with the desire to ingratiate himself with the princess while at the same time denigrating her jockey, and I wasn't certain that he couldn't cajole her into agreeing that yes, perhaps, on this one occasion, Kit Fielding had been too hard on her horse.

Well, they would find no weals on Cascade because I'd barely touched him with the whip. The other horse had been so close that when I'd raised my arm I found I couldn't bring my whip down without hitting him instead of Cascade. Maynard no doubt had seen my raised arm, but it was legs, feet, wrists and fury that had done the job. There might be whip marks in Cascade's soul, if he had one, but they wouldn't show on his hide.

Maynard deliberated for a lengthy time with pursed lips, shakes of the head and busy eyes, but in the end he bowed stiffly to the sweetly smiling princess, replaced his hat carefully and stalked disappointedly away.

Greatly relieved, I watched the princess join a bunch of her friends while Dusty with visible disapproval replaced the sweat-sheet and told the lad holding Cascade's bridle to lead him off to the stables. Cascade went tiredly, head low, all stamina spent. Sorry, I thought, sorry, old son. Blame it on Litsi.

The princess, I thought gratefully as I peeled off her colors to change into others for the next race, had withstood Maynard's persuasions and kept her reservations private. She knew how things stood between Maynard and myself because Bobby had told her one day back in November, and although she had never referred to it since, she had clearly not forgotten. I would have to do more than half kill her horse, it seemed, before she would deliver me to my enemy.

I rode the next race acutely conscious of him on the stands: two scampering miles over hurdles, finishing fourth. After that I changed back into the princess's colors and returned to the parade ring for the day's main event, a three-mile steeplechase regarded as a trial race for the Grand National.

Unusually, the princess wasn't already in the ring waiting, and I stood alone for a while watching her sturdy Cotopaxi being led round by his lad. Like many of her horses he bore the name of a mountain, and in his case it fitted aptly, as he was big, gaunt and craggy, a liver chestnut with splashes of gray on his quarters like dirty snow. At eight years old, he was coming satisfactorily to full uncompromising strength, and for once I really believed I might at last win the big one in a month's time.

I'd won almost every race in the calendar, except the Grand National. I'd been second, third, and fourth, but never first. Cotopaxi had it in him to change that, given the luck.

Dusty came across to disrupt the pleasant daydream. "Where's the princess?" he said.

"I don't know."

"She'd never miss old Paxi." Small, elderly, weather-beaten and habitually suspicious, he looked at me accusingly, as if I'd heard something I wasn't telling.

Dusty depended on me professionally, as I on him, but we'd never come to liking. He was apt to remind me that, champion jockey or not, I wouldn't get so many winners if it weren't for the hard work of the stable-lads, naturally including himself. His manner to me teetered sometimes on the edge of rudeness, never quite tumbling over, and I put up with it equably because he was in fact good at his job, and right about the lads, and besides that I hadn't much choice. Since Wykeham had stopped coming to the races, the horses' welfare away from home depended entirely upon Dusty, and the welfare of the horses was very basically my concern.

"Cascade," Dusty said, glowering, "can hardly put one foot in front of the other."

"He's not lame," I said mildly.

"He'll take weeks to get over it."

I didn't answer. I looked around for the princess, who still hadn't appeared. I'd wanted particularly to hear what Maynard had said to her, but it looked as if I would have to wait. And it was extraordinary that she hadn't come into the ring. Almost all owners liked to be in the parade ring before a race, and for the princess especially it was an unvarying routine. Moreover she was particularly proud and fond of Cotopaxi and had been talking all winter about his chances in the National.

The minutes ticked away, the signal was given for jockeys to mount, and Dusty gave me his usual adroit leg-up into the saddle. I rode out onto the course hoping nothing serious had happened, and had time, cantering down to the start, to look up to where the princess's private box was located, high on the stands, expecting anyway to see her there watching with her friends.

The balcony was, however, deserted, and I felt the first twinge of real concern. If she'd had to leave the racecourse suddenly I was sure she would have sent me a message, and I hadn't been exactly hard to find, standing there in the paddock. Messages, though, could go astray, and as messages went, "Tell Kit Fielding that Princess Casilia is going home" wouldn't have rated as emergency material.

I went on down to the start thinking that no doubt I would find out in time, and hoping that there hadn't been sudden bad news about the frail old chairbound husband she traveled home to every evening.

Cotopaxi, unlike Cascade, was positively bombarding me with information, mostly to the effect that he was feeling good, he didn't mind the cold weather, and he was glad to back on a racecourse for the first time since Christmas. January had been snowy and the first part of February freezing, and keen racers like Cotopaxi got easily bored by long spells in the stables.

Wykeham, unlike most of the daily press, didn't expect Cotopaxi to win at Newbury.

"He's not fully fit," he'd said on the previous evening. "He won't be wound up tight until Grand National day. Look after him, now, Kit, won't you?"

I'd said I would, and after Cascade I doubly meant it. Look after Cotopaxi, look out for Maynard Allardeck, bury Prince Litsi under the turf. Cotopaxi and I went round circumspectly, collectedly, setting ourselves right at every fence, jumping them all cleanly, enjoying the precision and wasting no time. I did enough stick-waving to give an impression of riding a flat-out finish, and we finished in un-disgraced third place, close enough to the winner to be encouraging. A good workout for Cotopaxi, a reassurance for Wykeham and a tremor of promise for the princess.

She hadn't been on her balcony during the race and she didn't appear in the unsaddling enclosure. Dusty muttered obscurely about her absence and I asked around in the weighing room for any message from her, with no results. I changed again to ride in the fifth race, and after that, in street clothes, decided to go up to her box anyway, as I did at the end of every racing afternoon, to see if the waitress who served there might know what had happened.

The princess rented a private box at several racecourses and had them all decorated alike with colors of cream, coffee and peach. In each was a dining table with chairs for lunch, with, beyond, glass doors to the viewing balcony. She entertained groups of friends regularly, but on that day even the friends had vanished.

I knocked briefly on the box door and, without waiting for any answer, turned the handle and walked in.

The table as usual had been pushed back against a wall after lunch to allow more space, and was familiarly set with the paraphernalia of tea: small sandwiches, small cakes, cups and saucers, alcohol to hand, boxes of cigars. That day they were all untouched, and there was no waitress pour-ing, offering me tea with lemon and a smile.

I had expected the box to be otherwise empty, but it wasn't.

The princess was in there, sitting down.

Near her, silent, stood a man I didn't know. Not one of her usual friends. A man of not much more than my own age, slender, dark-haired, with a strong nose and jaw.

"Princess . . ." I said, taking a step into the room.

She turned her head. She was still wearing the sable coat and the Russian hat, although she usually removed outdoor clothes in her box. Her eyes looked at me without expression, glazed and vacant, wide, blue and unfocused.

Shock, I thought.

"Princess," I said again, concerned for her.

The man spoke. His voice matched his nose and jaw, positive, noticeable, full of strength.

"Go away," he said.

2

I went.

I certainly didn't want to intrude uninvited into any private troubles in the princess's life, and it was that feeling that remained with me to ground level. I had been too long accustomed to our arm's-length relationship to think her affairs any of my business, except to the extent that she was Danielle's uncle's wife.

By the time I was walking out to my car I wished I hadn't left as precipitously without at least asking if I could help. There had been an urgent warning quality in the stranger's peremptory voice that had seemed to me at first to be merely protective of the princess, but in retrospect I wasn't so sure.

Nothing would be lost, I thought, if I waited for her to come down to return home, which she must surely do in the end, and made sure she was all right. If the stranger was still with her, if he was as dismissive as before, if she was looking to him for support, then at least I would let her know I would have assisted if she'd needed it.

I went through the paddock gate to the car park where her chauffeur, Thomas, was routinely waiting for her in her Rolls-Royce.

Thomas and I said hello to each other most days in car parks, he, a phlegmatic Londoner, placidly reading books and paying no attention to the sport going on around him. Large and dependable, he had been driving the princess for years, and knew her life and movements as well as anyone in her family.

He saw me coming and gave me a small wave. Normally, after I'd left her box, she would follow fairly soon, my appearance acting as a signal to Thomas to start the engine and warm the car.

I walked across to him, and he lowered a window to talk.

"Is she ready?" he asked.

I shook my head. "There's a man with her . . ." I paused. "Do you know a fairly young man, dark-haired, thin, prominent nose and chin?"

He pondered and said no one sprang to mind, and why was it worrying me.

"She didn't watch one of her horses race."

Thomas sat up straighter. "She'd never not watch."

"No. Well, she didn't."

"That's bad."

"Yes, I'd think so."

I told Thomas I would go back to make sure she was OK and left him looking as concerned as I felt myself.

The last race was over, the crowds leaving fast. I stood near the gate where I couldn't miss the princess when she came, and scanned faces. Many I knew, many knew me. I said goodnight fifty times and watched in vain for the fur hat.

The crowd died to a trickle and the trickle to twos and threes. I began to wander slowly back toward the stands, thinking in indecision that perhaps I would go up again to her box.

I'd almost reached the doorway to the private stand when she came out. Even from twenty feet I could see the glaze in her eyes, and she was walking as if she couldn't feel the ground, her feet rising too high and going down hard at each step.

She was alone, and in no state to be.

"Princess," I said, going fast to her side. "Let me help."

She looked at me unseeingly, swaying. I put an arm firmly round her waist, which I would never have done in ordinary circumstances, and felt her stiffen, as if to deny her need for support.

"I'm perfectly all right," she said, shakily.

"Yes . . . well, hold my arm." I let go of her waist and offered my arm for her to hold on to, which after a flicker of hesitation she accepted.

Her face was pale under the fur hat and there were trembles in her body. I walked with her slowly toward the gate, and through it, and across to where Thomas waited. He was out of the car, looking anxious, opening a rear door at our approach.

"Thank you," the princess said faintly, climbing in. "Thank you, Kit."

She sank into the rear seat, dislodging her hat on the way and apathetically watching it roll to the floor.

She peeled off her gloves and put one hand to her head, covering her eyes. "I think I . . ." She swallowed, pausing. "Do we have any water, Thomas?"

"Yes, madam," he said with alacrity, and went round to the trunk to fetch the small refreshment box he habitually took along. Sloe gin, champagne, and sparkling mineral water, the princess's favorites, were always to hand.

I stood by the car's open door, unsure how much help she would consider receiving. I knew all about her pride, her self-control, and her self-expectations. She wouldn't want anyone to think her weak.

Thomas gave her some mineral water in a cut-glass tumbler with ice tinkling, no mean feat. She took two or three small sips and sat staring vaguely into space.

"Princess," I said diffidently, "would it perhaps be of any use if I traveled with you to London?"

She turned her eyes my way and a sort of shudder shook her, rattling the ice.

"Yes," she said with clear relief. "I need someone to . . ." She stopped, not finding the words.

Someone to prevent her breaking down, I guessed. Not a shoulder to cry on but a reason for not crying.

Thomas, approving the arrangement, said to me prosaically, "What about your car?"

"It's in the jockeys' car park. I'll put it back by the racecourse stables. It'll be all right there."

He nodded, and we made a brief stop on our way out of the racecourse for me to move the Mercedes to a safe spot and tell the stable manager I'd be back for it later. The princess seemed not to notice any of these arrangements but continued staring vaguely at thoughts I couldn't imagine, and it wasn't until we were well on the way to London in the early dusk that she finally stirred and absentmindedly handed me the glass with the remains of bubbles and melted ice as a kind of preliminary to talking.

"I'm so sorry," she said, "to have given you trouble."

"But you haven't."

"I have had," she went on carefully, "a bad shock. And I cannot explain . . ." She stopped and shook her head, making hopeless gestures with her hands. It seemed to me all the same that she had come to a point where assistance of some sort might be welcomed.

"Is there anything I can do?" I said neutrally.

"I'm not sure how much I can ask."

"A great deal," I said bluntly.

The first signs of a smile crept back into her eyes, but faded again rapidly. "I've been thinking . . ." she said. "When we reach London, will you come into the house and wait while I talk to my husband?"

"Yes, of course."

"You can spare the time? Perhaps a few hours?"

"Any amount," I assured her wryly. Danielle had gone to Leonardo and time was a drag without her. I stifled in myself the acute lurch of unhappiness and wondered just what sort of shock the princess had suffered. Nothing, it seemed now, to do with Monsieur de Brescou's health. Something perhaps worse.

While it grew totally dark outside we traveled another long way in silence, with the princess staring again into space and sighing, and me wondering what to do about the tumbler.

As if reading my thoughts Thomas suddenly said, "There's a glass-holder, Mr. Fielding, located in the door below the ashtray," and I realized he'd noticed my dilemma via the rear-view mirror.

"Thank you, Thomas," I said to the mirror, and met his amused eyes. "Very thoughtful."

I hooked out what proved to be a chrome ring like a

toothmug holder, and let it embrace the glass. The princess, oblivious, went on staring at uncomfortable visions.

"Thomas," she said at length, "please will you see if Mrs. Jenkins is still in the house? If she is, would you ask her to see if Mr. Gerald Greening would be free to come round this evening?"

"Yes, madam," Thomas said, and pressed buttons on the car's telephone, glancing down in fractions while he drove.

Mrs. Jenkins worked for the princess and M. de Brescou as secretary and all-round personal assistant and was young, newly married and palely waiflike. She worked only weekdays and left promptly at five o'clock, which a glance at my watch put at only a few minutes ahead. Thomas caught her apparently on the doorstep and passed on the message, to the princess's satisfaction. She didn't say who Gerald Greening was, but went quietly back to her grim thoughts.

By the time we reached Eaton Square, she had physically recovered completely, and mentally to a great extent. She still looked pale and strained, though, and took Thomas's strong hand to help her from the car. I followed her onto the pavement, and she stood for a moment looking at Thomas and myself, as we stood there lit by the street-lamps.

"Well," she said thoughtfully, "thank you both."

Thomas looked as always as if he would willingly die for her besides driving her carefully to and from the races, but more mundanely at that moment walked across the pavement and with his bunch of keys opened the princess's front door.

She and I went in, leaving Thomas to drive away, and together walked up the wide staircase to the second floor.

The ground floor of the big old house consisted of offices, a guest suite, a library and a breakfast room. It was upstairs that the princess and her husband chiefly lived, with drawing room, sitting room and dining room on the second floor and bedrooms on three floors above. Staff lived in the semibasement, and there was an efficient elevator from top to bottom, installed in modern times to accommodate M. de Brescou's wheelchair.

"Will you wait in the sitting room?" she said. "Help yourself to a drink. If you'd like tea, ring down to Dawson . . ." The social phrases came out automatically, but her eyes were vague, and she was looking very tired.

"I'll be fine," I said.

"I'm afraid I may be a long time."

"I'll be here."

She nodded and went up the next broad flight of stairs to the floor above, where she and her husband each had a private suite of room, and where Roland de Brescou spent most of his time. I had never been up there, but Danielle had described his rooms as a minihospital, with besides his bedroom and sitting room, a physiotherapy room and a room for a male nurse.

"What's wrong with him?" I'd asked.

"Some frightful virus. I don't know exactly what, but not polio. His legs just stopped working, years ago. They don't say much about it, and you know what they're like, it feels intrusive to ask."

I went into the sitting room, which had become familiar territory, and phoned down to Dawson, the rather august butler, asking for tea.

"Certainly, sir," he said austerely. "Is Princess Casilia with you?"

"She's upstairs with Monsieur de Brescou."

He said, "Ah," and the line clicked off. He appeared in a short time, bearing a small silver tray with tea and lemon but no milk, no sugar and no biscuits.

"Did we have a successful afternoon, sir?" he asked, setting down his burden.

"A win and a third."

He gave me a small smile, a man nearing sixty, unextended and happy in his work. "Very gratifying, sir."

"Yes."

He nodded and went away, and I poured out and drank the tea and tried not to think of buttered toast. During the February freeze, I had somehow gained three pounds and was in consequence having a worse than usual battle against weight.

The sitting room was comfortable with flowered fabrics, rugs and pools of warm lamplight, altogether friendlier than the satins and gilt of the very French drawing room next door. I switched on the television to watch the news, and switched it off after, and wandered around looking for something to read. I also wondered fleetingly why the princess had wanted me to wait, and exactly what help it was that she might find too much to ask.

Reading materials seemed to be a straight choice between a glossy magazine about architecture in French and a worldwide airline timetable, and I was opting for the second when on a side table I came across a folded leaflet that announced "Master Classes in a Distinguished Setting," and found myself face to face with Danielle's weekend.

I sat in an armchair and read the booklet from front to back. The hotel, with illustrating photographs, was described as a country house refurbished in the grand manner, with soul-shaking views over fells and lakes and blazing log fires to warm the heart indoors.

The entertainments would begin with a reception on the Friday evening at six o'clock (which meant it was in progress as I read), followed by dinner, followed by Chopin sonatas performed in the gold drawing room.

On Saturday would come the lectures on "The Masters of the Italian Renaissance," given by the illustrious Keeper of Italian paintings in the Louvre. In the morning, "Botticelli, Leonardo da Vinci, Raphael: Master Works in the Louvre," and in the afternoon, "Giorgione's *Concert Champêtre* and Titian's *Laura Dianti*: the Cinquecento in Venice," all to be accompanied by slides illuminating points of brushwork and technique. These lectures, the leaflet said, represented a rare privilege seldom granted outside France by probably the world's greatest expert in Italian Renaissance art.

On Saturday evening there would be a grand Florentine banquet especially created by a master chef from Rome, and on Sunday visits would be arranged to the Lakeland houses of Wordsworth, Ruskin and (if desired) Beatrix Potter. Finally, afternoon tea would be served round the fire in the Great Hall, and everyone would disperse.

I seldom felt unsure either of myself or of my chosen way of life, but I put down the leaflet feeling helplessly inadequate.

I knew practically nothing of the Italian Renaissance and I couldn't reliably have dated da Vinci within a hundred years. I knew he painted the *Mona Lisa* and drew helicopters and submarines, and that was about all. Of Botticelli, Giorgione and Raphael I knew just as little. If Danielle's interests deeply lay with the Arts, would she ever come back to a man whose work was physical, philistine and insecure? To a man who'd liked biology and chemistry in his teens and not wanted to go to college? To someone who would positively have avoided going where she had gone with excitement?

I shivered. I couldn't bear to lose her, not to long-dead painters, nor to a live prince.

Time passed. I read the worldwide air timetables and found there were many places I'd never heard of, with people busily flying in and out of them every day. There were far too many things I didn't know.

Eventually, shortly after eight, the unruffled Dawson reappeared and invited me upstairs, and I followed him to the unfamiliar door of M. de Brescou's private sitting room.

"Mr. Fielding, sir," Dawson said, announcing me, and I walked into a room with gold-swagged curtains, dark-green walls and dark-red leather armchairs.

Roland de Brescou sat as usual in his wheelchair, and it was clear at once that he was suffering from the same severe shock that had affected the princess. Always weak-looking, he seemed more than ever to be on the point of expiring, his pale yellow-gray skin stretched over his cheekbones and the eyes gaunt and staring. He had been, I supposed, a good-looking man long ago, and he still retained a noble head of white hair and a naturally aristocratic manner. He wore, as ever, a dark suit and tie, making no concessions to illness. Old and frail he might be, but still his own master, unimpaired in his brain. Since my engagement to Danielle I had met him a few times, but although unfailingly courteous he was reclusive always, and as reticent as the princess herself.

"Come in," he said to me, his voice, always surprisingly

strong, sounding newly hoarse. "Good evening, Kit." The French echo in his English was as elusive as the princess's own.

"Good evening, monsieur," I said, making a small bow to him also, as he disliked shaking hands: his own were so thin that the squeezing of strangers hurt him.

The princess, sitting in one of the armchairs, raised tired fingers in a small greeting, and with Dawson withdrawing and closing the door behind me, she said apologetically, "We've kept you waiting so long . . ."

"You did warn me."

She nodded. "We want you to meet Mr. Greening."

Mr. Greening, I presumed, was the person standing to one side of the room, leaning against a green wall, hands in pockets, rocking on his heels. Mr. Greening, in dinner jacket and black tie, was bald, round-bellied and somewhere on the far side of fifty. He was regarding me with bright knowing eyes, assessing my age (thirty-one), height (five foot ten), clothes (gray suit, unremarkable) and possibly my income. He had the look of one used to making quick judgments and not believing what he was told.

"The jockey," he said in a voice that had been to Eton. "Strong and brave."

He was ironic, which I didn't mind. I smiled faintly, went through the obvious categories and came up with a possibility.

"The lawyer?" I suggested. "Astute?"

He laughed and peeled himself off the paintwork. "Gerald Greening," he said, nodding. "Solicitor. Would you be kind enough to witness some signatures to documents?"

I agreed, of course, reflecting that I wouldn't have expected the princess to ask me to wait so long just for that, but not protesting. Gerald Greening picked up a clipboard that had been lying on a coffee table, peeled a sheet of paper back over the clip and offered a pen to Roland de Brescou for him to sign the second page.

With a shaky flourish, the old man wrote his name beside a round red seal.

"Now you, Mr. Fielding." The pen and the clipboard came my way, and I signed where he asked, resting the board on my left forearm for support.

The whole two-page document, I noticed, was not typed, but handwritten in neat black script. Roland de Brescou's name and mine were both in the same black ink. Gerald Greening's address and occupation, when he added them at the bottom after his own signature, matched the handwriting of the text.

A rush job, I thought. Tomorrow could be too late.

"There isn't any necessity for you to know what's in the document you signed," Greening said to me easily, "but Princess Casilia insists that I tell you."

"Sit down, Kit," the princess said, "it'll take time."

I sat in one of the leather armchairs and glanced at Roland de Brescou, who was looking dubious, as if he thought telling me would be unproductive. He was no doubt right, I thought, but I was undeniably curious.

"Put simply," Greening said, still on his feet, "the document states that notwithstanding any former arrangements to the contrary, M. de Brescou may not make any business decisions without the knowledge, assent, and properly witnessed signatures of Princess Casilia, Prince Litsi"—he gave him at least half his full name—"and Miss Danielle de Brescou."

I listened in puzzlement. If there was nothing wrong with Roland de Brescou's competence, why the haste for him to sign away his authority?

"This is an interim measure," Gerald Greening went on. "A sandbag affair, one might say, to keep back the waters while we build the sea-wall." He looked pleased with the simile, and I had an impression he had used it before.

"And, er," I said, "does the tidal wave consist of anything in particular?" But it had to, of course, to have upset the princess so much.

Gerald Greening took a turn around the room, hands, complete with clipboard, clasped behind his back. A restless mind in a restless body, I thought, and listened to details about the de Brescous that neither the princess nor her husband would ever have told me themselves.

"You must understand," Greening said, impressing it upon me, "that M. de Brescou is of the ancient regime, from before the revolution. His is a patrician family, even though he himself bears no title. It's essential to understand that for him personal and family honor is of supreme importance."

"Yes," I said, "I understand that."

"Kit's own family," the princess said mildly, "stretches back through centuries of tradition."

Gerald Greening looked slightly startled, and I thought in amusement that the Fielding tradition of pride and hate wasn't exactly what he had in mind. He adjusted my status in his eyes to include ancestors, however, and went on with the story.

"In the mid-nineteenth century," he said, "M. de Brescou's great-grandfather was offered an opportunity to contribute to the building of bridges and canals and, in consequence, without quite meaning to, he founded one of France's great construction companies. He never worked in it himself—he was a landowner—but the business prospered hugely and with unusual resilience changed to fit the times. At the beginning of the twentieth century, M. de Brescou's grandfather agreed to merge the family business with another construction company whose chief interest was roads, not canals. The great canal-building era was ending, and cars, just appearing, needed better roads. M. de Brescou's grandfather retained fifty percent of the new company, an arrangement that gave neither partner outright control."

Gerald Greening's eyes gleamed with disapproval as he paced slowly round behind the chairs.

"M. de Brescou's father was killed in the Second World War without inheriting the business. M. de Brescou himself inherited it when his grandfather died, aged ninety, after the Second World War. Are you with me so far?"

"Yes," I said.

"Good." He went on pacing, setting out his story lucidly almost as if laying facts before a fairly dim jury. "The firm that had merged with that of M. de Brescou's grandfather was headed by a man called Henri Nanterre, who was also of aristocratic descent and high morals. The two men liked and trusted each other and agreed that their joint business should adhere to the highest principles. They installed managers of good reputation and sat back and . . . er . . increased their fortunes."

"Mm," I said.

"Before and during the Second World War, the firm went into recession, shrinking to a quarter of its former size, but it was still healthy enough to revive well in the

1950s, despite the deaths of the original managing friends. M. de Brescou remained on good terms with the inheriting Nanterre—Louis—and the tradition of employing top managers went on. And that brings us to three years ago, when Louis Nanterre died and left his fifty-percent share to his only son, Henri. Henri Nanterre is thirty-seven, an able entrepreneur, full of vigor, good at business. The profits of the company are annually increasing."

Both the princess and her husband listened gloomily to this long recital, which seemed to me to have been a success story of major proportions.

"Henri Nanterre," Greening explained carefully, "is of the modern world. That is to say, the old values mean little to him."

"He has no honor," Roland de Brescou said with distaste. "He disgraces his name."

I said slowly, to the princess, "What does he look like?"

"You saw him," she said simply. "In my box."

There was a brief silence, then the princess said to Greening, "Please go on, Gerald. Tell Kit what that . . . that wretched man wants, and what he said to me."

Roland de Brescou interrupted before he could speak, and, turning his wheelchair to face me directly, said, "I will tell him. I will tell you. I didn't think you should be involved in our affairs, but my wife wishes it . . ." He made a faint gesture with a thin hand, acknowledging his affection for her. ". . . and as you are to marry Danielle, well then, perhaps . . . But I will tell you myself." His voice was slow but stronger, the shock receding in him too, with perhaps anger taking its place.

"As you know," he said, "I have been for a long time . . ." He gestured down his body, not spelling it out. "We have lived also a long time in London. Far away from the business, you understand?"

I nodded.

"Louis Nanterre, he used to go there quite often to consult the managers. We would talk often on the telephone and he would tell me everything that was happening. We would decide together if it looked sensible to go in new directions. He and I, for instance, developed a factory to make things out of plastic, not metal, nor concrete. Things like heavy drainpipes that would not crack under roads, nor corrode. You understand? We developed new plastics, very tough."

He paused, more it seemed through lack of breath than of things to say. The princess, Greening and I waited until he was ready to go on.

"Louis," he said eventually, "used to come to London to this house twice a year, with auditors and lawyers—Gerald would be here—and we would discuss what had been done, and read the reports and suggestions from the boards of managers, and make plans." He sighed heavily. "Then Louis died, and I asked Henri to come over for the meetings, and he refused."

"Refused?" I repeated.

"Absolutely. Then suddenly I don't know any longer what is happening, and I sent Gerald over, and wrote to the auditors . . ."

"Henri had sacked the auditors," Gerald Greening said succinctly into the pause, "and engaged others of his own choice. He had sacked half the managers and was taking charge directly himself, and had branched out in directions that M. de Brescou knew nothing about."

"It's intolerable," Roland de Brescou said.

"And today?" I asked him tentatively. "What did he say at Newbury today?"

"To go to my wife!" He was quivering with fury. "To

threaten her. It's . . . disgraceful." There weren't words, it seemed, strong enough for his feelings.

"He told Princess Casilia," Gerald Greening said with precision, "that he needed her husband's signature on a document, that M. de Brescou did not want to sign, and that she was to make sure that he did."

"What document?" I asked flatly.

None of them, it seemed, was in a hurry to say, and it was Gerald Greening, finally, who shrugged heavily and said, "A French government form for a preliminary application for a license to manufacture and export guns."

"Guns?" I said, surprised. "What sort of guns?"

"Firearms for killing people. Small arms made of plastic."

"He told me," the princess said, looking hollow-eyed, "that it would be simple to use the strong plastics for guns. Many modern pistols and machine-guns can be made of plastic, he said. It is cheaper and lighter, he said. Production would be easy and profitable, once he had the license. And he said he would definitely be granted the license, he had done all the groundwork. He had had little difficulty because the de Brescou et Nanterre company is so reputable and respected, and all he needed was my husband's agreement."

She stopped in a distress that was echoed by her husband.

"Guns," he said. "I will never sign. It is dishonorable, do you understand, to trade nowadays in weapons of war. It is unthinkable. In Europe these days it is not a business of good repute. Especially guns made of plastic, which were invented so they could be carried through airports without being found. Of course, I know our plastics would be suitable, but never, never shall it happen that my name is used to sell guns that may find their way to terrorists. It is absolutely inconceivable."

I saw indeed that it was.

"One of our older managers telephoned me a month ago to ask if I truly meant to make guns," he said, outraged. "I had heard nothing of it. Nothing. Then Henri Nanterre sent a lawyer's letter, formally asking my assent. I replied that I would never give it, and I expected the matter to end there. There is no question of the company manufacturing guns without my consent. But to threaten my wife!"

"What sort of threats?" I asked.

"Henri Nanterre said to me," the princess said faintly, "that he was sure I would persuade my husband to sign, because I wouldn't want any accidents to happen to anyone I liked . . . or employed."

No wonder she had been devastated, I thought. Guns, threats of violence, a vista of dishonor: all a long way from her sheltered, secure and respected existence. Henri Nanterre, with his strong face and domineering voice, must have been battering at her for at least an hour before I arrived in her box.

"What happened to your friends at Newbury?" I asked her. "The ones in your box."

"He told them to go," she said tiredly. "He said he needed to talk urgently, and they were not to come back."

"And they went."

"Yes."

Well, I'd gone myself.

"I didn't know who he was," the princess said. "I was bewildered by him. He came bursting in and turned them out, and drowned my questions and protestations. I have not . . ." She shuddered. "I have never had to face anyone like that."

Henri Nanterre sounded pretty much a terrorist himself, I thought. Terrorist behavior, anyway: loud voice, hustle, threats.

"What did you say to him?" I asked, because if anyone could have tamed a terrorist with words, surely she could.

"I don't know. He didn't listen. He just talked over the top of anything I tried to say, until in the end I wasn't saying anything. It was useless. When I tried to stand up, he pushed me down. When I talked, he talked louder. He went on and on saying the same things over again . . . When you came into the box I was completely dazed."

"I should have stayed."

"No, much better that you didn't."

She looked at me calmly. Perhaps I would have had literally to fight him, I thought, and perhaps I would have lost, and certainly that would have been no help to anyone. All the same, I should have stayed.

Gerald Greening cleared his throat, put the clipboard down on a side table and went back to rocking on his heels against the wall behind my left shoulder.

"Princess Casilia tells me," he said, jingling coins in his pockets, "that last November her jockey got the better of two villainous press barons, one villainous asset stripper and various villainous thugs."

I turned my head and briefly met his glance, which was brightly empty of belief. A jokey man, I thought. Not what I would have chosen in a lawyer.

"Things sort of fell into place," I said neutrally.

"And are they all still after your blood?" There was a teasing note in his voice, as if no one could take the princess's story seriously.

"Only the asset stripper, as far as I know," I said.

"Maynard Allardeck?"

"You've heard of him?"

"I've met him," Greening said with minor triumph. "A sound and charming man, I would have said. Not a villain at all."

I made no comment. I avoided talking about Maynard whenever possible, not least because any slanderous thing I might say might drift back to his litigious ears.

"Anyway," Greening said, rocking on the edge of my vision, and with irony plain in his voice, "Princess Casilia would now like you to gallop to the rescue and try to rid M. de Brescou of the obnoxious Nanterre."

"No, no," the princess protested, sitting straighter. "Gerald, I said no such thing."

I stood slowly up and turned to face Greening directly, and I don't know exactly what he saw, but he stopped rocking and took his hands out of his pockets and said with an abrupt change of tone, "That's not what she said, but that's undoubtedly what she wants. And I'll admit that until this very moment I thought it all a bit of a joke." He looked at me uneasily. "Look, my dear chap, perhaps I got things wrong."

"Kit," the princess said behind me, "please sit down. I most certainly didn't ask that. I wondered only . . . oh, *do* sit down."

I sat, leaning forward toward her and looking at her troubled eyes. "It is," I said with acceptance, "what you want. It has to be. I'll do anything I can to help. But I'm still . . . a jockey."

"You're a Fielding," she said unexpectedly. "That's what Gerald has just seen. That something . . . Bobby told me you didn't realize . . ." She broke off in some confusion.

She never in normal circumstances spoke to me in that way. "I wanted to ask you," she said, with a visible return to composure, "to do what you could to prevent any 'accidents.' To think of what might happen, to warn us, advise us. We need someone like you, who can imagine . . ."

She stopped. I knew exactly what she meant, but I said, "Have you thought of enlisting the police?"

She nodded silently, and from behind me Gerald Greening said, "I telephoned them immediately Princess Casilia described to me what had happened. They said they had noted what I'd told them."

"No actual action?" I suggested.

"They say they are stretched with crimes that have actually happened, but they would put this house on their surveillance list."

"And you went pretty high up, of course?"

"As high as I could get this evening."

There was no possible way, I reflected, to guard anyone perpetually against assassination, but I doubted if Henri Nanterre meant to go that far, if only because he wouldn't necessarily gain from it. Much more likely that he thought he could put the frighteners quite easily on a paralyzed old man and an unworldly woman and was currently underestimating both the princess's courage and her husband's inflexible honor. To a man with few scruples, the moral opposition he expected might have seemed a temporary dislodgeable obstinacy, not an immovably embedded barrier.

I doubted if he were actually at that moment planning accidents. He would be expecting the threats to be enough. How soon, I wondered, would he find out that they weren't?

I said to the princess, "Did Nanterre give you any time

scale? Did he say when and where he expected Monsieur to sign the form?"

"I shall not sign it," Roland de Brescou murmured.

'No, monsieur, but Henri Nanterre doesn't know that yet."

"He said," the princess answered weakly, "that a notary would have to witness my husband signing. He said he would arrange it, and he would tell us when."

"A notary? A French lawyer?"

"I don't know. He was speaking in English to my friends, but when they'd gone he started in French, and I told him to speak English. I do speak French of course, but I prefer English, which is second nature to me, as you know."

I nodded. Danielle had told me that as neither the princess nor her husband preferred to chat in the other's native tongue, they both looked upon English as their chief language, and chose to live in England for that reason.

"What do you suppose Nanterre will do," I asked Greening, "when he discovers four people have to sign the application form now, not just Monsieur?"

He stared at me with shiny eyes. Contact lenses, I thought inconsequentially. "Consequences," he said, "are your particular field, as I understand it."

"It depends then," I said, "on how rich he is, how greedy, how power-hungry, how determined and how criminal."

"Oh, dear," the princess said faintly, "how very horrid this all is."

I agreed with her. At least as much as she, I would have preferred to be out on a windy racetrack where the rogues had four legs and merely bit.

"There's a simple way," I said to him, "to keep all your family safe and to preserve your good name."

"Go on," he said. "How?"

"Change the name of the company and sell your share."

He blinked. The princess put a hand to her mouth, and I couldn't see Greening's reaction, as he was behind me.

"Unfortunately," Roland de Brescou said eventually, "I cannot do either without Henri Nanterre's agreement. The original partnership was set up in that way." He paused. "It is of course possible that he would agree to such changes if he could set up a consortium to acquire the whole, with himself to be at its head with a majority vote. He could then, if he wished, manufacture guns."

"It does seem a positive solution," Gerald Greening said judiciously from the rear. "You would be free of trouble, monsieur. You would have your money out. Yes, certainly a proposal to be considered."

Roland de Brescou studied my face. "Tell me," he said, "would you personally follow that course?"

Would I? I thought. Would I, if I were old and paralyzed? Would I if I knew the result would be a load of new guns in a world already awash with them? If I knew I was backing away from my principles? If I cared for my family's safety?

"I don't know, monsieur," I said.

He smiled faintly and turned his head toward the princess. "And you, my dear? Would you?"

Whatever answer she would have given him was interrupted by the buzz of the house's intercom system, a recent installation that saved everyone a lot of walking. The princess picked up the handset, pressed a button, and said "Yes?" She listened. "Just a minute." She looked at her husband, saying, "Are you expecting visitors? Dawson says two men have called, saying they have an appointment. He's shown them into the library."

Roland de Brescou was shaking his head doubtfully when there was an audible squawk from the handset. "What?" asked the princess, returning it to her ear. "What did you say, Dawson?" She listened but seemed to hear nothing. "He's gone," she said, puzzled. "What do you suppose has happened?"

"I'll go and see, if you like," I said.

"Yes, Kit, please do."

I rose and went as far as the door, but before I could touch it it opened abruptly to reveal two men walking purposefully in. One unmistakably was Henri Nanterre: the other, a pace behind, a pale sharp-featured young man in a narrow black suit, carrying a briefcase.

Dawson, out of breath, appeared with a rush behind them, mouth open in horror at the unceremonious breaking of his defenses.

"Madam," he was saying helplessly, "they simply ran past me . . ."

Henri Nanterre rudely shut the door on his explanations and turned to face the roomful of people. He seemed disconcerted to find Gerald Greening there, and he took a second sharp look at me, remembering where he'd seen me before and not particularly liking that, either. I guessed that he had come expecting only the princess and her husband, reckoning he had softened them both up enough for his purpose.

His beaky nose looked somewhat diminished against the darker walls, nor did his aggression seem as concentrated as it had been in the smaller box, but he was still forceful, both in his loud voice and in the total rejection of the good manners he should have inherited.

He clicked his fingers to his companion, who removed a single beige-colored sheet of paper from the briefcase and handed it to him, and then he said something long and clearly objectionable to Roland de Brescou in French. His target leaned backward in his wheelchair as if to retreat from unpleasantness, and into the first available pause said testily, "Speak English."

Henri Nanterre waved the paper and poured out another lengthy burst of French, drowning de Brescou's attempts to interrupt him. The princess made a helpless gesture with her hand to me, indicating that that was exactly what had happened to her also.

"Nanterre!" Gerald Greening said peremptorily, and got a glance but no pause in the tirade. I went back to the armchair I'd occupied before and sat down there, crossing my legs and swinging my foot. The motion irritated Nanterre into breaking off and saying something to me that might have been *"et qui êtes-vous?"* though I couldn't be sure. My sketchy French had mostly been learned on the racecourses of Auteuil and Cagnes sur Mer, and chiefly consisted of words like *courants* (runners), *haies* (fences) and *piste* (track).

I stared mildly at Nanterre and went on swinging my foot.

Greening took the opportunity of the brief silence to say rather pompously, "Monsieur de Brescou has no power to sign any paper whatsoever."

"Don't be ridiculous," Nanterre said, at last speaking English, which like many French businessmen, he proved to know fluently. "He has too much power. He is out of touch with the modern world, and his obstructive attitude must cease. I require him to make a decision that will bring new impetus and prosperity to a company that is ageing and suffering from out-of-date methods. The period of road-building is over. We must look to new markets. I have found such a market, which is uniquely suited to the plastic materials we are accustomed to make use of, and no stupidly old-fashioned ideas shall stand in the way."

"Monsieur de Brescou has relinquished his power to make solo decisions," Greening said. "Four people besides yourself must now put their names to any change of company policy."

"That is absolutely untrue," Nanterre said loudly. "De Brescou has total command."

"No longer. He has signed it away."

Nanterre looked flummoxed, and I began to think that Greening's sandbags might actually hold against the flood when he made the stupid error of glancing smugly in the direction of the downturned clipboard. How could he be so damned silly, I thought, and had no sympathy for him when Nanterre followed the direction of his eyes and moved like lightning to the side table, reaching it first.

"Put that down," Greening said furiously, but Nanterre was skimming the page and handing it briskly to his pale acolyte.

"Is that legal?" he demanded.

Gerald Greening was advancing to retrieve his property, the unintroduced Frenchman backing away while he read and holding the clipboard out of reach. "*Oui*," he said finally. "Yes. Legal."

"In that case . . ." Nanterre snatched the clipboard out of his grasp, tore the handwritten pages off it and ripped them across and across. "The document no longer exists."

"Of course it exists," I said. "Even in pieces, it exists. It was signed and it was witnessed. Its intention remains a fact, and it can be written again."

Nanterre's gaze sharpened in my direction. "Who are you?" he demanded.

"A friend."

"Stop swinging that foot."

I went on swinging it. "Why don't you just face the fact that Monsieur de Brescou will never let his company sell arms?" I said. "Why, if that's what you want to do, don't you agree to dissolve the existing company, and with your proceeds set up again on your own?"

He narrowed his eyes at me, everyone in the room waiting for an answer. When it came, it was grudging, but clearly the truth. Bad news, also for Roland de Brescou.

"I was told," Nanterre said with cold anger, "that only if de Brescou applied personally would I be granted the facility. I was told it was essential to have the backing of his name."

It struck me that perhaps someone in the French background didn't want Nanterre to make guns, and was taking subtle steps to prevent it while avoiding making a flat and perhaps politically embarrassing refusal. To insist on a condition that wouldn't be fulfilled would be to lay the failure of Nanterre's plans solely and neatly at de Brescou's feet.

"Therefore," Nanterre went on ominously, "de Brescou will sign. With or without trouble." He looked at the torn pages he was still grasping and held them out to his assistant. "Go and find a bathroom," he said. "Get rid of these pieces. Then return."

The pale young man nodded and went away. Gerald

Greening made several protestations, which had no effect on Nanterre. He was looking as though various thoughts were occurring to him that gave him no pleasure, and he interrupted Greening, saying loudly, "Where are the people whose names were on the agreement?"

Greening, showing the first piece of lawyerly sense for a long time, said he had no idea.

"Where are they?" Nanterre demanded of Roland de Brescou. For answer, a Gallic shrug.

He shouted the question at the princess, who gave a silent shake of the head, and at me, with the same result. "Where are they?"

They would be listening to the sweet chords of Chopin, I supposed, and wondered if they even knew of the agreement's existence.

"What are their names?" Nanterre said.

No one answered. He went to the door and shouted loudly down the hallway. "Valery. Come here at once. Valery! Come here."

The man Valery hurried back empty-handed. "The agreement is finished," he said reassuringly. "All gone down the drain."

"You read the names on it, didn't you?" Nanterre demanded. "You remember those names?"

Valery swallowed. "I didn't, er . . ." he stuttered. "I didn't study the names. Er . . . the first was Princess Casilia . . ."

"And the others?"

Valery shook his head, eyes wide. He as well as Nanterre saw too late that they had thrown away knowledge they might have used. Pressure couldn't be applied to people one couldn't identify. Bribes and blandishments could go nowhere.

Nanterre transmitted his frustration into an increase of aggression, thrusting the application form again toward Roland de Brescou and demanding he sign it.

Monsieur de Brescou didn't even bother to shake his head. Nanterre was losing it, I thought, and would soon retire. I was wrong.

He handed the form to Valery, put his right hand inside his jacket, and from a hidden holster produced a black and businesslike pistol. With a gliding step he reached the princess and pressed the end of the barrel against her temple, standing behind her and holding her head firmly with his left hand under the chin.

"Now," he said gratingly to de Brescou, "sign the form."

Into an electrified atmosphere I said plainly, "Don't be ridiculous."

"Stop swinging that foot," Nanterre said furiously.

I stopped swinging it. There was a time for everything.

"If you shoot Princess Casilia," I said calmly, "Monsieur de Brescou will not sign the form."

The princess had her eyes shut and Roland de Brescou looked frail to fainting. Valery's wide eyes risked popping out altogether and Gerald Greening, somewhere behind me, was saying "Oh, my God," incredulously under his breath.

I said, my mouth drier than I liked, "If you shoot Princess Casilia, we are all witnesses. You would have to kill us all, including Valery."

Valery moaned.

"Monsieur de Brescou would not have signed the form,"

I said. "You would end up in jail for life. What would be the point?"

He stared at me with hot dark eyes, the princess's head firm in his grip.

After a pause that lasted a couple of millennia, he gave the princess's head a shake and let her go.

"There are no bullets," he said. He shoved the gun back into its holster, holding his jacket open for the purpose. He gave me a bitter glance as if he would impress my face on his memory forever and without another word walked out of the room.

Valery closed his eyes, opened them a slit, ducked his head and scuttled away in his master's wake, looking as if he wished he were anywhere else.

The princess with a small sound of great distress slid out of her chair onto her knees beside the wheelchair and put her arms round her husband, her face turned to his neck, her shining dark hair against his cheek. He raised a thin hand to stroke her head, and looked at me with somber eyes.

"I would have signed," he said.

"Yes, monsieur."

I felt sick myself and could hardly imagine their turmoil. The princess was shaking visibly, crying, I thought.

I stood up. "I'll wait downstairs," I said.

He gave the briefest of nods, and I followed where Nanterre had gone, looking back for Gerald Greening. Numbly he came after me, closing the door, and we went down to the sitting room where I'd waited before.

"You didn't know," he said croakily, "that the gun was empty, did you?"

"No."

"You took a terrible risk." He made straight for the tray of bottles and glasses, pouring brandy with a shaking hand. "Do you want some?"

I nodded and sat rather weakly on one of the chintz sofas. He gave me a glass and collapsed in much the same fashion.

"I've never liked guns," he said hollowly.

"I wonder if he meant to produce it?" I said. "He didn't mean to use it or he'd have brought it loaded."

"Then why carry it at all?"

"A prototype, wouldn't you say?" I suggested. "His plastic equalizer, demonstration model. I wonder how he got it into England. Through airports undetected, would you say? In pieces?"

Greening made inroads into his brandy and said, "When I met him in France I thought him bombastic but shrewd. But these threats . . . tonight's behavior . . ."

"Not shrewd but crude," I said.

He gave me a glance. "Do you think he'll give up?"

"Nanterre? No, I'm afraid he won't. He must have seen he came near tonight to getting what he wanted. I'd say he'll try again. Another way, perhaps."

"When you aren't there." He said it as a statement, all the former doubts missing. If he wasn't careful, I thought, he'd persuade himself too far the other way. He looked at his watch, sighing deeply. "I told my wife I'd be slightly delayed. Slightly! I'm supposed to be meeting her at a dinner." He paused. "If I go in a short while, will you make my apologies?"

"OK," I said, a shade surprised. "Aren't you going . . . er . . . to reinstate the sandbags?"

It took him a moment to see what I meant, and then he

said he would have to ask M. de Brescou what he wanted.

"It might safeguard him as you intended, don't you think?" I said. "Especially as Nanterre doesn't know who else to put pressure on." I glanced at the Master Classes leaflet that still lay on the coffee table. "Did Danielle and Prince Litsi know their names had been used?"

He shook his head. "Princess Casilia couldn't remember the name of the hotel. It didn't affect the legality of the document. Their assent at that stage wasn't necessary."

A few steps down the road, though, after Nanterre's show of force, I reckoned it was no longer fair to embroil them without their consent, and I was on the point of saying so when the door quietly opened and Princess Casilia came in.

We stood up. If she had been crying, there was no sign of it, although she did have the empty-eyed look and the pallor of people stretched into unreality.

"Gerald, we both want to thank you for coming," she said, her voice higher in pitch than usual. "We are so sorry about your dinner."

"Princess," he protested. "My time is yours."

"My husband asks if you could return tomorrow morning."

Greening gave a small squirm as if jettisoning his Saturday golf and asked if ten o'clock would suit, and with evident relief took his departure.

"Kit . . ." The princess turned to me. "Will you stay here in the house, tonight? In case . . . just in case . . ."

"Yes," I said.

She closed her eyes and opened them again. "It has been such a dreadful day." She paused. "Nothing seems real."

"Can I pour you a drink?"

"No. Ask Dawson to bring you some food. Tell him you'll sleep in the bamboo room." She looked at me without intensity, too tired for emotion. "My husband wants to see you in the morning."

"Fairly early," I suggested. "I have to be at Newbury for the first race."

"Goodness! I'd forgotten." Some of the faraway look left her eyes. "I didn't even ask how Cotopaxi ran."

"He was third. Ran well." It seemed a long time ago. "You'll see it on the video."

Like many owners she bought videotapes of most of her horses' races, to watch and re-enjoy their performances over and over.

"Yes, that'll be nice."

She said goodnight much as if she hadn't had a gun aimed closely against her head half an hour earlier, and with upright carriage went gently away upstairs.

A remarkable woman, I thought, not for the first time, and descended to the basement in search of Dawson, who was sitting, jacket off, in front of the television drinking beer. The butler, slightly abashed by having let the uninvited guests outrush him, made no demur at checking with me through the house's defenses. Window locks, front door, rear door, basement door, all secure.

John Grundy, the male nurse, he said, would arrive at ten, assist Monsieur to bed, sleep in the room next to him, and in the morning help him bathe, shave and dress. He would do Monsieur's laundry and be gone by eleven.

Only Dawson and his wife (the princess's personal maid) slept in the basement, he said: all the rest of the staff came in by day. Prince Litsi, who was occupying the guest suite on the ground floor, and Miss de Brescou, whose room was beyond the princess's suite, were away, as I knew.

His eyebrows shot up at the mention of the bamboo room, and when he took me by lift to the floor above the princess and her husband, I could see why. Palatial, pale blue, gold and cream, it looked fit for the noblest of visitors, the bamboo of its name found in the pattern of the curtains and the pale Chinese-Chippendale furniture. There was a vast double bed, a dressing room, a bathroom, and an array of various drinks and a good television set hidden behind discreet louvered doors.

Dawson left me there, and I took the opportunity to make my regular evening telephone call to Wykeham, to tell him how his horses had run. He was pleased, he said, about Cotopaxi, but did I realize what I'd done to Cascade? Dusty, he said, had told him angrily all about the race, including Maynard Allardeck's inspection afterward.

"How is Cascade?" I asked.

"We weighed him. He's lost thirty pounds. He can hardly hold his head up. You don't often send horses back in that state."

"I'm sorry," I said.

"There's winning and winning," he said testily. "You've ruined him for Cheltenham."

"I'm sorry," I said again, contritely. Cheltenham, two and a half weeks ahead, was of course the top meeting of the jumping year, its races loaded with prestige and prizes. Wykeham liked above all to have successes there, as indeed did I and every jump jockey riding. Missing a winner there would serve me right, I supposed, for letting unhappiness get the better of me, but I was genuinely sorry for Wykeham's sake.

"Don't do anything like that tomorrow with Calgoorlie," he said severely.

I sighed. Calgoorlie had been dead for years. Wykeham's memory was apt to slip cogs to the point that sometimes I couldn't work out what horse he was referring to.

"Do you mean Kinley?" I suggested.

"What? Yes, of course, that's what I said. You give him a nice ride, now, Kit."

At least, I thought, he knew who he was talking to: he still on the telephone called me often by the name of the jockey who'd had my job ten years earlier.

I assured him I would give Kinley a nice ride.

"And win, of course," he said.

"All right." A nice ride and a win couldn't always be achieved together, as Cascade very well knew. Kinley however was a white-hot hope for Cheltenham, and if he didn't win comfortably at Newbury the expectations could cool to pink.

"Dusty says the princess didn't come into the ring before Cotopaxi's race, or see him afterward. He says it was because she was angry about Cascade." Wykeham's old voice was full of displeasure. "We can't afford to anger the princess."

"Dusty's wrong," I said. "She wasn't angry. She had some trouble with . . . er . . . a visitor in her box. She explained to me after . . . and invited me to Eaton Square, which is where I am now."

"Oh," he said, mollified. "All right, then. Kinley's race is televised tomorrow," he said, "so I'll be watching."

"Great."

"Well then . . . Goodnight, Paul."

"Goodnight, Wykeham," I said.

Wryly I telephoned to the answering machine in my own house, but there was nothing much in the way of messages, and presently Dawson returned with a supper of chicken soup, cold ham and a banana (my choice).

Later, together, we made another tour of the house, meeting John Grundy, a sixty-year-old widower, on his way to his own room. Both men said they would be undisturbed to see me wandering around now and then in the small hours, but although I did prowl up and down once or twice, the big house was silent all night, its clocks ticking in whispers. I slept on and off between linen sheets under a silk coverlet in pajamas thoughtfully supplied by Dawson, and in the morning was ushered in to see Roland de Brescou.

He was alone in his sitting room, freshly dressed in a city suit with a white shirt and foulard tie. Black shoes, brilliantly polished. White hair, neatly brushed. No concessions to his condition, no concession to weekends.

His wheelchair was unusual in having a high back—and I'd often wondered why more weren't designed that way—so that he could rest his head if he felt like dozing. That morning, although he was awake, he was resting his head anyway.

"Please sit down," he said civilly, and watched me take the same place as the evening before, in the dark-red leather armchair. He looked if possible even frailer, with gray shadows in his skin, and the long hands that lay quiet on the padded armrests had a quality of transparency, the flesh thin as paper over the bones.

I felt almost indecently strong and healthy in contrast, and asked if there were anything I could fetch and carry for him.

He said no with a twitch of eye muscle that might have been interpreted as an understanding smile, as if he were accustomed to such guilt reactions in visitors.

"I wish to thank you," he said, "for coming to our defense. For helping Princess Casilia."

He had never in my presence called her "my wife," nor would I ever have referred to her in that way to him. His formal patterns of speech were curiously catching.

"Also," he said, as I opened my mouth to demur, "for giving me time to consider what to do about Henri Nanterre." He moistened his dry lips with the tip of an apparently desiccated tongue. "I have been unable to sleep . . . I cannot risk harm to Princess Casilia or anyone around us. It is time for me to relinquish control. To find a successor . . . but I have no children, and there are few de Brescous left. It isn't going to be easy to find any family member to take my place."

Even the thought of the discussions and decisions such a course would lead to seemed to exhaust him.

"I miss Louis," he said unexpectedly. "I cannot continue without him. It is time for me to retire. I should have seen . . . When Louis died . . . it was time." He seemed to be talking to himself as much as me, clarifying his thoughts, his eyes wandering.

I made a nondescript noise of nothing much more than interest. I would have agreed that the time to retire was long past, though, and it almost seemed he caught something of that thought, because he said calmly, "My grandfather was in total command at ninety. I expected to die also at the head of the company, as I am the chairman."

"Yes, I see."

His gaze steadied on my face. "Princess Casilia will go to

the races today. She hopes you will go with her in her car."
He paused. "May I ask you to defend her from harm?"

"Yes," I said matter-of-factly, "with my life."

It didn't even sound melodramatic after the past evening's events, and he seemed to take it as a normal remark. He merely nodded a fraction and I thought that in retrospect I would be hotly embarrassed at myself. But then, I probably meant it, and the truth pops out.

It seemed anyway what he wanted to hear. He nodded again a couple of times slowly as if to seal the pact, and I stood up to take my leave. There was a briefcase, I saw, lying half under one of the chairs between me and the door, and I picked it up to ask him where he would like it put.

"It isn't mine," he said, without much interest. "It must be Gerald Greening's. He's returning this morning."

I had a sudden picture, however, of the pathetic Valery producing the handgun application form from that case, and of him scuttling away empty-handed at the end. When I explained to Roland de Brescou, he suggested I take the case downstairs to the hall, so that when its owner called back to collect it, he wouldn't need to come up.

I took the case away with me but, lacking de Brescou's incurious honesty, went up to the bamboo room, not down.

The case, black leather, serviceable, unostentatious, proved to be unlocked and unexciting, containing merely what looked like a duplicate of the form that Roland de Brescou hadn't signed.

On undistinguished buff paper, mostly in small badly printed italics, and of course in French, it hardly looked worth the upheaval it was causing. As far as I could make out it wasn't specifically to do with armaments, but had many dotted-line spaces needing to be filled in. No one had filled in anything on the duplicate, although presumably the one Valery had taken away with him had been ready for signing.

I put the form in a drawer of a bedside table and took the briefcase downstairs, meeting Gerald Greening as he arrived. We said good mornings with the memory of last night's violence hovering, and he said he had not only rewritten the sandbags but had had the document properly typed and provided with seals. Would I be so good as to repeat my services as witness?

We returned to Roland de Brescou and wrote our names, and I mentioned again about telling Danielle and Prince Litsi. I couldn't help thinking of them. They would be starting about now on "The Master Works of Leonardo . . ." Dammit, dammit.

"Yes, yes," Greening was saying, "I understand they return tomorrow evening. Perhaps you could inform them yourself."

"Perhaps."

"And now," Greening said, "to update the police."

He busied himself on the telephone, reaching yesterday's man and higher, obtaining the promise of a CID officer's attentions, admitting he didn't know where Nanterre could be found. "Immediately he surfaces again we will inform you," he was saying, and I wondered how immediately would be immediately, should Nanterre turn up with bullets.

Roland de Brescou, however, showed approval, not dismay, and I left them beginning to discuss how best to find a de Brescou successor. I made various preparations for the day, and I was waiting in the hall when the princess came down to go to the races, with Dawson hovering and Thomas, alerted by telephone, drawing smoothly to a halt outside. She was wearing a cream-colored coat, not the sables, with heavy gold earrings and no hat, and although she seemed perfectly calm she couldn't disguise apprehensive glances up and down the street as she was seen across the pavement by her three assorted minders.

"It is important," she said conversationally as soon as she was settled and Thomas had centrally locked all the doors, "not to let peril deter one from one's pleasures."

"Mm," I said noncommittally.

She smiled sweetly. "You, Kit, do not."

"Those pleasures earn me my living."

"Peril should not, then, deter one from one's duty." She sighed. "So stuffy, don't you think, put that way? Duty and pleasure so often coincide, deep down, don't you think?"

I did think, and I thought she was probably right. She was no mean psychologist, in her way.

"Tell me about Cotopaxi," she commanded, and listened contentedly, asking questions when I paused. After that, we discussed Kinley, her brilliant young hurdler, and after that her other runner for the day, Hillsborough, and it wasn't until we were nearing Newbury that I asked if she would mind if Thomas accompanied her into the meeting and stayed at her side all afternoon.

"Thomas?" she said, surprised. "But he doesn't like racing. It bores him, doesn't it Thomas?"

"Ordinarily, madam," he said.

"Thomas is large and capable," I said, pointing out facts, "and Monsieur de Brescou asked that you should enjoy the races unmolested."

"Oh," she said, disconcerted. "How much . . . did you tell Thomas?"

"To look out for a frog with a hawk's nose and keep him from annoying you, madam," Thomas said.

She was relieved, amused and, it seemed to me, grateful.

Back at the ranch, whether she knew it or not, John Grundy was sacrificing his Saturday afternoon to remain close to Roland de Brescou, with the number of the local police station imprinted on his mind.

"They already know there might be trouble," I'd told him. "If you call them, they'll come at once."

John Grundy, tough for his years, had commented merely that he'd dealt with fighting drunks often enough, and to leave it to him. Dawson, whose wife was going out with her sister, swore he would let no strangers in. It seemed unlikely, to my mind, that Nanterre would actually attempt another head-on attack, but it would be foolish to risk being proved wrong with everything wide open.

Thomas, looking all six foot three a bodyguard, walked a pace behind the princess all afternoon, the princess behaving most of the time as if unaware of her shadow. She hadn't wanted to cancel her afternoon party because of the five friends she'd invited to lunch, and she requested them, at my suggestion, to stay with her whatever happened and not to leave her alone unless she herself asked it.

Two of them came into the parade ring before the first of her two races, Thomas looming behind, all of them forming a shield when she walked back toward the stands. She was a far more likely target than de Brescou himself, I thought uneasily, watching her go as I rode Hillsborough out onto the course: her husband would never sign away his honor to save his own life, but to free an abducted wife . . . very likely.

He could repudiate a signature obtained under threat. He could retract, kick up a fuss, could say, "I couldn't help it." The guns might not then be made, but his health would deteriorate and his name could be rubble. Better to prevent than to rescue, I thought, and wondered what I'd overlooked.

Hillsborough felt dull in my hands and I knew going down to the start that he wouldn't do much good. There were none of the signals that horses feeling well and ready to race give, and although I tried to jolly him along once we'd started, he was as sluggish as a cold engine.

He met most of the fences right but lost ground on landing through not setting off again fast, and when I tried to make him quicken after the last he either couldn't or wouldn't, and lost two places to faster finishers, trailing in eighth of the twelve runners.

It couldn't be helped: one can't win them all. I was irritated, though, when an official came to the changing room afterward and said the Stewards wanted to see me immediately, and I followed him to the Stewards' Room with more seethe than resignation, and there, as expected, was Maynard Allardeck, sitting at a table with two others, looking as impartial and reasonable as a saint. The Stewards said they wanted to know why my well-backed mount had run so badly. They said they were of the opinion that I hadn't ridden the horse out fully or attempted to win, and would I please give them an explanation.

Maynard was almost certainly the instigator, but not the spokesman. One of the others, a man I respected, had said for openers, "Mr. Fielding, explain the poor showing of Hillsborough."

He had himself ridden as an amateur in days gone by, and I told him straightforwardly that my horse had seemed not to be feeling well and hadn't been enjoying himself. He had been flat-footed even going down to the start and during the race I'd thought once or twice of pulling him up altogether.

The Steward glanced at Allardeck and said to me, "Why didn't you use your whip after the last fence?"

The phrase "flogging a dead horse" drifted almost irresistibly into my mind but I said only, "I gave him a lot of signals to quicken, but he couldn't. Beating him wouldn't have made any difference."

"You appeared to be giving him an easy ride," he said, but without the aggression of conviction. "What's your explanation?"

Giving a horse an easy ride was an euphemism for "not trying to win," or even worse, for "trying not to win," a loss-of-license matter. I said with some force, "Princess Casilia's horses are always doing their best. Hillsborough was doing his best, but he was having an off day."

There was a shade of amusement in the Steward's eyes. He knew, as everyone in racing knew, how things stood between Allardecks and Fieldings; Stewards' inquiries had for half a century sorted out the fiery accusations flung at Maynard's father by my grandfather, and at my grandfather by Maynard's father, both of them training Flat racers in Newmarket. The only new twist to the old battle was the recent Allardeck presence on the power side of the table, no doubt highly funny to all but myself.

"We note your explanation," the Steward said dryly, and told me I could go.

I went without looking directly at Maynard. Twice in two days I'd wriggled off his hooks, and I didn't want him to think I was gloating. I went back fast to the changing room to exchange the princess's colors for those of another owner and to weigh out, but even so I was late into the parade ring for the next race (and one could be fined for that also).

I walked in hurriedly to join the one hopeful little group without a jockey, and saw, thirty feet away, Henri Nanterre.

He was standing in another group of owners, trainer and jockey, and was looking my way as if he'd been watching my arrival.

Unwelcome as he was, however, I had to postpone thoughts of him on account of the excited questions of the tubby enthusiastic couple whose dreams I was supposed to make come true within the next ten minutes; and anyway, the princess, I hoped, was safely surrounded upstairs.

The Dream, so named, had been a winner on the Flat and was having his first run over hurdles. He proved to be fast, all right, but he hadn't learned the knack of jumping: he rattled the first three flights ominously and put his feet straight through the fourth, and that was as far as we went. The Dream galloped away loose in fright, I picked myself up undamaged from the grass and waited resignedly for wheels to roll along to pick me up. One had to expect a fall every ten or eleven rides, and mostly they were easy, like that, producing a bruise at worst. The bad ones turned up perhaps twice a year, always unexpected.

I checked in with the doctor, as one had to after every fall, and while changing for the next race made time to talk to the jockey from the group with Nanterre: Jamie Fingall, long a colleague, one of the crowd.

"French guy with the beaky nose? Yeah, well, the guvnor introduced him but I didn't pay much attention. He owns horses in France, something like that."

"Um . . . Was he with your guvnor, or with the owners?"

"With the owners, but it sounded to me like the guvnor was trying to sweet-talk the Frenchie into sending him a horse over here."

"Thanks, then."

"Be my guest."

Jamie Fingall's guvnor, Basil Clutter, trained in Lambourn about a mile down the road from my house, but there wasn't time to seek him out before the next race, the three-mile 'chase, and after that I had to change again and go out to meet the princess in the parade ring, where Kinley was already stalking round.

As before, she was well guarded and seemed almost to be enjoying it, and I didn't know whether or not to alarm her with news of Nanterre. In the end I said only to Thomas, "The frog is here. Stay close to her," and he gave a sketchy thumbs-up, and looked determined. Thomas looking determined, I thought, would deter Attila the Hun.

Kinley made up for an otherwise disgusting afternoon, sending my spirits soaring from depths to dizzy heights.

The rapport between us, established almost instantly during his first hurdle race the previous November, had deepened in three succeeding outings so that by February he seemed to know in advance what I wanted him to do, as I knew what he wanted to do before he did it. The result was racing at its sublime best, an unexplainable synthesis at a primitive level and undoubtedly a shared joy.

Kinley jumped hurdles with a surge that had almost left me behind the first time I felt it, and even though every time since I'd know what was going to happen, I hadn't outgrown the surprise. The first hurdle left me gasping as usual, and by the end I reckoned we'd stolen twenty clean lengths in the air. He won jauntily and at a canter and I hoped Wykeham, watching on the box, would think it "a nice ride" and forgive me Cascade. Maynard Allardeck, I grimly thought, walking Kinley back along the path to the unsaddling enclosure, could find no vestige of an excuse that time to carp or cavil, and I realized that he and Kinley and Nanterre among them had at least stopped me brooding over Botticelli, Giorgione, Titian and Raphael.

The princess had her best stars in her blue eyes, looking as if guns hadn't been invented. I slid to the ground and we smiled in shared triumph, and I refrained with an effort from hugging her.

"He's ready for Cheltenham," she said, sticking out a glove to pat lightly the dark hide. "He's as good as Sir Ken."

Sir Ken had been an all-time star in the 1950s, winning three Champion Hurdles and numerous other top hurdling events. Owning a horse like Sir Ken was the ultimate for many who'd seen him, and the princess, who had, referred to him often.

"He has a long way to go," I said, unbuckling the girths. "He's still so young."

"Oh, yes," she said happily. "But . . ." She stopped abruptly, with a gasp. I looked at her and saw her eyes widen as she looked with horror above my right shoulder, and I whipped round fast to see what was there.

Henri Nanterre was there, staring at her.

I stood between them. Thomas and the friends were behind her, more occupied with avoiding Kinley's light-hearted hooves than with guarding their charge in the safest and most public of places.

Henri Nanterre momentarily transferred his gaze to my face and then, with shock, stared at me with his mouth opening.

I'd thought in the parade ring that since he'd been watching me, he'd found out who I was, but realized in that second that he'd thought of me then simply as the princess's jockey. He was confounded, it seemed, to identify me from the evening before.

"You're . . ." he said, for once at a loss for loud words. "You . . ."

"That's right," I said. "What do you want?"

He recovered with a snap from his surprise, narrowed his eyes at the princess, and said distinctly, "Jockeys can have accidents."

"So can people who carry guns," I said. "Is that what you came to say?"

It appeared, actually, that it more or less was.

"Go away," I said, much as he'd said it to me a day earlier up in the box, and to my complete astonishment, he went.

"Hey," Thomas said agitatedly, "that was . . . that was . . . wasn't it?"

"Yes, it was," I said, looping the girths round my saddle.

"Now you know what he looks like."

"Madam!" Thomas said penitently, "where did he come from?"

"I didn't see," she said, slightly breathless. "He was just in there."

"Fella moves like an eel," one of her friends said; and certainly there had been a sort of gliding speed to his departure.

"Well, my dears," the princess said to her friends, laughing a trifle shakily, "let's go up and celebrate this lovely win. And Kit . . . come up soon."

"Yes, Princess."

I weighed in and, as it was my last ride of the day, changed into street clothes. After that I made a detour over to the saddling boxes because Basil Clutter, as Jamie had told me, would be there, saddling up his runner for the last race.

Trainers in those places never had time to talk, but he did manage an answer or two, grudgingly, while he settled weight cloth, number cloth and saddle onto his restless charge's back.

"Frenchman? Nanterre, yes. Owns horses in France, trained by Villon. Industrialist of some sort. Where's he staying? How should I know? Ask the Roquevilles, he was with them. Roquevilles? Look, stop asking questions, ring me tonight, right?"

"Right," I said, sighing, and left him sponging out his horse's mouth so he should look clean and well-groomed before the public. Basil Clutter was hard-working and always bustling, saving money by doing Dusty's job, being his own traveling head-lad.

I went up to the princess's box, drank tea with lemon,

and relived for her and the friends the glories of Kinley's jumping. When it was time to go she said, "You will come back with me, won't you?" as if it were natural for me to do so, and I said, "Yes, certainly," as if I thought so too.

I picked up from my still parked car the overnight bag I habitually carried with me for contingencies, and we traveled without much trouble back to Eaton Square where I telephoned to Wykeham from the bamboo room. He was pleased, he said, about Kinley, but annoyed about Hillsborough. Dusty had told him I'd made no show and been hauled in by the Stewards for it, and what did I think I was doing, getting into trouble two days in a row?

I could strangle Dusty, I thought, and told Wykeham what I'd told the Stewards. "They accepted the explanation," I said. "Maynard Allardeck was one of them, and he's after me whatever I do."

"Yes, I suppose he is." He cheered up a good deal and even chuckled. "Bookmakers are taking bets on when— not whether—he'll get you suspended."

"Very funny," I said, not amused. "I'm still at Eaton Square, if you want me."

"Are you?" he said. "All right then. Goodnight, Kit."

"Goodnight, Wykeham."

I got through next to Basil Clutter, who told me the Roquevilles' number, and I caught the Roquevilles on their return from Newbury.

No, Bernard Roqueville said, he didn't know where Henri Nanterre was staying. Yes, he knew him, but not well. He'd met him in Paris at the races, at Longchamp, and Nanterre had renewed the acquaintanceship by inviting him and his wife for a drink at Newbury. Why was I interested? he asked.

I said I was hoping to locate Nanterre while he was in England. Bernard Roqueville regretted he couldn't help, and that was that.

A short lead going nowhere, I thought resignedly, putting down the receiver. Maybe the police would have better luck, although I feared that finding someone to give him a finger-wagging for waving an empty gun at a foreign princess wouldn't exactly have brought them out steaming in a full-scale manhunt.

I went downstairs to the sitting room and discussed Hillsborough's fall from grace over a drink with the princess, and later in the evening she, Roland de Brescou and I ate dinner together in the dining room, served by Dawson; and I thought only about twenty times of the Florentine Banquet up north.

It wasn't until after ten, saying goodnight, that she spoke about Nanterre.

"He said, didn't he, that jockeys have accidents."

"That's what he said. And so they do, pretty often."

"That wasn't what he meant."

"Perhaps not."

"I couldn't forgive myself if because of us you came to harm."

"That's what he's counting on. But I'll take my chance, and so will Thomas." And privately I thought that if her husband hadn't cracked instantly with a gun to his wife's head, he was unlikely to bend because of a whole barrage pointed at ours.

She said, remembering with a shiver, "Accidents would happen to those I liked . . . and employed."

"It's only noise. He won't do anything," I said encouragingly, and she said quietly that she hoped not, and went to bed.

I wandered again round the big house, checking its defenses, and wondered again what I'd overlooked.

In the morning, I found out.

I was already awake at seven when the intercom buzzed, and when I answered, a sleepy-voiced Dawson asked me to pick up the ordinary telephone as there was an incoming call for me. I picked up the receiver and found it was Wykeham on the line.

Racing stables wake early on Sundays, as on other days, and I was used to Wykeham's dawn thoughts, as he woke always by five. His voice that day, however, was as incoherently agitated as I'd ever heard it, and at first I wondered wildly what sins I might have committed in my sleep.

"D—did you hear what I s—said?" he stuttered. "Two of them! T—two of the p—princess's horses are d—dead."

"Two?" I said, sitting bolt upright in bed and feeling cold. "How? I mean . . . which two?"

"They're dead in their boxes. Stiff. They've been dead for hours . . ."

"Which two?" I said again, fearfully.

There was a silence at the other end. He had difficulty remembering their names at the best of times, and I could imagine that at that moment a whole roll-call of long-gone heroes was fumbling on his tongue.

"The two," he said in the end, "that ran on Friday."

I felt numb.

"Are you there?" he demanded.

"Yes . . . Do you mean . . . Cascade . . . and Cotopaxi?"

He *couldn't* mean it, I thought. It couldn't be true. Not Cotopaxi . . . not before the Grand National.

"Cascade," he said. "Cotopaxi."

Oh, no . . . "How?" I said.

"I've got the vet coming," he said. "Got him out of bed. I don't know how. That's his job. But two! One might die, I've known it happen, but not two . . . Tell the princess, Kit."

"That's your job," I protested.

"No, no, you're there . . . Break it to her. Better than on the phone. They're like children to her."

People she liked . . . Jesus Christ.

"What about Kinley?" I asked urgently.

"What?"

"Kinley . . . yesterday's hurdle winner."

"Oh, yes, him. He's all right. We checked all the others when we found these two. Their boxes were next to each other, I expect you remember . . . Tell the princess soon, Kit, won't you? We'll have to move these horses out. She'll have to say what she wants done with the carcasses. Though if they're poisoned . . ."

"Do you think they're poisoned?" I said.

"Don't know. Tell her now, Kit." He put his receiver down with a crash, and I replaced mine feeling I would burst with ineffectual anger.

To kill her horses! If Henri Nanterre had been there at that moment I would have stuffed his plastic gun down his loud-voiced throat. Cascade and Cotopaxi . . . people I knew, had known for years. I grieved for them as for friends.

Dawson agreed that his wife would wake the princess and tell her I had some sad news of one of her horses, and would wait for her in the sitting room. I dressed and went down there, and presently she came, without makeup and with anxious eyes.

"What is it?" she asked. "Which one?"

When I told her it was two, and which two, I watched her horror turn to horrified speculation.

"Oh, no, he couldn't," she exclaimed. "You don't think, do you . . ."

"If he has," I said, "he'll wish he hadn't."

She decided that we should go down to Wykeham's stable immediately, and wouldn't be deterred when I tried to persuade her not to.

"Of course I must go. Poor Wykeham, he'll need comforting. I should feel wrong if I didn't go."

Wykeham needed comforting less than she did, but by eight-thirty we were on the road, the princess in lipstick and Thomas placidly uncomplaining about the loss of his free day. My offer of driving the Rolls instead of him had been turned down like an improper suggestion.

Wykeham's establishment, an hour's drive south of London, was outside a small village on a slope of the Sussex Downs. Sprawling and complex, it had been enlarged haphazardly at intervals over a century, and was attractive to owners because of its maze of unexpected little courtyards, with eight or ten boxes in each, and holly bushes in red-painted tubs. To the stable staff, the picturesque convolution meant a lot of fetching and carrying, a lot of time wasted.

The princess's horses were spread through five of the courtyards, not filling any of them. Wykeham, like many trainers, preferred to scatter an owner's horses about rather than to clump them all together, and Cascade and Cotopaxi, as it happened, had been the only two belonging to the princess to be housed in the courtyard nearest the entrance drive.

One had to park in a central area and walk through

archways into the courtyards, and when he heard us arrive, Wykeham came out of the first courtyard to meet us.

He looked older by the week, I thought uneasily, watching him roguishly kiss the princess's hand. He always half flirted with her, with twinkling eyes and the remnants of a powerful old charm, but that morning he simply looked distracted, his white hair blowing when he removed his hat, his thin old hands shaking.

"My dear Wykeham," the princess said, alarmed. "You look so cold."

"Come into the house," he said, moving that way. "That's best."

The princess hesitated. "Are my poor horses still here?"

He nodded miserably. "The vet's with them."

"Then I think I'll see them," she said simply, and walked firmly into the courtyard, Wykeham and I following, not trying to dissuade her.

The doors of two of the boxes stood open, the interiors beyond lit palely with electric light, although there was full daylight outside. All the other boxes were firmly closed, and Wykeham was saying, "We've just left the other horses here in their boxes. They don't seem to be disturbed, because there's no blood. That's what would upset them, you know . . ."

The princess, only half listening, walked more slowly across to where her horses lay on the dark-brown peat on the floor of their boxes, their bodies silent humps, all flashing speed gone.

They had died with their night rugs on, but either the vet or Wykeham or the lads had unbuckled those and rolled them back against the walls. We looked in silence at the revealed dark sheen of Cascade and the snow-splashed chestnut of Cotopaxi.

Robin Curtiss, the tall and gangling boyish vet, had met the princess occasionally on other mornings, and me more often. Dressed in green protective overalls, he nodded to us both and excused himself from shaking hands, saying he would need to wash first.

The princess, acknowledging his greeting, asked at once and with composure, "Please tell me . . . how did they die?"

Robin Curtiss glanced at Wykeham and me, but neither of us would have tried to stop him answering, so he looked back to the princess and told her straight.

"Ma'am, they were shot. They knew nothing about it. They were shot with a humane killer. With a bolt."

6

Cascade was lying slantwise across the box, his head in shadow but not far from the door. Robin Curtiss stepped onto the peat and bent down, picking up the black forelock of hair that fell naturally forward from between the horse's ears.

"You can't clearly see, ma'am, as he's so dark, but there's the spot, right under his forelock, where the bolt went in." He straightened up, dusting his fingers on a handkerchief. "Easy to miss," he said. "You can't see what happened unless you're looking for it."

The princess turned away from her dead horse with a glitter of tears but a calm face. She stopped for a minute at the door of the next box, where Cotopaxi's rump was nearest, his head virtually out of sight near the manger.

"He's the same," Robin Curtiss said. "Under the forelock, almost invisible. It was expert, ma'am. They didn't suffer."

She nodded, swallowing, then, unable to speak, put one hand on Wykeham's arm and with the other waved toward the arch of the courtyard and Wykeham's house beyond. Robin Curtiss and I watched them go and he sighed in sympathy.

"Poor lady. It always takes them hard."

"They were murdered," I said. "That makes it harder."

"Yeah, they sure were murdered. Wykeham's called the police, though I told him it wasn't strictly necessary. The law's very vague about killing animals. But with them belonging to Princess Casilia, I suppose he thought it best. And he's in a tizzy about moving the bodies as soon as possible, but we don't know where he stands with the insurance company . . . whether in a case like this they have to be told first . . . and it's Sunday . . ." He stopped rambling and said more coherently, "You don't often see wounds like these, nowadays."

"What do you mean?" I asked.

"Captive bullets are old hat. Almost no one uses them now."

"Captive bullets?"

"The bolt. Called captive because the killing agent doesn't fly free of the gun, but is retracted back into it. Surely you know that?"

"Yes. I mean, I know the bolt retracts. I saw one, close to, years ago. I didn't know they were old hat. What do you use now, then?"

"You must have seen a horse put down," he said, astonished. "All those times, out on the course, when your mount breaks a leg . . ."

"It's only happened to me twice," I said. "And both times I took my saddle off and walked away."

I found myself thinking about it, trying to explain. "One moment you're in partnership with that big creature, and maybe you like him, and the next moment he's going to die . . . So I've not wanted to stay to watch. It may be odd to you, especially as I was brought up in a racing stable, but I never have seen the gun actually put to the head, and I've always vaguely imagined it was shot from the side, like through a human temple."

"Well," he said, still surprised and mildly amused, "you'd better get educated. You of all people. Look," he said, "look at Cotopaxi's head." He picked his way over the stiff chestnut legs until he could show me what he wanted. Cotopaxi's eyes were half open and milky, and although Robin Curtiss was totally unmoved, to me it was still no everyday matter.

"A horse's brain is only the size of a bunched fist," he said. "I suppose you know that?"

"Yes, I know it's small."

He nodded. "Most of a horse's head is empty space, all sinuses. The brain is up between the ears, at the top of the neck. The bone in that area is pretty solid. There's only the one place where you can be sure a bolt will do the job." He picked up Cotopaxi's forelock and pointed to a small disturbance of the pale hairs. "You take a line from the right ear to the left eye," he said, "and a line from the left ear to the right eye. Where the lines cross, that's the best . . . more or less the only . . . place to aim. And see? The bolt went into Cotopaxi at that exact spot. It wasn't any old haphazard job. Whoever did this knew exactly what to do."

"Well," I said thoughtfully, "now you've told me, I'd know what to do."

"Yes, but don't forget you have to get the angle right as well as the place. You have to aim straight at the spot where the spinal cord and the brain meet. Then the result's instantaneous and, as you can see, there's no blood."

"And meanwhile," I suggested ironically, "the horse is simply standing still letting all this happen?"

"Funnily enough, most of them do. Even so, I'm told that for short people it's difficult to get the hand up to the right angle at the right height."

"Yes, I'm sure," I said. I looked down at the waste of the great racing spirit. I'd sat on that back, shared that mind, felt the fluid majesty of those muscles, enjoyed his triumphs, schooled him as a young horse, thrilled to his growing strengths.

I made my way back to the outside air and Robin Curtiss followed me out, still matter-of-factly continuing my education.

"Apart from the difficulty of hitting the right spot, the bolt has another disadvantage, which is that although it retracts at once, the horse begins to fall just as quick, and the hard skull bones tend to bend the bolt after a lot of use, and the gun no longer works."

"So now you use something else?"

"Yes," he nodded. "A free bullet. I'll show you, if you like. I've a pistol in my car."

We walked unhurriedly out of the courtyard to where his car was parked not far from the princess's Rolls. He unlocked the trunk, and in there unlocked an attaché case, and from it produced a brown cloth, which he unwrapped.

Inside lay an automatic Luger-type pistol, which looked ordinary except for its barrel. Instead of the straight narrow barrel one would expect, there was a wide bulbous affair with a slanted oval opening at the end.

"This barrel sends the bullet out spinning in a spiral," he explained.

"Any old bullet?"

"It has to be the right caliber, but yes, any old bullet, and any old gun. That's one big advantage, you can weld a barrel like this onto any pistol you like. Well, the bullet leaves the gun with a lot of short-range energy, but because it's going in a spiral, almost any obstruction will stop it. So if you shoot a horse, the bullet will stop in its head. Mostly, that is." He smiled cheerfully. "Anyway, you don't have to be so accurate, as with a bolt, because the wobbling bullet does a lot more damage."

I looked at him thoughtfully. "How can you be so sure those two were killed with a bolt?"

"Oh, with the free bullet you get powder burns at the entry, and also blood coming down the nose, and probably also from the mouth. Not much, sometimes, but it's there, because of the widespread damage done inside, you see."

"Yes," I said, sighing, "I see." I watched him wrap up his gun again and said, "I suppose you have to have a license for that."

"Sure. And for the captive bullet also."

There must be thousands of humane killers about, I reflected. Every vet would have one. Every knackers' yard. A great many sheep and cattle farmers. The huntsman of every pack of hounds. People dealing with police horses . . . the probabilities seemed endless.

"So I suppose there are hundreds of the old bolt types lying around out of date and unused?"

"Well," he said, "under lock and key."

"Not last night."

"No."

"What time last night, would you say?"

He completed the stowing and locking away of his own pistol.

"Early," he said positively. "Not much after midnight. I know it was a cold night, but both horses were stone cold this morning. No internal temperature. That takes hours . . . and they were found at half six." He grinned. "The knackermen don't like fetching horses that have been dead that long. They have difficulty moving them when they're stiff, and getting them out of the boxes is a right problem." He peeled off his overalls and put them in the trunk. "There'll have to be post-mortems. The insurance people insist on it." He closed the car trunk and locked it. "We may as well go into the house."

"And leave them there?" I gestured back toward the courtyard.

"They're not going anywhere," he said, but he went back and shut the boxes' doors, in case, he said, any owners turned up for a nice Sunday look-round and had their sensibilities affronted. Robin's own sensibilities had been sensibly dumped during week one of his veterinary training, I guessed, but he didn't need a bedside manner to be a highly efficient minister to Wykeham's jumpers.

We went into Wykeham's house, ancient and rambling to match the yard, and found him and the princess consoling themselves with tea and memories, she at her most sustaining, he looking warmer and more in command, but puzzled.

He rose to his feet at our appearance and bustled me out of his sitting room making some flimsy remark about showing me where to make hot drinks, which I'd known for ten years.

"I don't understand," he said, leading the way into the kitchen. "Why doesn't she ask who killed them? It's the first thing I'd want to know. She hasn't mentioned it once. Just talks about the races in that way she has, and asking about the others. Why doesn't she want to know who killed them?"

"Mm," I said. "She suspects she knows."

"What? For God's sake then, Kit . . . who?"

I hesitated. He looked thin and shaky, with lines cut deep in the wrinkled old face, the dark freckles of age standing out starkly. "She'd have to tell you herself," I said, "but it's something to do with her husband's business. For what it's worth, I don't think you need worry about a traitor in your own camp. If she hasn't told you who she thinks it is, she won't tell anyone until she's discussed it with her husband, and they might decide to say nothing even then, they hate publicity so much."

"There's going to be publicity anyway," he said worriedly. "The ante-post cofavorite for the Grand National shot in his box. Even if we try, we can't keep that out of the papers."

I rattled about making fresh tea for Robin and myself, not relishing any more than he did the fuss lying ahead.

"All the same," I said, "your main worry isn't who. Your main worry is keeping all the others safe."

"Kit!" He was totally appalled. "B–bloody hell, K–Kit." He was back to stuttering. "It w–won't happen again."

"Well," I said temperately, but there was no way to soften it, "I'd say they're all at risk. The whole lot of her horses. Not immediately, not today. But if the princess and her husband decide on one particular course of action, which they may do, then they'll all be at risk, Kinley, perhaps, above all. So the thing to do is to apply our minds to defensive action."

"But Kit—"

"Dog patrols," I said.

"They're expensive . . ."

"The princess," I remarked, "is rich. Ask her. If she doesn't like the expense, I'll pay for them myself." Wykeham's mouth opened and closed again when I pointed out, "I've already lost the best chance I ever had of winning the Grand National. Her horses mean almost as much to me as they do to her and to you, and I'm damned well not going to let anyone pick them off two by two. So you get the security people here by tonight, and make sure there's someone about in the stable the whole time from now on, patrolling all the courtyards night and day."

"All right," he said slowly. "I'll fix it . . . If I knew who'd killed them, I'd kill him myself."

It sounded extraordinary, said that way, without anger, more as an unexpected self-discovery. What I'd wished I could do in fury, he proposed as a sane course of action; but people say these things, not meaning them, and he wouldn't have a mouse's chance physically, I thought regretfully, against the hawklike Nanterre.

Wykeham had been a Hercules in his youth, he'd told me, a powerhouse on legs with the joy of life pumping through his veins. "Joy of life," he'd said to me several times, "that's what I have. That's what you have. No one gets anywhere without it. Relish the struggle, that's the way."

He'd been an amateur jockey of note, and he'd dazzled and married the daughter of a mediumly successful trainer whose horses had started winning from the day Wykeham stepped into the yard. Now, fifty years on, with his strength gone, his wife dead and his own daughters grandmothers, he retained only the priceless ability to put the joy of life into his horses. He thought of little besides his horses, cared for little else, walked round at evening stables talking to each as a person, playing with some, admonishing others, coaxing a few, ignoring none.

I'd ridden for him from when I was nineteen, a fact he was apt to relate with complacency. "Spot 'em young," he'd told sundry owners. "That's the thing. I'm good at that." And he'd steadfastly given me, I sometimes reflected, exactly what he gave his charges; opportunity, trust and job-satisfaction.

He had trained a winner of the Grand National twice when I'd been at school, and in my time had come close, but it was only recently I'd realized how deeply he longed for a third slice of glory. The dead horse outside was for all of us a sickening, dragging, deflating disappointment.

"Cotopaxi," he said intensely, for once getting the name right, "was the one I would have saved first in a fire."

The princess and I traveled back to London without waiting for the police, the insurers or the slaughterer's men. ("So horrid, all of that.")

I'd expected her to talk as usual chiefly about her horses, but it was of Wykeham, it seemed, that she was thinking.

"Thirty-five years ago, before you were born," she said, "when I first went racing, Wykeham strode the scene like a Colossus. He was almost everything he says he was, a Hercules indeed. Powerful, successful, enormously attractive. Half the women swooning over him with their husbands spluttering . . ." She smiled at this memory. "I suppose it's hard for you to picture, Kit, knowing him only now, when he's old, but he was a splendid man. He still is, of course. I felt privileged, long ago, when he agreed to train my horses."

I glanced in fascination at her serene face. In the past I'd seen her often with Wykeham at the races, always deferring to him, tapping him playfully on the arm. I hadn't realized how much she must miss him now he stayed at home, how much she must regret the waning of such a titan.

A contemporary of my grandfather (and of Maynard Allardeck's father), Wykeham had been already a legend to me when he'd offered me the job. I'd accepted, almost dazed, and grown up fast, mature at twenty from the demands and responsibility he'd thrust on me. Hundreds of thousands of pounds' worth of horseflesh in my hands all the time, the success of the stable on my shoulders. He'd given me no allowances for youth, told me in no uncertain terms from the beginning that the whole enterprise rested finally on its jockey's skill, cool head and common sense, and told me if I didn't measure up to what was needed, too bad, but bye bye.

Shaken to my soul I'd wholeheartedly embraced what he offered, knowing there weren't two such chances in any life, and it had worked out fine, on the whole.

The princess's thoughts were following my own. "When Paul Peck had that dreadful fall and decided to retire," she said, "there we were at the height of the season with no stable jockey and all the other top jockeys signed up elsewhere. Wykeham told me and the other owners that there was this young Fielding boy in Newmarket who had been

riding as an amateur since he'd left school a year earlier . . ." She smiled. "We were very doubtful. Wykeham
said to trust him, he was never wrong. You know how
modest he is!" She paused, considering. "How long ago
was that?"

"Ten years last October."

She sighed. "Time goes so fast."

The older the faster . . . and for me also. Time no longer
stretched out to infinity. My years in the saddle would end,
maybe in four years, maybe five, whenever my body
stopped mending fast from the falls, and I was far from
ready to face the inexorability of the march of days. I intensely loved my job and dreaded its ending: anything
after, I thought, would be unutterably dreary.

The princess was silent for a while, her thoughts revert-
ing to Cascade and Cotopaxi.

"That bolt," she said tentatively, "I didn't like to ask
Robin . . . I really don't know what a humane killer looks
like."

"Robin says the bolt type isn't much used nowadays," I
said, "but I saw one once. My grandfather's vet showed
me. It looked like an extra-heavy pistol with a very thick
barrel. The bolt itself is a metal rod that slides inside the
barrel. When the trigger is pulled, the metal rod shoots
out, but because it's fixed inside to a spring, it retracts
immediately into the barrel again." I reflected. "The
rod . . . the bolt . . . is a bit thicker than a pencil, and
about four inches of it shoots out into . . . er . . . whatever
it's aimed at."

She was surprised. "So small? I'd thought, somehow,
you know, that it would be much bigger. And I didn't
know until today that it was . . . from in front."

She stopped talking abruptly and spent a fair time concentrating on the scenery. She had agreed without reserve to the dog patrols and had told Wykeham not to economize, the vulnerability of her other horses all too clearly understood.

"I had so been looking forward to the Grand National," she said eventually. "So very much."

"Yes, I know. So had I."

"You'll ride something else. For someone else."

"It won't be the same."

She patted my hand rather blindly. "It's such a waste," she said passionately. "So stupid. My husband would never trade in guns to save my horses. Never. And I wouldn't ask it. My dear, dear horses."

She struggled against tears and with a few sniffs and swallows won the battle, and when we reached Eaton Square she said we would go into the sitting room for a drink "to cheer ourselves up."

This good plan was revised, however, because the sitting room wasn't empty. Two people, sitting separately in armchairs, stood up as the princess walked in; and they were Prince Litsi and Danielle.

"My dear aunt," the prince said, bowing to her, kissing her hand, kissing her also on both cheeks. "Good morning."

"Good morning," she said faintly, and kissed Danielle. "I thought you were returning late this evening."

"The weather was frightful." The prince shook my hand. "Rain. Mist. Freezing. We decided yesterday we'd had enough and left early today, before breakfast."

I kissed Danielle's smooth cheek, wanting much more. She looked briefly into my eyes and said Dawson had told them I was staying in the house. I hadn't seen her for three weeks and I didn't want to hear about Dawson. Around the princess, however, one kept raw emotions under wraps, and I heard myself asking if she'd enjoyed the lectures, as if I hoped she had.

"They were great."

The princess decided that Prince Litsi, Danielle and myself should have the drinks, while she went upstairs to see her husband.

"You pour them," she said to her nephew. "And you, Kit, tell them everything that's been happening, will you? My dears . . . such horrid troubles." She waved a hand vaguely and went away, her back straight and slender, a statement in itself.

"Kit," the prince said, transferring his attention.

"Sir."

We stood as if assessing each other, he taller, ten years older, a man of a wider world. A big man, Prince Litsi, with heavy shoulders, a large head, full mouth, positive nose and pale intelligent eyes. Light-brown hair had begun to recede with distinction from his forehead, and a strong neck rose from a cream open-necked shirt. He looked as impressive as I'd remembered. It had been a year or more since we'd last met.

From his point of view I suppose he saw brown curly hair, light-brown eyes and a leanness imposed by the weights allocated to racehorses. Perhaps he saw also the man whose fiancée he had lured away to esoteric delights, but to do him justice there was nothing in his face of triumph or amusement.

"I'd like a drink," Danielle said abruptly. She sat down, waiting. "Litsi . . ."

His gaze lingered my way for another moment, then he turned to busy himself with the bottles. We had talked only on racecourses, I reflected, politely skimming the surface with postrace chit-chat. I knew him really as little as he knew me.

Without inquiring he poured white wine for Danielle and Scotch for himself and me.

"OK?" he said, proffering the glass.

"Yes, sir."

"Call me Litsi," he said easily. "All this protocol . . . I drop it in private. It's different for Aunt Casilia, but I never knew the old days. There's no throne anymore. I'll never be king. I live in the modern world . . . so will you let me?"

"Yes," I said. "If you like."

He nodded and sipped his drink. "You call Aunt Casilia 'Princess,' anyway," he pointed out.

"She asked me to."

"There you are, then." He waved a large hand, the subject closed. "Tell us what has been disturbing the household."

I looked at Danielle, dressed that day in black trousers, white shirt, blue sweater. She wore the usual pink lipstick, her cloudy dark hair held back in a blue band, everything known and loved and familiar. I wanted fiercely to hold her and feel her warmth against me, but she was sitting very firmly in an armchair built for one, and she would only meet my eyes for a flicker or two between concentrations on her drink.

I'm losing her, I thought, and couldn't bear it.

"Kit," the prince said, sitting down.

I took a slow breath, returned my gaze to his face, sat

down also, and began the long recital, starting chronologically with Henri Nanterre's bullying invasion on Friday afternoon and ending with the dead horses in Wykeham's stable that morning.

Litsi listened with increasing dismay, Danielle with simpler indignation.

"That's horrible," she said. "Poor Aunt Casilia." She frowned. "I guess it's not right to knuckle under to threats, but why is Uncle Roland so against guns? They're made all over the place, aren't they?"

"In France," Litsi said, "for a man of Roland's background to deal in guns would be considered despicable."

"But he doesn't live in France," Danielle said.

"He lives in himself." Litsi glanced my way. "You understand, don't you, why he can't?"

"Yes," I said.

He nodded. Danielle looked from one of us to the other and sighed. "The European mind, I guess. Trading in arms in America isn't unacceptable."

I thought it was probably less acceptable than she realized, and from his expression Litsi thought so too.

"Would the old four hundred families trade in arms?" he asked, but if he expected a negative he didn't get it.

"Yes, sure, I guess so," Danielle said. "I mean, why would it worry them?"

"Nevertheless," Litsi said, "for Roland it is impossible."

A voice on the stairs interrupted the discussion: a loud female voice, coming nearer.

"Where is everyone? In there?" She swept into view in the sitting-room doorway. "Dawson says the bamboo room is occupied. That's ridiculous. I always have the bamboo room. I've told Dawson to remove the things of whoever is in there."

Dawson gave me a bland look from over her shoulder and continued on his way to the floor above, carrying a suitcase.

"Now then," said the vision in the doorway. "Someone fix me a 'bloody.' The damn plane was two hours late."

"Good grief," Danielle said faintly, as all three of us rose to our feet. "Aunt Beatrice."

Aunt Beatrice, Roland de Brescou's sister, spoke with a slight French accent heavily overlaid with American. She had a mass of cloudy hair, not dark and long like Danielle's, but white going on pale orange. This framed and rose above a round face with round eyes and an expression of habitual determination.

"Danielle!" Beatrice said, thin eyebrows rising. "What are you doing here?"

"I work in England." Danielle went to her aunt to give her a dutiful peck. "Since last fall."

"Nobody tells me anything."

She was wearing a silk jersey suit—her outdoor mink having gone upstairs over Dawson's arm—with a heavy seal on a gold chain shining in front. Her fistful of rings looked like ounce-heavy nuggets, and a crocodile had passed on for her handbag. Beatrice, in short, enjoyed her cash.

She was clearly about to ask who Litsi and I were when the princess entered, having come downstairs, I reckoned, at record speed.

"Beatrice," she said, advancing with both hands outstretched and a sugar-substitute smile, "what a delightful surprise." She grasped Beatrice's arm and gave her two welcoming kisses, and I saw that her eyes were cold with dismay.

"Surprise?" Beatrice said, as they disengaged. "I called on Friday and spoke to your secretary. I told her to be sure to give you the message, and she said she would leave a note."

"Oh." A look of comprehension crossed the princess's face. "Then I expect it's down in the office, and I've missed it. We've been . . . rather busy."

"Casilia, about the bamboo room . . ." Beatrice began purposefully, and the princess with dexterity interrupted her.

"Do you know my nephew, Litsi?" she said, making sociable introductions. "Litsi, this is Roland's sister, Beatrice de Brescou Bunt. Did you leave Palm Beach last evening, Beatrice? Such a long flight from Miami."

"Casilia . . ." Beatrice shook hands with Litsi. "The bam—"

"And this is Danielle's fiancé, Christmas Fielding." The princess went on obliviously. "I don't think you've met him either. And now, my dear Beatrice, some tomato juice and vodka?"

"Casilia!" Beatrice said, sticking her toes in. "I always have the bamboo room."

I opened my mouth to say obligingly that I didn't mind moving, and received a rapid look of pure steel from the princess. I shut my mouth, amazed and amused, and held my facial muscles in limbo.

"Mrs. Dawson is unpacking your things in the rose room, Beatrice," the princess said firmly. "You'll be very comfortable there."

Beatrice, furious but outmaneuvered, allowed a genial Litsi to concoct her a bloody mary, she issuing sharp instructions about shaking the tomato juice, about how much Worcestershire sauce, how much lemon, how much ice. The princess watched with a wiped-clean expression of vague benevolence and Danielle was stifling her laughter.

"And now," Beatrice said, the drink finally fixed to her satisfaction, "what's all this rubbish about Roland refusing to expand the business?"

After a frosty second of immobility, the princess sat collectedly in an armchair, crossing her wrists and ankles in artificial composure.

Beatrice repeated her question insistently. She was never, I discovered, one to give up. Litsi busied himself with offering her a chair, smoothly settling her into it, discussing cushions and comfort and giving the princess time for mental remustering.

Litsi sat in a third armchair, leaning forward to Beatrice with smothering civility, and Danielle and I took places on a sofa, although with half an acre of flowered chintz between us.

"Roland is being obstructionist and I've come to tell him I object. He must change his mind at once. It is ridiculous not to move with the times and it's time to look for new markets."

The princess looked at me, and I nodded. We had heard much the same thing, even some of the identical phrases, from Henri Nanterre on Friday evening.

"How do you know of any business proposals?" the princess asked.

"That dynamic young son of Louis Nanterre told me, of course. He made a special journey to see me, and explained the whole thing. He asked me to persuade Roland to drag himself into the twentieth century, let alone the twenty-first, and I decided I would come over here myself and insist on it."

"You do know," I said, "that he's proposing to make and export guns?"

"Of course," she said. "But only plastic parts of guns. Roland is old-fashioned. I've a good friend in Palm Beach whose husband's corporation makes missiles for the Defense Department. Where's the difference?" She paused. "And what business is it of yours?" Her gaze traveled to Danielle, and she remembered. "I suppose if you're engaged to Danielle," she said grudgingly, "then it's marginally your business. I didn't know Danielle was engaged. Nobody tells me anything."

Henri Nanterre, I thought, had told her a great deal too much.

"Beatrice," the princess said, "I'm sure you'll want to wash after your journey. Dawson is arranging a late lunch for us, although as we didn't know there would be so many . . ."

"I want to talk to Roland," Beatrice said obstinately.

"Yes, later. He's resting just now." The princess stood, and we also, waiting for Danielle's aunt to be impelled upstairs by the sheer unanimity of our expectant good manners; and it was interesting, I thought, that she gave in, put down her unfinished drink and went, albeit grumbling as she departed that she expected to be reinstated in the bamboo room by the following day at the latest.

"She's relentless," Danielle said as her voice faded away. "She always gets what she wants. And anyway, the bamboo room's empty, isn't it? How odd of Aunt Casilia to refuse it."

"I've slept in there the last two nights," I said.

"Have you indeed!" Litsi's voice answered. "In accommodation above princes."

"That's not fair," Danielle said. "You said you preferred those rooms on the ground floor because you could go in and out without disturbing anyone."

Litsi looked at her fondly. "So I do. I only meant that Aunt Casilia must esteem your fiancé highly."

"Yes," Danielle said, giving me an embarrassed glance. "She does."

We all sat down again, though Danielle came no nearer to me on the sofa.

Litsi said, "Why did Henri Nanterre recruit your aunt Beatrice so diligently? She won't change Roland's mind."

"She lives on de Brescou money," Danielle said unexpectedly. "My parents do now as well, now that my black sheep of a father has been accepted back into the fold. Uncle Roland set up generous trusts for everybody out of the revenues from his land, but for as long as I've known my aunt she's complained he could afford more."

"For as long as you've known her?" Litsi echoed. "Haven't you always known her?"

She shook her head. "She disapproved of Dad. He left home originally under the heaviest of clouds, though what exactly he did, he's never told me; he just laughs if I ask, but it must have been pretty bad. It was a choice, Mom says, between exile and jail, and he chose California. She and I came on the scene a lot later. Anyway, about eight years ago Aunt Beatrice suddenly swooped down on us to see what had become of her disgraced little brother, and I've seen her several times since then. She married an American businessman way way back, and it was after he died she set out to track Dad down. It took her two years—the United States is a big country—but she looks on persistence as a prime virtue. She lives in a marvelous Spanish-style house in Palm Beach—I stayed there for a few days one spring break—and she makes trips to New York, and every summer she travels in Europe and spends some time in 'our chateau,' as she calls it."

Litsi was nodding. "Aunt Casilia has been known to visit me in Paris when her sister-in-law stays too long. Aunt Casilia and Roland," he explained to me unnecessarily, "go to the chateau for six weeks or so around July and August, to seek some country air and play their part as landowners. Did you know?"

"They mention it sometimes," I said.

"Yes, of course."

"What's the chateau like?" Danielle asked.

"Not a Disney castle," Litsi answered, smiling. "More like a large Georgian country house, built of light-colored stone, with shutters on all the windows. Chateau de Brescou. The local town is built on land south of Bordeaux mostly owned by Roland, and he takes moral and civic pride in its well-being. Even without the construction company, he could fund a mini-Olympics on the income he receives in rents, and his estates are run as the company used to be, with good managers and scrupulous fairness."

"He *cannot*," I commented, "deal in arms."

Danielle sighed. "I do see," she admitted, "that with all that old aristocratic honor, he simply couldn't face it."

"But I'm really surprised," I said, "that Beatrice could face it quite easily. I would have thought she would have shared her brother's feelings."

"I'll bet," Danielle said, "that Henri Nanterre promised her a million-dollar handout if she got Uncle Roland to change his mind."

"In that case," I suggested mildly, "your uncle could offer her double to go back to Palm Beach and stay there."

Danielle looked shocked. "That wouldn't be right."

"Morally indefensible," I agreed, "but pragmatically an effective solution."

Litsi's gaze was thoughtful on my face. "Do you think she's such a threat?"

"I think she could be like water dripping on a stone, wearing it away. Like water dripping on a man's forehead, driving him mad."

"The water torture," Litsi said. "I'm told it feels like a red-hot poker after a while, drilling a hole into the skull."

"She's just like that," Danielle said.

There was a short silence while we contemplated the boring capacities of Beatrice de Brescou Bunt, and then Litsi said consideringly, "It might be a good idea to tell her about the document you witnessed. Tell her the bad news that all four of us would have to agree to the guns, and assure her that even if she drives Roland to collapse, she'll still have to deal with me."

"Don't tell her," Danielle begged. "She'll give none of us any peace."

Neither of them had objected to the use made of them in their absence; on the contrary, they had been pleased. "It makes us a family," Danielle had said, and it was I, the witness, who had felt excluded.

"Upstairs," I said, reflecting, "I've got what I think is a duplicate of the form Henri Nanterre wanted Monsieur de Brescou to sign. It is in French. Would you like to see it?"

"Very much," Litsi said.

"Right."

I went upstairs to fetch it and found Beatrice Bunt in my bedroom.

"What are you doing here?" she demanded.

"I came to fetch something," I said.

She was holding the bright-blue running shorts I usually slept in, which I had stored that morning in the bedside table drawer on top of Nanterre's form. The drawer was open, the paper presumably inside.

"These are yours?" she said in disbelief. "*You* are using this room?"

"That's right." I walked over to her, took the shorts from her hand and returned them to the drawer. The form, I was relieved to see, lay there undisturbed.

"In that case," she said with triumph, "there's no problem. I shall have this room, and you can have the other. I always have the bamboo suite, it's the accepted thing. I see some of your things are in the bathroom. It won't take long to switch them over."

I'd left the door open when I went in and, perhaps hearing her voice, the princess came inquiringly to see what was going on.

"I've told this young man to move, Casilia," Beatrice said, "because of course this is my room, naturally."

"Danielle's fiancé," the princess said calmly, "stays in this room as long as he stays in this house. Now come along, Beatrice, do, the rose room is extremely comfortable, you'll find."

"It's half the size of this one, and there's no dressing room."

The princess gave her a bland look, admirably concealing irritation. "When Kit leaves, you shall have the bamboo room, of course."

"I thought you said his name was Christmas."

"So it is," the princess agreed. "He was born on Christmas Day. Come along, Beatrice, let's go down for this very delayed lunch." She positively shepherded her sister-in-law out into the passage, and returned a second later for one brief and remarkable sentence, half instruction, half entreaty.

"Stay in this house," she said, "until she is gone."

After lunch, Litsi, Danielle and I went up to the disputed territory to look at the form, Litsi observing that his money was on Beatrice to winkle me out of all this splendor before tomorrow night.

"Did you see the dagger looks you were getting across the mousse."

"Couldn't miss them."

"And those pointed remarks about good manners, unselfishness, and the proper precedence of rank?"

The princess had behaved as if she hadn't heard, sweetly making inquiries about Beatrice's health, her dogs and the weather in Florida in February. Roland de Brescou, as very often, had remained upstairs for lunch, his door barricaded, I had no doubt. The princess with soft words would defend him.

"Well," I said, "here's this form."

I retrieved it from under my blue shorts and gave it to Litsi, who wandered with it over to a group of comfortable chairs near the window. He read it attentively, sitting down absentmindedly, a big man with natural presence and unextended power. I liked him and because of Danielle feared him, a contradictory jumble of emotion, but I also trusted his overall air of amiable competence.

I moved across the room to join him, and Danielle also, and after a while he raised his head and frowned.

"For a start," he said, "this is not an application form for a license to make or export arms. Are you sure that's what Nanterre said it was?"

I thought back. "As far as I remember, it was the lawyer Gerald Greening who said it was a government form for preliminary application for a license. I understood that that was what Henri Nanterre had told the princess in her box at Newbury."

"Well, it isn't a government form at all. It isn't an application for any sort of license. What it is is a very vague and general form that would be used by simple people to draw up a contract." He paused. "In England I believe one can buy from stationers' shops a printed form for making a will. The legal words are all there to ensure that the will is properly executed. One simply inserts in the spaces what one wants done, like leaving the car to one's grandson. It's what's written into the spaces that really counts. Well, this form is rather like that. The legal form of words is correct, so that this would be a binding document, if properly signed and properly witnessed." He glanced down at the paper. "It's impossible to tell of course how Henri Nanterre had filled in all the spaces, but I would guess that overall it would say merely that the parties named in the contract had agreed on the course of action outlined by the accompanying documents. I would think that this form would be attached to, and act as page one of, a bulk of papers that would include all sorts of things like factory capacity, overseas sales forces, preliminary orders from customers and the specifications of the guns proposed to be manufactured. All sorts of things. But this simple form with Roland's signature on it would validate the whole presentation. It would be taken very seriously indeed as a full statement of intent. With this in his hands Henri Nanterre could apply for his license immediately."

"And get it," I said. "He was sure of it."

"Yes."

"But Uncle Roland could say he was forced into signing," Danielle said. "He could repudiate it, couldn't he?"

"He might have been able to nullify an application form quite easily, but with a contract it's much more difficult. He could plead threats and harassment, but the legal position might be that it was too late to change his mind, once he'd surrendered."

"And if he did get the contract overthrown," I said reflectively, "Henri Nanterre could start his harassment over again. There could be no end to it, until the contract was re-signed."

"But all four of us have to sign now," Danielle said. "What if we all say we won't?"

"I think," I said, "if your uncle decided to sign, you would all follow his lead."

Litsi nodded. "The four-signature agreement is a delaying tactic, not a solution."

"And what," Danielle said flatly, "is a solution?"

Litsi looked my way. "Put Kit to work on it." He smiled. "Danielle told me you tied all sorts of strong men into knots last November. Can't you do it again?"

"This is a bit different," I said.

"What happened last time?" he asked. "Danielle told me no details."

"A newspaper was giving my sister, Holly, and her husband a lot of unearned bad publicity—he's a racehorse trainer and they said he was going broke—and basically I got them to apologize and pay Bobby some compensation."

"And Bobby's appalling father," Danielle said, "tell Litsi about him."

She could look at me, now, as if everything were the same. I tried with probably little success to keep my general anxiety about her from showing too much and told the story to Litsi.

"The real reason for the attacks on Bobby was to get at his father, who'd been trying to take over the newspaper. Bobby's father, Maynard Allardeck, was in line for a knighthood, and the newspaper's idea was to discredit him so that he shouldn't get one. Maynard was a real pain, a ruthless burden on Bobby's back. So I . . . er . . . got him off."

"How?" Litsi asked curiously.

"Maynard," I said, "makes fortunes by lending money to dicky businesses. He puts them straight and then calls in the loan. The businesses can't repay him, so he takes over the businesses, and shortly after sells off their assets, closing them down. The smiling shark comes along and gobbles up the grateful minnows, who don't discover their mistake until they're half digested."

"So what did you do?" Litsi said.

"Well, I went around filming interviews with some of the people he had damaged. They were pretty emotional stuff. An old couple he'd cheated out of a star racehorse, a man whose son committed suicide when he lost his business, and a foolish boy who'd been led into gambling away half his inheritance."

"I saw the film," Danielle said. "It hit like hammers. It made me cry. Kit threatened to send videotape copies to all sorts of people if Maynard did any more harm to Bobby. And you've forgotten to say," she said to me, "that Maynard tried to get Bobby to kill you."

Litsi blinked. "To kill . . ."

"Mm," I said. "He's paranoid about Bobby marrying my sister. He's been programmed from birth to hate all Fieldings . . . he told Bobby when he was a little boy that if he was ever naughty the Fieldings would eat him."

I explained about the depth and bitterness of the old Fielding-Allardeck feud.

"Bobby and I," I said, "have made it up and are friends, but his father can't stand that."

"Bobby thinks," Danielle said to me, "that Maynard also can't stand you being successful. He wouldn't feel so murderous if you'd been a lousy jockey."

"Maynard," I told Litsi, smiling, "is a member of the Jockey Club and also now turns up quite often as a Steward at various racecourses. He would dearly like to see me lose my license."

"Which he can't manage unfairly," Litsi said thoughtfully, "because of the existence of the film."

"It's a standoff," I agreed equably.

"OK," Litsi said, "then how about a standoff for Henri Nanterre?"

"I don't know enough about him. I'd known Maynard all my life. I don't know anything about arms or anyone who deals in them."

Litsi pursed his lips. "I think I could arrange that," he said.

I telephoned to Wykeham later that Sunday afternoon and listened to the weariness in his voice. His day had been a procession of frustrations and difficulties that were not yet over. The dog-patrol man, complete with dog, was sitting in his kitchen drinking tea and complaining that the weather was freezing. Wykeham was afraid most of the patrolling would be done all night indoors.

"Is it freezing really?" I asked. Freezing was always bad news because racing would be abandoned, frosty ground being hard, slippery and dangerous.

"Two degrees off it."

Wykeham kept thermometers above the outdoor water taps so he could switch on low-powered battery heaters in a heavy freeze and keep the water flowing. His whole stable was rich with gadgets he'd adopted over the years, like infrared lights in the boxes to keep the horses warm and healthy.

"A policeman came," Wykeham said. "A detective constable. He said it was probably some boys' prank. I ask you! I told him it was no prank to shoot two horses expertly, but he said it was amazing what boys got up to. He said he'd seen worse things. He'd seen ponies in fields with their eyes gouged out. It was c–c–crazy. I said Cotopaxi was no pony, he was cofavorite for the Grand National, and he said it was b–bad luck on the owner."

"Did he promise any action?"

"He said he would come back tomorrow and take statements from the lads, but I don't think they know anything. Pete, who looked after Cotopaxi, has been in tears and the others are all indignant. It's worse for them than having one killed accidentally."

"For us all," I said.

"Yes." He sighed. "It didn't help that the slaughterers had so much trouble getting the bodies out. I didn't watch. I couldn't. I l–loved both those horses."

To the slaughterers, of course, dead horses were just so much dogmeat, and although it was perhaps a properly unsentimental way of looking at it, it wasn't always possible for someone like Wykeham, who had cared for them, talked to them, planned for them and lived through their lives. Trainers of steeplechasers usually knew their charges for a longer span than Flat-race trainers, ten years or more sometimes as opposed to three or four. When Wykeham said he loved a horse, he meant it.

He wouldn't yet have the same feeling for Kinley, I thought. Kinley, the bright star, young and fizzing. Kinley was excitement, not an old buddy.

"Look after Kinley," I said.

"Yes, I've moved him. He's in the corner box."

The corner box, always the last to be used, couldn't be

reached directly from any courtyard but only through another box. Its position was a nuisance for lads, but it was also the most secret and safe place in the stable.

"That's great," I said with relief, "and now, what about tomorrow?"

"Tomorrow?"

"Plumpton races."

There was a slight silence while he reorganized his thoughts. He always sent a bunch of horses to go-ahead Plumpton because it was one of his nearest courses, and as far as I knew I was riding six of them.

"Dusty has a list," he said eventually.

"OK."

"Just ride them as you think best."

"All right."

"Goodnight, then, Kit."

"Goodnight, Wykeham."

At least he'd got my name right, I thought, disconnecting. Perhaps all the right horses would arrive at Plumpton.

I went down there on the train the next morning, feeling glad, as the miles rolled by, to be away from the Eaton Square house. Even diluted by the princess, Litsi and Danielle, an evening spent with Beatrice de Brescou Bunt had opened vistas of social punishment I would as soon have remained closed. I had excused myself early, to openly reproachful looks from the others, but even in sleep I seemed to hear that insistent complaining voice.

When I'd left in the morning Litsi had said he would himself spend most of the day with Roland after John Grundy had left. The princess and Danielle would occupy Beatrice. Danielle, working evening shifts in her television news company, would have to leave it all to the princess from soon after five-thirty. I had promised to return from Plumpton as soon as possible, but truthfully I was happy to be presented with a very good reason not to, in the shape of a message awaiting me in the changing room. Relayed from the stable manager at Newbury racecourse, the note requested me to remove my car from where I'd left it, as the space was urgently required for something else.

I telephoned to Eaton Square, and as it happened Danielle answered.

I explained about the car. "I'll get a lift from Plumpton to Newbury. I think I'd better sleep at home in Lambourn, though, as I've got to go to Devon to race tomorrow. Will you apologize to the princess? Tell her I'll come back tomorrow night, after racing, if she'd like."

"Deserter," Danielle said. "You sound suspiciously pleased."

"It does make sense in terms of miles," I said.

"Tell it to the marines."

"Look after yourself," I said.

She said, "Yes," on a sigh after a pause, and put the phone down. Sometimes it seemed that everything was the same between us, and then, on a sigh, it wasn't. Without much enthusiasm, I went in search of Dusty, who had arrived with the right horses, the right colors for me to wear and a poor opinion of the detective constable for trying to question the lads while they were working. No one knew anything, anyway, Dusty said, and the lads were in a mood for the lynching of any prowling stranger. The head-lad (not Dusty, who was the traveling head-lad) had looked round the courtyards as usual at about eleven on Saturday night, when all had appeared quiet. He hadn't looked into all the eighty boxes, only one or two whose inmates weren't well, and he hadn't looked at either Cascade or Cotopaxi. He'd looked in on Kinley and Hillsborough to make sure they'd eaten their food after racing, and he'd gone home to bed. What more could anyone do? Dusty demanded.

"No one's blaming anybody," I said.

He said, "Not so far," darkly, and took my saddle away to put it on the right horse for the first race.

We stage-managed the afternoon between us, as so often, he producing and saddling the horses, I riding them, both of us doing a public relations job on the various owners, congratulating, commiserating, explaining and excusing. We ended with a typical day of two winners, a second, two also-rans and a faller, the last giving me a soft landing and no problems.

"Thanks, Dusty," I said at the end. "Thanks for everything."

"What do you mean?" he said suspiciously.

"I just meant, six races is a busy day for you, and it all went well."

"It would have gone better if you hadn't fallen off in the fifth," he said sourly.

I hadn't fallen off. The horse had gone right down under me, leaving grass stains on its number cloth. Dusty knew it perfectly well.

"Well," I said. "Thanks, anyway."

He gave me an unsmiling nod and hurried off, and in essential discord we would no doubt act as a team at Newton Abbot the next day and at Ascot the next, effective but cold.

Two other jockeys who lived in Lambourn gave me a lift back to Newbury, and I collected my car from its extended parking there and drove home to my house on the hill.

I lit the log fire to cheer things up a bit, ate some grilled chicken and telephoned to Wykeham.

He'd had another wearing day. The insurers had been questioning his security, the detectives had annoyed all the lads, and the dog-patrol man had been found asleep in the hay barn by the head-lad when he arrived at six in the morning. Wykeham had informed Weatherbys, the Jockey Club secretariat, of the horses' deaths (a routine obligation) and all afternoon his telephone had been driving him mad as one newspaper after another had called up to ask if it were true that they'd been murdered.

Finally, he said, the princess had rung to say she'd canceled her visit to her friends at Newton Abbot and wouldn't be there to watch her horses, and please would Wykeham tell Kit that yes, she did very definitely want him to return to Eaton Square as soon as he could.

"What's going on there?" Wykeham asked, without pressing interest. "She sounds unlike herself."

"Her sister-in-law arrived unexpectedly."

"Oh?" He didn't pursue it. "Well done, today, with the winners."

"Thanks." I waited, expecting to hear that Dusty had said I'd fallen off, but I'd misjudged the old crosspatch. "Dusty says Torquil went down flat in the fifth. Were you all right?"

"Not a scratch," I said, much surprised.

"Good. About tomorrow, then . . ."

We discussed the next day's runners and eventually said goodnight, and he called me Kit, which made it twice in a row. I would know things were returning to normal, I thought, when he went back to Paul.

I played back all the messages on my answering machine and found most of them echoes of Wykeham's: a whole column of pressmen wanted to know my feelings on the loss of Cotopaxi. Just as well, I thought, that I hadn't been at home to express them.

There was an inquiry from a Devon trainer as to whether I could ride two for him at Newton Abbot, his own jockey having been hurt: I looked up the horses in the form book, telephoned to accept, and peacefully went to bed.

The telephone woke me at approximately two-thirty.

"Hello," I said sleepily, squinting at the unwelcome news on my watch. "Who is it?"

"Kit . . ."

I came wide awake in a split second. It was Danielle's voice, very distressed.

"Where are you?" I said.

"I . . . oh . . . I need . . . I'm in a shop."

"Did you say shock or shop?" I said.

"Oh . . ." She gulped audibly. "Both, I suppose."

"What's happened? Take a deep breath. Tell me slowly."

"I left the studio . . . ten after two . . . started to drive home." She stopped. She always finished at two, when the studio closed and all the American news-gatherers left for the night, and drove her own small Ford car back to the garage behind Eaton Square where Thomas kept the Rolls.

"Go on," I said.

"A car seemed to be following me. Then I had a flat tire. I had to stop. I . . . ." She swallowed again. "I found . . . I had two tires almost flat. And the other car stopped and a man got out . . . He was wearing . . . a hood."

Jesus Christ, I thought.

"I ran," Danielle said, audibly trying to stifle near-hysteria. "He started after me . . . I ran and ran . . . I saw this shop . . . it's open all night . . . and I ran in here. But the man here doesn't like it. He let me use his telephone . . . but I've no money, I left my purse and my coat in the car . . and I don't know . . . what to do . . ."

"What you do," I said, "is stay there until I reach you."

"Yes, but . . . the man here doesn't want me to . . . and somewhere outside . . . I can't . . . I simply can't go outside. I feel so stupid . . . but I'm frightened."

"Yes, you've good reason to be. I'll come at once. You let me talk to the man in the shop . . . and don't worry, I'll be there in under an hour."

She said, "All right," faintly, and in a few seconds an Asian-sounding voice said, "Hello?"

"My young lady," I said, "needs your help. You keep her warm, give her a hot drink, make her comfortable until I arrive, and I'll pay you."

"Cash," he said economically.

"Yes, cash."

"Fifty pounds," he said.

"For that," I said, "you look after her very well indeed. And now tell me your address. How do I find you?"

He gave me directions and told me earnestly he would look after the lady, I wasn't to hurry, I would be sure to bring the cash, wouldn't I, and I assured him again that yes, I would.

I dressed, swept some spare clothes into a bag, locked the house and broke the speed limit to London. After a couple of wrong turns and an inquiry from an unwilling night-walker I found the street and the row of dark shops, with one brightly lit near the end next to the Undergound station. I stopped with a jerk on double yellow lines and went inside.

The place was a narrow minisupermarket with a take-away hot-food glass cabinet near the door, the whole of the rest of the space packed to the ceiling with provisions smelling subtly of spices. Two customers were choosing hot food, a third further down the shop looking at tins, but there was no sign of Danielle.

The Asian man serving, smoothly round of face, plump of body and drugged as to eye, gave me a brief glance as I hurried in, and went back methodically to picking out the customers' choices, chapatis and sausage rolls, with tongs.

"The young lady," I said.

He behaved as if he hadn't heard, wrapping the purchases, adding up the cost.

"Where is she?" I insisted, and might as well not have spoken. The Asian talked to his customers in a language I'd never heard; took their money, gave them change, waited until they had left.

"Where is she?" I said forcefully, growing anxious.

"Give me the money." His eyes spoke eloquently of his need for cash. "She is safe."

"Where?"

"At the back of the shop, behind the door. Give me the money."

I gave him what he'd asked, left him counting it, and fairly sprinted where he'd pointed. I reached a back wall stocked from floor to ceiling like the rest, and began to feel acutely angry before I saw that the door, too, was covered with racks.

In a small space surrounded by packets of coffee I spotted the doorknob; grasped it, turned it, pushed the door inward. It led into a room piled with more stock in brown cardboard boxes, leaving only a small space for a desk, a chair and a single-bar electric fire.

Danielle was sitting on the chair, huddled into a big dark masculine overcoat, trying to keep warm by the inadequate heater and staring blindly into space.

"Hi," I said.

The look of unplumbable relief on her face was as good, I supposed, as a passionate kiss, which actually I didn't get. She stood, though, and slid into my arms as if coming home, and I held her tight, not feeling her much through the thick coat, smelling the musky Eastern fragrance of the dark material, smoothing Danielle's hair and breathing deeply with content.

She slowly disengaged herself after a while, though I could have stood there for hours.

"You must think I'm stupid," she said shakily, sniffing and wiping her eyes on her knuckles. "A real fool."

"Far from it."

"I'm so glad to see you." It was heartfelt: true.

"Come on, then," I said, much comforted. "We'd best be going."

She slid out of the oversize overcoat and laid it on the chair, shivering a little in her shirt, sweater and trousers. The chill of shock, I thought, because neither the shop nor the storeroom was actively cold

"There's a rug in my car," I said. "And then we'll go and fetch your coat."

She nodded, and we went up through the shop toward the street door.

"Thank you," I said to the Asian.

"Did you switch the fire off?" he demanded.

I shook my head. He looked displeased.

"Goodnight," I said, and Danielle said, "Thank you."

He looked at us with the drugged eyes and didn't an-

swer, and after a few seconds we left him and crossed the
pavement to the car.

"He wasn't bad, really," Danielle said, as I draped the
rug round her shoulders. "He gave me some coffee from
that hot counter, and offered me some food, but I couldn't
eat it."

I closed her into the passenger seat, went round and slid
behind the wheel, beside her.

"Where's your car?" I said.

She had difficulty in remembering, which wasn't surprising considering the panic of her flight.

"I'd gone only two miles, I guess, when I realized I had a
flat. I pulled in off the highway. If we go back toward the
studio . . . but I can't remember . . ."

"We'll find it," I said. "You can't have run far." And we
found it in fact quite easily, its rear pointing toward us
down a seedy side turning as we coasted along.

I left her in my car while I took a look. Her coat and
handbag had vanished, also the windshield wipers and the
radio. Remarkable, I thought, that the car itself was still
there, despite the two flat tires, as the keys were still in the
ignition. I took them out, locked the doors and went back
to Danielle with the bad news and the good.

"You still have a car," I said, "but it could be stripped or
gone by morning if we don't get it towed."

She nodded numbly and stayed in the car again when I
found an all-night garage with a tow truck, and negotiated
with the incumbents. Sure, they said lazily, accepting the
car's keys, registration number and whereabouts. Leave it
to them, they would fetch it at once, fix the tires, replace
the windshield wipers, and it would be ready for collection
in the morning.

It wasn't until we were again on our way toward Eaton Square that Danielle said any more about her would-be attacker, and then it was unwillingly.

"Do you think he was a rapist?" she said tautly.

"It seems . . . well . . . likely, I'm afraid." I tried to picture him. "What sort of clothes was he wearing? What sort of hood?"

"I didn't notice," she began, and then realized that she remembered more than she'd thought. "A suit. An ordinary man's suit. And polished leather shoes. The light shone on them, and I could hear them tapping on the ground. How odd. The hood was . . . a woolen hat, dark, pulled down, with holes for eyes and mouth."

"Horrible," I said with sympathy.

"I think he was waiting for me to leave the studio." She shuddered. "Do you think he fixed my tires?"

"Two flat at once is no coincidence."

"What do you think I should do?"

"Tell the police?" I suggested.

"No, certainly not. They think any young woman driving alone in the middle of the night is asking for trouble."

"All the same . . ."

"Do you know," she said, "that a friend of a friend of mine—an American—was driving along in London, like I was, doing absolutely nothing wrong, when she was stopped by the police and taken to the police station? They stripped her! Can you believe it? They said they were looking for drugs or bombs. There was a terrorist scare on, and they thought she had a suspicious accent. It took her ages to get people to wake up and say she was truly going home after working late. She's been a wreck ever since, and gave up her job."

"It does seem unbelievable," I agreed.

"It happened," she said.

"They're not all like that," I said mildly.

She decided nevertheless to tell only her colleagues in the studio, saying they should step up security round the parked cars.

"I'm sorry I made you come so far," she said, not particularly sounding it. "But I didn't want the police, and otherwise it meant waking Dawson and getting someone there to come for me. I felt shattered . . . I knew you would come."

"Mm."

She sighed, some of the tension at last leaving her voice. "There wasn't much in my purse, that's one good thing. Just lipstick and a hairbrush, not much money. No credit cards. I never take much with me to work."

I nodded. "What about keys?"

"Oh . . ."

"The front-door key of Eaton Square?"

"Yes," she said, dismayed. "And the key to the back door of the studios, where the staff go in. I'll have to tell them in the morning, when the day shift gets there."

"Did you have anything with you that had the Eaton Square address on it?"

"No," she said positively. "I cleaned the whole car out this afternoon . . . I did it really to evade Aunt Beatrice . . . and I changed purses. I had no letters or anything like that with me."

"That's something," I said.

"You're so practical."

"I would tell the police," I said neutrally.

"No. You don't understand, you're not female."

There seemed to be no reply to that, so I pressed her no

further. I drove back to Eaton Square as I'd done so many times before, driving her home from work, and it wasn't until we were nearly there that I wondered whether the hooded man could possibly have been not a rapist at all, but Henri Nanterre.

On the face of it, it didn't seem possible, but coming at that particular time it had to be considered. If it in fact were part of the campaign of harassment and accidents, then we would hear about it, as about the horses also: no act of terrorism was complete without the boasting afterward.

Danielle had never seen Henri Nanterre and wouldn't have known his general shape, weight, and way of moving. Conversely, nor would he have turned up in Chiswick when he had no reason to know she was in England, even if he knew of her actual existence.

"You're very quiet all of a sudden," Danielle said, sounding no longer frightened but consequently sleepy. "What are you thinking?"

I glanced at her softening face, seeing the taut lines of strain smoothing out. Three or four times we'd known what the other was thinking, in the sort of telepathic jump that sometimes occurred between people who knew each other well, but not on a regular basis, and not lately. I was glad at that moment that she couldn't read my thoughts, not knowing if she would be more or less worried if she did.

"Tomorrow evening," I said, "get Thomas to drive you to work. He's not going to Devon now . . . and I'll fetch you."

"But if you're riding in Devon . . ."

"I'll go down and back on the train," I said. "I should be back in Eaton Square by nine."

"All right, I guess . . . thanks."

I parked my car where hers stood usually, and took my bag from the trunk, and with Danielle swathed in the rug as if in an oversized shawl we walked round to the front door in Eaton Square.

"I hope you have a key?" she said, yawning. "We'll look like gypsies if you don't."

"Dawson lent me one."

"Good . . . I'm asleep on my feet."

We went indoors and quietly up the stairs. When we reached her floor I put my arms round her, rug and all, again holding her close, but there was no clinging relief-driven response this time, and when I bent to kiss her it was her cheek she offered, not her mouth.

"Goodnight," I said. "Will you be all right?"

"Yes." She would hardly meet my eyes. "I truly thank you."

"You owe me nothing," I said.

"Oh . . ." She looked at me briefly, as if confused. Then she dropped the rug, which she had been holding close round her like a defensive stockade, put her arms round my neck and gave me a quick kiss at least reminiscent of better times, even if it landed somewhere on my chin.

"Goodnight," she said lightly, and walked away along the passage to her room without looking back, and I picked up my bag and the rug and went on upstairs feeling a good deal better than the day before. I opened the door of the bamboo room half expecting to find Beatrice snoring blissfully between my sheets, but the linen was smooth and vacant, and I plummeted there into dreamland for a good two hours.

9

Around seven-fifteen in the morning I knocked on Litsi's ground-floor door until a sleepy voice said, "Who is it?"

"Kit."

A short silence, then, "Come in, then."

The room was dark, Litsi leaning up on one elbow and stretching to switch on a bedside lamp. The light revealed a large oak-paneled room with a four-poster bed, brocade curtaining and ancestral paintings: very suitable, I thought, for Litsi.

"I thought you weren't here," he said, rubbing his eyes with his fingers. "What day is it?"

"Tuesday. I came back here before five this morning, and that's what I've come to tell you about."

He went from leaning to sitting up straight while he listened.

DICK FRANCIS

"Do you think it really was Nanterre?" he said when I'd finished.

"If it was, perhaps he wanted only to catch her and frighten her. Tell her what could happen if her uncle didn't give in. She must have surprised whoever it was by running so fast. She wears trainers to work . . . running shoes, really . . . and she's always pretty fit. Maybe he simply couldn't catch her."

"If he meant a warning he couldn't deliver, we'll hear from him."

"Yes. And about the horses, too."

"He's unhinged," Litsi said, "if it was him."

"Anyway," I said, "I thought I'd better warn you."

I told him about Danielle's handbag being missing. "If it was an ordinary thief, it would be all right because there was no connecting address, but if Nanterre took it, he now has a front-door key to this house. Do you think you could explain to the princess and get the lock changed? I'm off to Devon to ride a few races, and I'll be here again this evening. I'm picking Danielle up when she finishes work, but if I miss the train back, will you make sure she gets home safely? If you need a car, you can borrow mine."

"Just don't miss the train."

"No."

His eyebrows rose and fell. "Give me the keys, then," he said.

I gave them to him. "See if you can find out," I said, "if Danielle told her aunt Beatrice where she works and at what time she leaves."

He blinked.

"Henri Nanterre," I reminded him, "has a spy right in this house."

"Go and break your neck."

I smiled and went away, and caught the train to Devon. I might be a fool, I thought, entrusting Danielle to Litsi, but she needed to be safe, and one short ride in my Mercedes, Litsi driving, was unlikely to decide things one way or another.

For all the speed and risks of the job, jump jockeys were seldom killed: it was more dangerous, for instance, to clean windows for a living. All the same, there were occasional days when one ended in hospital, always at frustrating and inconvenient moments. I wouldn't say that I rode exactly carefully that day at Newton Abbot, but it was certainly without the reckless fury of the past two weeks.

Maybe she would finally come back to me, maybe she wouldn't: I had a better chance right under her eyes than two hundred miles away in traction.

The chief topic of conversation all afternoon on the racecourse as far as I was concerned was the killing of Cascade and Cotopaxi. I read accounts in the sports pages of two papers on the train and saw two others in the changing room, all more speculation and bold headlines than hard fact. I was besieged by curious and sympathetic questions from anyone I talked to, but could add little except that yes, I had seen them in their boxes, and yes, of course the princess was upset, and yes, I would be looking for another ride in the Grand National.

Dusty, from his thunderstorm expression, was putting up with much the same barrage. He was slightly mollified when one of the princess's runners won, greeted by clapping and cheers that spoke of her public popularity. The clerk of the course and the chairman of the board of directors called me into the directors' room, not to complain of my riding but to commiserate, asking me to pass on their regrets to the princess and to Wykeham. They clapped me gruffly on the shoulder and gave me champagne, and it was all a long way from Maynard Allardeck.

I caught the return train on schedule, dined on a railway sandwich, and was back at Eaton Square before nine. I had to get Dawson to let me in because the lock had indeed been changed, and I went up to the sitting room, opening the door there on the princess, Litsi and Beatrice Bunt, all sitting immobile in private separate silences, as if they were covered by vacuum bell jars and couldn't hear each other speak.

"Good evening," I said, my voice sounding loud.

Beatrice Bunt jumped because I'd spoken behind her. The princess's expression changed from blank to welcoming, and Litsi came alive as if one had waved a wand over a waxwork.

"You're back!" he said. "Thank God for that at least."

"What's happened?" I asked.

None of them was quite ready to say.

"Is Danielle all right?" I said.

The princess looked surprised. "Yes, of course. Thomas drove her to work." She was sitting on a sofa, her back straight, her head high, every muscle on the defensive and no ease anywhere. "Come over here"—she patted the cushions beside her—"and tell me how my horses ran."

It was her refuge, I knew, from unpleasant reality: she'd talked of her runners in the direst of moments in the past, clinging to a rock in a tilting world.

I sat beside her, willingly playing the game.

"Bernina was on the top of her form, and won her hurdle race. She seems to like it in Devon, that's the third time she's won down there."

"Tell me about her race," the princess said, looking both pleased and in some inner way still disorientated, and I told her about the race without anything in her expression changing. I glanced at Litsi and saw that he was listening in the same detached way, and at Beatrice, who appeared not to be listening at all.

I passed on the messages of sympathy from the directors, and said how pleased the crowd had been that she'd had a winner.

"How kind," she murmured.

"What's happened?" I said again.

It was Litsi who eventually answered. "Henri Nanterre telephoned here about an hour ago. He wanted to speak to Roland, but Roland refused, so he asked for me by name."

My eyebrows rose.

"He said he knew my name as one of the three others who had to sign business directives with Roland. He said Danielle and the princess were the others: his notary had remembered."

I frowned. "I suppose he might have remembered if someone had told him the names . . . he might have recognized them."

Litsi nodded. "Henri Nanterre said that his notary had left his briefcase in Roland's sitting room. In the briefcase could be found a form of contract with spaces at the bottom for signatures and witnesses. He says all four of us are to sign this form in the presence of his notary, in a place that he will designate. He said he would telephone each morning until everyone was ready to agree."

"Or else?" I said.

"He mentioned," Litsi said evenly, "that it would be a shame for the princess to lose more of her horses needlessly, and that young women out alone at night were al-

ways at risk." He paused, one eyebrow lifting ironically.
"He said that princes weren't immune from accidents, and
that a certain jockey, if he wished to stay healthy, should
remove himself from the household and mind his own
business."

"His exact words?" I asked interestedly.

Litsi shook his head. "He spoke in French."

"We have asked Beatrice," the princess said with brittle
veneer politeness, "if she has spoken with Henri Nanterre
since her arrival in this house on Sunday, but she tells us
she doesn't know where he is."

I looked at Beatrice, who stared implacably back. It
wasn't necessary to know where someone actually was if he
had a telephone number, but there seemed to be no point
in making her upgrade the evasion into a straightforward
lie, which the boldness in her eyes assured me we would
get.

The princess said that her husband had asked to talk to
me on my return, and suggested that I might go at this
point. I went, sensing the three of them stiffening back
into their bell jars, and upstairs knocked on Roland de
Brescou's door.

He bade me come in and sit down, and asked with nicely
feigned interest about my day's fortunes. I said Bernina
had won and he said "Good" absentmindedly, while he
arranged in his thoughts what to say next. He was looking,
I thought, not so physically frail as on Friday and Saturday,
but not as determined either.

"It is going to take time to arrange my retirement," he
said, "and as soon as I make any positive moves, Henri
Nanterre will find out. Gerald Greening thinks that when
he does find out, he will demand I withdraw my intention,

under pain of more and more threats and vicious actions."
He paused. "Has Litsi told you about Nanterre's telephone
call?"

"Yes, monsieur."

"The horses . . . Danielle . . . my wife . . . Litsi . . .
yourself . . . I cannot leave you all open to harm. Gerald
Greening advises now that I sign the contract, and then as
soon as Nanterre gets his firearms approval, I can sell all
my interest in the business. Nanterre will have to agree. I
shall make it a condition before signing. Everyone will
guess I have sold because of the guns . . . some at least of
my reputation may be salvaged." A spasm of distress
twisted his mouth. "It is of the greatest conceivable personal disgrace that I sign this contract, but I see no other
way."

He fell silent but with an implied question, as if inviting
my comment; and after a short pause I gave it.

"Don't sign, monsieur," I said.

He looked at me consideringly, with the first vestige of a
smile.

"Litsi said you would say that," he said.

"Did he? And what did Litsi himself say?"

"What would you think?"

"Don't sign," I said.

"You and Litsi." Again the fugitive smile. "So different.
So alike. He described you as—and these are his words,
not mine—'a tough devil with brains,' and he said I should
give you and him time to think of a way of deterring Nanterre permanently. He said that only if both of you failed
and admitted failure should I think of signing."

"And . . . did you agree?"

"If you yourself wish it, I will agree."

A commitment of positive action, I thought, was a lot different from raising defenses; but I thought of the horses, and the princess, and Danielle, and really there was no question.

"I wish it," I said.

"Very well, but I do hope nothing appalling will happen."

I said we would try our best to prevent it, and asked if he would mind having a guard in the house every day during John Grundy's off-duty hours.

"A guard?" He frowned.

"Not in your rooms, monsieur. Moving about. You would hardly notice him, but we'd give you a walkie-talkie so you could call him if you needed. And may we also install a telephone that records what's said?"

He lifted a thin hand an inch and let it fall back on the arm of the wheelchair.

"Do what you think best," he said, and then, with an almost mischievous smile, the only glimpse I'd ever had of the lighter side within, he asked, "Has Beatrice got you out of the bamboo room yet?"

"No, monsieur," I said cheerfully.

"She was up here this morning demanding I move you," he said, the smile lingering. "She insists also that I allow Nanterre to run the business as he thinks best, but truly I don't know which of her purposes obsesses her most. She switched from one to the other within the same sentence." He paused. "If you can defeat my sister," he said, "Nanterre should be easy."

By the following midmorning I'd been out to buy a recording telephone, and the guard had been installed, in the unconventional form of a springy twenty-year-old who had learned karate in the cradle.

Beatrice predictably disapproved, both of his looks and of his presence, particularly as he nearly knocked her over on one of the landings, while proving he could run from the basement to the attic faster than the elevator could travel the same distance.

He told me his name was Sammy (this week), and he was deeply impressed by the princess, whom he called "Your Regal Highness," to her discreet and friendly amusement.

"Are you sure?" she said to me tentatively, when he wasn't listening.

"He comes with the very highest references," I assured her. "His employer promised he could kick a pistol out of anyone's hand before it was fired."

Sammy's slightly poltergeist spirits seemed to cheer her greatly, and with firmness she announced that all of us, of course including Beatrice, should go to Ascot races. Lunch was already ordered there, and Sammy would guard her husband: she behaved with the gaiety sometimes induced by risk-taking, which to Litsi and Danielle at least proved infectious.

Beatrice, glowering, complained she didn't like horse-racing. Her opinion of me had dropped as low as the Marianas Trench since she'd discovered I was a professional jockey. "He's the *help*," I overheard her saying in outrage to the princess. "Surely there are some rooms in the attic."

The "attic," as it happened, was an unused nursery suite, cold and draped in dust-sheets, as I'd discovered on my night prowls. The room I could realistically have expected to have been given lay beside the rose room, sharing the rose room's bathroom, but it, too, was palely shrouded.

"I didn't know you were coming, Beatrice, dear," the princess reminded her. "And he's Danielle's fiancé."

"But *really* . . ."

She did go to the races, though, albeit with ill grace, presumably on the premise that even if she gained access again to her brother, and even if she wore him to exhaustion, she couldn't make him sign the contract, because first, he didn't have it (it was now in Litsi's room in case she took the bamboo room by force) and second, his three cosigners couldn't be similarly coerced. Litsi had carefully told her, after Nanterre's telephone call and before my return from Devon, that the contract form was missing.

"Where is it?" she had demanded.

"My dear Beatrice," Litsi had said blandly, "I have no idea. The notary's briefcase is still in the hall awaiting collection, but there is no paper of any sort in it."

And it was after he'd told me of this exchange, before we'd gone to bed on the previous evening, that I'd taken the paper downstairs for his safekeeping.

Beatrice went to Ascot with the princess in the Rolls; Danielle and Litsi came with me.

Danielle, subdued, sat in the back. She had been quiet when I'd fetched her during the night, shivering now and again from her thoughts, even though the car had been warm. I told her about Nanterre's telephone call and also about her uncle's agreement with Litsi and me, and although her eyes looked huge with worry, all she'd said was, "*Please* be careful. Both of you . . . be careful."

At Ascot it was with unmixed feelings of jealousy that I watched Litsi take her away in the direction of the princess's lunch while I peeled off, as one might say, to the office.

I had four races to ride: one for the princess, two others for Wykeham, one for a Lambourn trainer. Dusty was in a bad mood, Maynard Allardeck had again turned up as a Steward, and the tree of my favorite lightweight saddle, my valet told me, had disintegrated. Apart from that it was bitterly cold, and apart from that I had somehow gained another pound, probably via the railway sandwich.

Wykeham's first runner was a four-year-old ex–Flat racer out for his first experience over hurdles, and although I'd schooled him a few times over practice jumps on Wykeham's gallops, I hadn't been able to teach him courage. He went round the whole way letting me know he hated it, and I had difficulty thinking of anything encouraging to say to his owners afterward. A horse that didn't like racing was a waste of time, a waste of money and a waste of emotion: better to sell him quick and try again. I put it as tactfully as possible, but the owners shook their heads doubtfully and said they would ask Wykeham.

The second of Wykeham's runners finished nowhere also, not from unwillingness, as he was kind-hearted and sure-footed, but from being nowhere near fast enough against the opposition.

I went out for the princess's race with a low *joie de vivre* rating, a feeling not cured by seeing Danielle walk into the parade ring holding on to Litsi's arm and laughing.

The princess, who had been in the ring first, after seeing her horse saddled, followed my gaze and gently tapped my arm.

"She's in a muddle," she said distinctly. "Give her time."

I looked at the princess's blue eyes, half hidden as usual behind reticent lashes. She must have felt very strongly that I needed advice, or she wouldn't have given it.

I said, "All right" with an unloosened jaw, and she briefly nodded, turning to greet the others.

"Where's Beatrice?" she asked, looking in vain behind them. "Didn't she come down?"

"She said it was too cold. She stayed up in the box," Litsi said, and to me, he added, "Do we put our money on?"

Col, the princess's runner, was stalking round in his navy-blue gold-crested rug, looking bored. He was a horse of limited enthusiasm, difficult to ride because if he reached the front too soon he would lose interest and stop, and if one left the final run too late and got beaten, one looked and felt a fool.

"Don't back him," I said. It was that sort of day.

"Yes, back him," the princess said simultaneously.

"Frightfully helpful," Litsi commented, amused.

Col was a bright chestnut with a white blaze down his nose and three white socks. As with most of the horses Wykeham was particularly hoping to win with at Cheltenham, Col probably wouldn't reach his absolute pinnacle of fitness until the National Hunt Festival in another two weeks, but he should be ready enough for Ascot, a slightly less testing track.

At Cheltenham he was entered for the Gold Cup, the top event of the meeting, and although not a hot fancy, as Cotopaxi had been for the Grand National, he had a realistic chance of being placed.

"Do your best," the princess said, as she often did, and as usual I said yes, I would. Dusty gave me a leg-up and I cantered Col down to the start trying to wind up a bit of life-force for us both. A gloomy jockey on a bored horse might as well go straight back to the stable.

By the time we started I was telling him we were out there to do a job of work, and to take a little pride in it, talking to myself as much as him; and by the third of the twenty-two fences there were some faint stirrings in both of us of the ebb turning to flood.

Most of the art of jump racing lay in presenting a horse at a fence so that he could cross it without slowing. Col was one of the comparatively rare sort that could judge distances on his own, leaving his jockey free to worry about tactics, but he would never quicken unless one insisted, and had no personal competitive drive.

I'd ridden and won on him often and understood his needs, and knew that by the end I'd have to dredge up the one wild burst of all-out urging that might wake up his phlegmatic soul.

I daresay that from the stands nothing looked wrong. Even though to me Col seemed to be plodding, his plod was respectably fast. We traveled most of the three miles in fourth or fifth place and came up into third on the last bend when two of the early leaders tired.

There were three fences still to go, with the 240-yard run-in after. One of the horses ahead was still chock-full of running: it was his speed Col would have to exceed. The jockey on the other already had his whip up and was no doubt feeling the first ominous warning that the steam was running out of the boiler. I gave Col the smallest of pulls to steady him in third place for the first of the three fences in the straight. This he jumped cleanly and was going equally well within himself as we crossed the next, passing that jockey with his whip up before we reached the last.

Too much daylight, I thought. He liked ideally to jump the last with two or three others still close ahead. He jumped the last with a tremendous leap, though, and it was no problem after all to stoke up the will-win spirit and tell him that now . . . now . . . was the time.

Col put his leading foot to the ground and it bent and buckled under him. His nose went down to the grass. The reins slid through my fingers to their full extent and I leaned back and gripped fiercely with my legs, trying not to be thrown off. By some agile miracle, his other foreleg struck the ground solidly, and with all his half-ton weight on that slender fetlock Col pushed himself upright and kept on going.

I gathered the reins. The race had to be lost, but the fire, so long arriving, couldn't easily be put out. Come on, now, you great brute, I was saying to him: now's the time, there is one to beat, get on with it, now show me, show everyone you can do it, you still can do it.

As if he understood every word he put his head forward and accelerated in the brief astonishing last-minute spurt that had snatched last-second victories before from seeming impossibilities.

We nearly made it that time, very nearly. Col ate up the lengths he'd lost and I rode him almost as hard as Cascade but without the fury, and we were up with the other horse's rump, up with the saddle, up with the neck . . . and the winning post flashed back three strides too soon.

The princess had said she wouldn't come down to the unsaddling enclosure unless we won, as it was a long way from her box.

Maynard was there, however, balefully staring at me as I slid to the ground, his eyes dark and his face tight with hate. Why he came near me I couldn't understand. If I'd hated anyone that much I would have avoided the sight of him as much as possible: and I did loathe Maynard for what he'd tried to do to Bobby, to brainwash his own son into killing.

Dusty put the sheet over Col's heaving chestnut sides with a studied lack of comment on the race's result, and I went and weighed in with much of the afternoon's dissatisfaction drifting around like a cloud.

I rode the next race for the Lambourn trainer and finished third, a good way back, and with a feeling of having accomplished nothing, changed into street clothes, done for the day.

On my way out of the weighing room, en route to the princess's box, a voice said, "Hey, Kit," behind me, and I turned to find Basil Clutter walking quickly in my wake.

"Are you still looking for Henri Nanterre?" he said, catching me up.

"Yes, I am." I stopped and he stopped also, although almost jogging from foot to foot, as he could never easily stand still.

"The Roquevilles are here today; they had a runner in the first race. They've someone with them who knows Henri Nanterre quite well. They said if you were still interested perhaps you'd like to meet her."

"Yes, I would."

He looked at his watch. "I'm supposed to be joining them in the owners' and trainers' bar for a drink now, so you'd better come along."

"Thank you," I said, "very much."

I followed him to the bar and, armed with Perrier to their port, met the Roquevilles' friend, who was revealed as small and French-looking, with a gamine chic that had outlasted her youth. The elfin face bore wrinkles, the club-cut black hair showed grayish roots, and she wore high-heeled black boots and a smooth black leather trouser-suit with a silk scarf knotted at the back of her neck, cowboy fashion.

Her speech, surprisingly, was straightforward earthy racecourse English, and she was introduced to me as Madame Madeleine Darcy, English wife of a French racehorse trainer.

"Henri Nanterre?" she said with distaste. "Of course I know the bastard. We used to train his horses until he whisked them away overnight and sent them to Villon."

10

She talked with the freedom of pique and the pleasure of entertaining an attentive audience.

"He's a cock," she said, "with a very loud crow. He struts like a rooster. We have known him since he was young, when the horses belonged to his father, Louis, who was a very nice man, a gentleman."

"So Henri inherited the horses?" I said.

"But yes, along with everything else. Louis was soft-headed. He thought his son could do no wrong. So stupid. Henri is a greedy bully. Villon is welcome to him."

"In what way is he a greedy bully?" I asked.

Her plucked eyebrows rose. "We bought a yearling filly with nice bloodlines that we were going to race ourselves and breed from later. Henri saw her in the yard—he was always poking round the stables—and said he would buy her. When we said we didn't want to sell, he said that unless we did, he would take all his horses away. He had eight . . . we didn't want to lose them. We were furious. He made us sell him the filly at the price we'd paid for her . . . and we'd kept her for months. Then a few weeks later, he telephoned one evening and said horse-boxes would be arriving in the morning to collect his horses. And pouf, they were gone."

"What happened to the filly?" I said.

Her mouth curved with pleasure. "She contracted navicular and had to be put down, poor little bitch. And do you know what that bastard Nanterre did?"

She paused for effect. About four voices, mine included, said, "What?"

"Villon told us. He was disgusted. Nanterre said he didn't trust the knackers not to patch up the filly, pump her full of painkillers and sell her, making a profit at his expense, so he insisted on being there. The filly was put down on Villon's land with Nanterre watching."

Mrs. Roqueville looked both sick and disappointed. "He seemed a pleasant enough man when we met him at Longchamp, and again at Newbury."

"I expect the Marquis de Sade was perfectly charming on the racecourse," Madeleine said sweetly. "It is where anyone can pretend to be a gentleman."

After a respectful pause I said, "Do you know anything of his business affairs?"

"Business." She wrinkled her nose. "He is the de Brescou et Nanterre construction company. I don't know anything about his business, only about his horses. I wouldn't trust him in business. As a man deals with his racehorse trainer, so will he deal in business. The honorable will be honorable. The greedy bully will run true to form."

"And . . . do you know where I could find him in England?"

"I wouldn't look, if I were you." She gave me a bright smile. "He'll bring you nothing but trouble."

I relayed the conversation to Litsi and Danielle up in the princess's box.

"What's navicular?" Litsi said.

"A disease of the navicular bone in a horse's foot. When it gets bad, the horse can't walk."

"That Nanterre," Danielle said disgustedly, "is gross."

The princess and Beatrice, a few feet away at the balcony end of the box, were talking to a tall, bulky man with noticeably light-gray eyes in a big bland face.

Litsi, following my gaze, said, "Lord Vaughnley. He came to commiserate with Aunt Casilia over Col not winning. Do you know him? He's something in publishing, I think."

"Mm," I said neutrally. "He owns the *Towncrier* newspaper."

"Does he?" Litsi's agile mind made the jump. "Not the paper that attacked Bobby?"

"No, that was the *Flag*."

"Oh." Litsi seemed disappointed. "Then he isn't one of the two defeated press barons after all."

"Yes, he is." Lord Vaughnley's attention was switching my way. "I'll tell you about it, some time," I said to Litsi, and watched Lord Vaughnley hesitate, as he always did, before offering his hand for me to shake: yet he must have known he would meet me in that place, as my being there at the end of each day's racing was a ritual well known to him.

"Kit," he said, grasping the nettle, "a great race . . . such bad luck."

"The way it goes," I said.

"Better luck in the Gold Cup, eh?"

"It would be nice."

"Anything I can do for you, my dear fellow?"

It was a question he asked whenever we met, though I could see Litsi's astonishment out of the side of my eyes. Usually I answered that there wasn't, but on that day thought there was no harm in trying a flier. If one didn't ask, one would never learn.

"Nothing, really," I said, "except . . . I suppose you've never come across the name of Henri Nanterre?"

Everyone watched him while he pondered, the princess with rapidly sharpening interest, Litsi and Danielle with simple curiosity, Beatrice with seeming alarm. Lord Vaughnley looked around at the waiting faces, frowned, and finally answered with a question of his own.

"Who is he?" he asked.

"My husband's business partner," the princess said. "Dear Lord Vaughnley, do you know of him?"

Lord Vaughnley was puzzled but slowly shook his big head. "I can't recall ever . . ."

"Could you . . . er . . . see if the *Towncrier* has a file on him?" I asked.

He gave me a resigned little smile, and nodded. "Write the name down for me," he said. "In caps."

I fished out a pen and small notepad and wrote both the name and that of the construction company, in capital letters as required.

"He's French," I said. "Owns horses. He might be on the racing pages, or maybe business. Or even gossip."

"Anything you want specifically?" he said, still smiling.

"He's over in England just now. Ideally, we'd like to know where he's staying."

Beatrice's mouth opened and closed again with a snap. She definitely knows, I thought, how to reach him. Perhaps we could make use of that, when we had a plan.

Lord Vaughnley tucked the slip of paper away in an inner pocket, saying he would get the names run through the computer that very evening, if it was important to the princess.

"Indeed it is," she said with feeling.

"Any little fact," I said, "could be helpful."

"Very well." He kissed the princess's hand and made general farewells, and to me he said as he was going, "Have you embarked on another crusade?"

"I guess so."

"Then God help this Nanterre."

"What did he mean by that?" Beatrice demanded as Lord Vaughnley departed, and the princess told her soothingly that it was a long story that wasn't to interfere with my telling her all about Col's race. Lord Vaughnley, she added, was a good friend she saw often at the races, and it was perfectly natural for him to help her in any way.

Beatrice, to do her justice, had been a great deal quieter since Nanterre's telephone call the evening before. She had refused to believe he had killed the horses ("It must have been vandals, as the police said") until he had himself admitted it, and although she was still adamant that Roland should go along with Nanterre in business, we no longer heard praise of him personally.

Her hostility toward me, on the other hand, seemed to have deepened, and on my account of the race she passed her own opinion.

"Rubbish. You didn't lose the race at the last fence. You

were too far back all along. Anyone could see that." She picked up a small sandwich from the display on the table and bit into it decisively, as if snapping off my head.

No one argued with her pronouncement and, emboldened, she said to Danielle with malice, "Your fortune-hunter isn't even a good jockey."

"Beatrice," the princess immediately said, unruffled. "Kit has a fortune of his own, and he is heir to his grandfather, who is rich."

She glanced at me briefly, forbidding me to contradict. Such fortune as I had I'd earned, and although my grandfather owned several chunks of Newmarket, their liquidity was of the consistency of bricks.

"And Aunt Beatrice," Danielle said, faintly blushing, "I am poor."

Beatrice ate her sandwich, letting her round eyes do the talking. Her pale-orange hair, I thought inconsequentially, was almost the same color as the hessian-covered walls.

The sixth and last race was already in progress, the commentary booming outside. Everyone except Beatrice went on the balcony to watch, and I wondered whether a putative million dollars was worth an unquiet mind. "It's nice to be nice," our grandmother had said often enough to Holly and me, bringing us up, and "Hate curdles your brains." Grandfather, overhearing her heresies, had tried to undo her work with anti-Allardeck slogans, but in the end it was she who'd prevailed. Holly had married Bobby, and apart from the present state of affairs with Danielle and other various past hard knocks, I had grown up, and remained, basically happy. Beatrice, for all her mink/crocodile/Spanish-house indulgences in Palm Beach, hadn't been so lucky.

When it came to going home, Beatrice again went with the princess in the Rolls. I had hoped Litsi would join them, as I was detouring to Chiswick to deliver Danielle to the studio, but he took Danielle's arm and steered her and himself, chatting away, in the direction of the jockeys' car park as if there had never been any question. Litsi had his aunt's precious knack of courteously and covertly getting his own way. He would have made a great king, I thought wryly, given the chance.

We dropped Danielle off (she waved to both of us and kissed neither) and I drove the two of us back to Eaton Square. Beatrice, naturally enough, came into the conversation.

"You were shocked," Litsi said, amused, "when she called you a fortune-hunter. You hadn't even thought of Danielle's prospects."

"She called me a bad jockey," I said.

"Oh, sure." He chuckled. "You're a puritan."

"Danielle has the money she earns," I said. "As I do."

"Danielle is Roland's niece," he said as if teaching an infant. "Roland and Aunt Casilia are fond of her, and they have no children."

"I don't want that complication."

He grunted beside me and said no more on the subject, and after a while I said, "Do you know why they have no children? Is it choice, or his illness? Or just that they couldn't?"

"His illness, I've always supposed, but I've never asked. He was about forty, I think, when they married, about fifteen years older than her, and he caught the virus not very long after. I can't remember ever seeing him walk, though he was a good skier, I believe, in his time."

"Rotten for them," I said.

He nodded. "He was lucky in some respects. Some people who get that virus—and thank God it's rare—lose the use of their arms as well. They never speak of it much, of course."

"How are we going to save his honor?"

"You invent," Litsi said lazily, "and I'll gofer."

"Gofer a lever," I said absentmindedly.

"A lever?"

"To move the world."

He stretched contentedly. "Do you have any ideas at all?"

"One or two. Rather vague."

"Which you're not sharing?"

"Not yet. Have to think a bit first." I told him I'd bought a recording telephone that morning. "When we get back, we'll rig it and work out a routine."

"He said he would ring again this evening."

No need to say who "he" was.

"Mm," I said. "The phone I bought is also a conference phone. It has a loudspeaker, so that everyone in the room can hear what the caller's saying. You don't need the receiver. So when he rings, if it's you that answers, will you get him to speak in English?"

"Perhaps you'd better answer, then he'd have to."

"All right. And the message we give is no dice?"

"You couldn't just string him along?"

"Yeah, maybe," I said, "but to fix him we've got to find him, and he could be anywhere. Beatrice knows where he is, or at least how to reach him. If we get him out in the open . . ." I paused. "What we ideally need is a tethered goat."

"And just who," Litsi inquired ironically, "are you electing for that dead-end job?"

I smiled. "A stuffed goat with a mechanical bleat. All real goats must be guarded or careful."

"Aunt Casilia, Roland and Danielle, guarded."

"And the horses," I said.

"OK. And the horses guarded. And you and I . . ."

I nodded. "Careful."

Neither of us mentioned that Nanterre had specifically threatened each of us as his next targets: there was no point. I didn't think he would actually try to kill either of us, but the damage would have to be more than a pinprick to expect a result.

"What's he like?" Litsi said. "You've met him. I've never seen him. Know your enemy . . . the first rule for combat."

"Well, I think he got into all this without thinking it out first," I said. "Last Friday, I think he believed he had only to browbeat the princess heavily enough, and Roland would collapse. That's also very nearly what happened."

"As I understand it, it didn't happen because you were there."

"I don't know. Anyway, on Friday night when he pulled the gun out that had no bullets in . . . I think that may be typical of him. He acts on impulse, without thinking things through. He's used to getting his own way easily because of his hectoring manner. He's used to being obeyed. Since his father died—and his father had customarily indulged him—he has run the construction company pretty well as he likes. I'd say he's quite likely reached the stage where he literally can't believe he can be defied, and especially not by an old, ill man long out of touch with the world.

When Roland rejected him by post, I'd guess he came over thinking 'I'll soon change all that.' I think in some ways he's childish, which doesn't make him less destructive: more so, probably."

I paused, but Litsi made no comment.

"Attacking Danielle," I said. "He thought again that he would have it all his own way. I'll bet it never once occurred to him that she could run faster than he could. He turned up there in a city suit and polished leather shoes. It was a sort of arrogance, an assumption that he would naturally be faster, stronger, dominant. If he'd had any doubts at all, he'd have worn a jogging suit, something like that, and faster shoes."

"And the horses?" Litsi said.

I hated to think of the horses. "They were vulnerable," I said. "And he knew how to kill them. I don't know where he would get a humane killer, but he does deal in guns. He carries one. They attract him, otherwise he wouldn't be wanting to make them. People mostly do what their natures urge, don't they? He may have a real urge to see things die. Wanting to make sure the slaughterers didn't cheat him could be just the only acceptable reason he could give for a darker desire. People always think up reasonable reasons for doing what they want."

"Do you?" he asked curiously.

"Oh, sure. I say I race for the money."

"And you don't?"

"I'd do it for nothing, but being paid is better."

He nodded, having no difficulty in understanding. "So what do you expect next from Nanterre?" he asked.

"Another half-baked attack on one of us. He won't have planned properly for contingencies, but we might find ourselves in nasty spots nevertheless."

"Charming," he said.

"Don't go down dark alleys to meet strangers."

"I never do."

I asked him rather tentatively what he did do, back in Paris, where he lived.

"Frightfully little, I'm afraid," he said. "I have an interest in an art gallery. I spend a good deal of my life looking at paintings. The Louvre expert Danielle and I went to listen to is a very old acquaintance. I was sure she would enjoy . . ." He paused. "She did enjoy it."

"Yes."

I could feel him shift in the passenger seat until he could see me better.

"There was a group of us," he said. "We weren't alone."

"Yes, I know."

He didn't pursue it. He said unexpectedly instead, "I have been married, but we are separated. Technically I am still married. If either of us wished to remarry, there would be a divorce. But she has lovers, and I also . . ." He shrugged. "It's common enough, in France."

I said, "Thank you," after a pause, and he nodded; and we didn't speak of it again.

"I would like to have been an artist," he said after a while. "I studied for years. I can see the genius in great paintings, but for myself . . . I can put paint on canvas, but I haven't the great gift. And you, my friend Kit, are damn bloody lucky to have been endowed with the skill to match your desire."

I was silent; silenced. I'd had the skill from birth, and one couldn't say where it came from; and I hadn't much thought what it would be like to be without it. I looked at life suddenly from Litsi's point of view, and knew that I was in truth damn bloody lucky, that it was the root of my basic happiness, and that I should be humbly grateful.

When we got to Eaton Square I suggested dropping him at the front door while I went to park the car, but he wouldn't hear of it. Dark alleys, he reminded me, and being careful.

"There's some light in the mews," I said.

"All the same, we'll park the car together and walk back together, and take our own advice."

"OK," I said, and reflected that at one-thirty, when I went to fetch Danielle, I would be going alone into the selfsame dark alley, and it would be then that I'd better be careful.

Litsi and I let ourselves in, Dawson meeting us in the hall saying the princess and Beatrice had vanished to their rooms to change and rest.

"Where is Sammy?" I said.

Sammy, Dawson said with faint disapproval, was walking about, and was never in any place longer than a minute. I went upstairs to fetch the new telephone and found Sammy coming down the stairs from the top floor.

"Did you know there's another kitchen up there?" he said.

"Yes, I looked."

"And there's a skylight or two. I rigged a nice little pair of booby traps under those. If you hear a lot of old brass firearms crashing around up there, you get the force here pronto."

I assured him I would, and took him downstairs with me to show him, as well as Dawson and Litsi, how the recording telephone worked.

The normal telephone arrangements in that house were both simple and complicated: there was only one line, but about a dozen scattered instruments.

Incoming calls rang in only three of those: the one in the sitting-room, one in the office where Mrs. Jenkins worked by day, and one in the basement. Whoever was near one of those instruments when a call came in would answer, and if it were for someone else, reach that person via the intercom, as Dawson had reached me when Wykeham rang the previous Sunday. This arrangement was to save six or more people answering whenever the telephone rang.

From each guest bedroom outgoing calls could be directly made, as from the princess's rooms, and her husband's. The house was rarely as full as at present, Dawson said, and the telephone was seldom busy. The system normally worked smoothly.

I explained that to work the new telephone one had simply to unplug the ordinary instrument and plug in the new one.

"If you press that button," I said, pointing, "the whole conversation will be recorded. If you press that one, everyone in the room can hear what's being said."

I plugged the simple box of tricks into the sitting-room socket. "It had better be in here while we are all around. During the day, if everyone's out, like today, it can go to Mrs. Jenkins's office, and at night, if Dawson wouldn't mind, in the basement. It doesn't matter how many calls are unnecessarily recorded, we can scrub them out, but every time . . . if one could develop the habit?"

They all nodded.

"Such an uncouth man," Dawson commented. "I would know that loud voice anywhere."

"It's a pity," Litsi said, when Dawson and Sammy had gone, "that we can't somehow tap Beatrice's phone and record what she says."

"Anytime she's upstairs, like now, we can just lift the receiver and listen."

We lifted the receiver, but no one in the house was talking. We could wait and listen for hours, but meanwhile no outside calls could come in. Regretfully Litsi put the receiver back again, saying we might be lucky, he would try every few minutes; but by the time Beatrice reappeared for dinner the intermittent vigil had produced no results.

I had meanwhile talked to Wykeham and collected the messages off my answering machine, neither a lengthy event, and if anyone had inadvertently broken in on the calls, I'd heard no clicks on the line.

Beatrice came down demanding her "bloody" in a flattering white dress covered in sunflowers, Litsi fussing over her with amiable solicitude, and refusing to be disconcerted by ungraciousness.

"I know you don't want me here," she said bluntly, "but until Roland signs on the dotted line, I'm staying."

The princess came down to dinner, but not Roland, and on our return to the sitting room afterward Litsi, without seeming to, maneuvered everyone around so that it was I who ended up sitting by the telephone. He smiled over his coffee cup, and everyone waited.

When the bell finally rang, Beatrice jumped.

I picked up the receiver, pressing both the recorder and conference buttons; and a voice spoke French loudly into our expectations.

Litsi rose immediately to his feet, came over to me and made gestures for me to give him the phone.

"It isn't Nanterre," he said.

He took the receiver, disengaged the conference button and spoke privately in French. "*Oui . . . Non . . . Certainement . . . Ce soir . . . Oui . . . Merci.*"

He put down the receiver and almost immediately the bell rang again. Litsi picked up the receiver again, briefly listened, grimaced, pressed the record and conference buttons again, and passed the buck to me.

"It's him," he said succinctly, and indeed everyone could hear the familiar domineering voice saying words that meant nothing to me at all.

"Speak English, please," I said.

"I said," Nanterre said in English, "I wish to speak to Prince Litsi and he is to be brought to the telephone immediately."

"He isn't available," I said. "I can give him a message."

"Who are you?" he said. "I know who you are. You are the jockey."

"Yes."

"I left instructions for you to leave the house."

"I don't obey your instructions."

"You'll regret it."

"In what way?" I asked, but he wouldn't be drawn into a specific threat; quite likely, I supposed, because he hadn't yet thought up a particular mayhem.

"My notary will arrive at the house tomorrow morning at ten o'clock," he said. "He will be shown to the library, as before. He will wait there. Roland de Brescou and Princess Casilia will go down there when he arrives. Also Prince Litsi and Danielle de Brescou will go down. All will sign the form that is in the notary's briefcase. The notary will witness each signature, and carry the document away in his briefcase. Is this understood?"

"It is understood," I said calmly, "but it's not going to happen."

"It must happen."

"There's no document in the briefcase."

It stopped him barely a second. "My notary will bring a paper bearing the same form of words. Everyone will sign the notary's document."

"No, they aren't ready to," I said.

"I have warned what will happen if the document is not signed."

"What will happen?" I asked. "You can't make people behave against their consciences."

"Every conscience has its price," he said furiously, and instantly disconnected. The telephone clicked a few times and came forth with the dialing tone, and I put the receiver back in its cradle to shut it off.

Litsi shook his head regretfully. "He's being cautious. Nothing he said can be presented to the police as a threat requiring action on their part."

"You should all sign his document," Beatrice said aggrievedly, "and be done with all this obstruction to expanding his business."

No one bothered to argue with her: the ground had already been covered too often. Litsi then asked the princess if she would mind if he and I went out for a little while. Sammy was still in the house to look after things until John Grundy came, and I would be back in good time to fetch Danielle.

The princess acquiesced to this arrangement while looking anything but ecstatic over further time alone with Beatrice, and it was with twinges of guilt that I happily followed Litsi out of the room.

"We'll go in a taxi," he said, "to the Marylebone Plaza hotel."

"That's not your sort of place," I observed mildly.

"We're going to meet someone. It's his sort of place."

"Who?"

"Someone to tell you about the arms trade."

"Really?" I said, interested. "Who is he?"

"I don't precisely know. We are to go to room eleven twelve and talk to a Mr. Mohammed. That isn't his real name, which he would prefer we didn't know. He will be helpful, I'm told."

"How did you find him?" I asked.

Litsi smiled. "I didn't exactly. But I asked someone in France who would know . . . who could tell me what's going on in the handguns world. Mr. Mohammed is the result. Be satisfied with that."

"OK."

"Your name is Mr. Smith," he said. "Mine is Mr. Jones."

"Such stunning originality."

The Marylebone Plaza hotel was about three miles distant from Eaton Square geographically and in a different world economically. The Marylebone Plaza was frankly a bare-bones overnight stopping place for impecunious travelers, huge, impersonal, a shelter for the anonymous. I'd passed it fairly often but never been through its doors before, nor, it was clear, had Litsi. We made our way however across an expanse of hard gray mottled flooring, and took an elevator to the eleventh floor.

Upstairs the passages were narrow, though carpeted; the lighting economical. We peered at door numbers, found 1112, and knocked.

The door was opened to us by a swarthy-skinned man in a good suit with a white shirt, gold cuff links, and an impassive expression.

"Mr. Jones and Mr. Smith," Litsi said.

The man opened the door further and gestured to us to go in, and inside we found another man similarly dressed, except that he wore also a heavy gold ring inset with four diamonds arranged in a square.

"Mohammed," he said, extending the hand with the ring to be shaken. He nodded over our shoulders to his friend, who silently went out the door, closing it behind him.

Mohammed, somewhere between Litsi's age and mine, I judged, had dark hair, dark eyes, olive skin and a heavy dark mustache. The opulence of the ring was echoed in the leather suitcase lying on the bed and in his wristwatch, which looked like gold nuggets strung together round his wrist.

He was in good humor, and apologized for meeting us "where no one would know any of us."

"I am legitimately in the arms trade," he assured us. "I will tell you anything you want to know, as long as you do not say who told you."

He apologized again for the fact that the room was furnished with a single chair, and offered it to Litsi. I perched against a table, Mohammed sat on the bed. There were reddish curtains across the window, a brown patterned carpet on the floor, a striped cotton bedspread; all clean-looking and in good repair.

"I will leave in an hour," Mohammed said, consulting the nuggets. "You wish to ask about plastic guns. Please go ahead."

"Er . . ." Litsi said.

"Who makes them?" I asked.

Mohammed switched his dark gaze my way. "The best-known," he said straightforwardly, "are made by Glock of Austria. The Glock 17." He reached unhurriedly toward the suitcase and unclipped the locks. "I brought one to show you."

Beneath his educated English there was an accent I couldn't place. Arab, in some way, I thought. Definitely Mediterranean, not Italian, perhaps French.

"The Glock 17," he was saying, "is mostly plastic but has metal parts. Future guns of this sort can be made entirely from plastic. It's a matter of a suitable formula for the material."

From the suitcase he produced a neat square black box.

"This handgun is legitimately in my possession," he said.

"Despite the manner of our meeting, I am a reputable dealer."

We assured him that we hadn't thought otherwise.

He nodded in satisfaction and took the lid off the box. Inside, packed in a molded tray, like a toy, lay a black pistol, an ammunition clip, and eighteen golden bullets, flat caps uppermost, points invisible, arranged neatly in three horizontal rows of six.

Mohammed lifted the weapon out of the box.

"This pistol," he said, "has many advantages. It is light, it is cheaper and easier to make than all-metal guns, and also it is more accurate."

He let the information sink into our brains in true salesman fashion.

"It pulls apart." He showed us, snapping off the entire top of the pistol, revealing a metal rod lying within. "This is the metal barrel." He picked it out. "There is also a metal spring. The bullets also are metal. The butt and the ammunition clip are plastic. The pieces pop back together again very easily." He reassembled the pistol fast, closing its top into place with a snap. "Extremely easy, as you see. The clip holds nine bullets at a time. People who use this weapon, including some police forces, consider it a great advance, the forerunner of a whole new concept of handguns."

"Aren't they trying to ban it in America?" Litsi said.

"Yes." Mohammed shrugged. "Amendment 4194 to Title 18, forbidding the import, manufacture and sale of any such gun made after January 1, 1986. It is because the plastic is undetectable by X-ray scanners. They fear the guns will be carried through airports and into government buildings by terrorists."

"And won't they?" I said.

"Perhaps." He shrugged. "Approximately two million private citizens in America own handguns," he said. "They believe in the right to carry arms. This Glock pistol is the beginning of the future. It may result in the widespread development of plastic-detectors. And perhaps in the banning of all hand luggage on airplanes except small ladies' handbags and flat briefcases that can be searched by hand." He looked from me to Litsi. "Is terrorism your concern?"

"No," Litsi said. "Not directly."

Mohammed seemed relieved. "This gun wasn't invented as a terrorist weapon," he said. "It is seriously a good pistol, better all round."

"We understand that," I said. "How profitable is it?"

"To whom?"

"To the manufacturer."

"Ah." He cleared his throat. "It depends." He considered. "It costs less to make and is consequently cheaper in price than metal guns. The profit margin may not be so very different overall, but the gross profit of course depends on the number of items sold." He smiled cheerfully. "It's calculated that most of the two million people already owning guns in America, for instance, will want to upgrade to the new product. The new is better and more prestigious, and so on. Also their police forces would like to have them. Apart from there, the world is thirsty for guns for use—private Americans, you understand, own them mostly for historical reasons, for sport, for fantasy, for the feeling of personal power, not because they intend to kill people—but in many many places, killing is the purpose. Killing, security and defense. The market is wide open for really cheap good reliable new pistols. For a while at least, until the demand is filled, manufacturers could make big honest money fast."

Litsi and I listened to him with respect.

"What about dishonest money?" I asked.

He paused only momentarily. "It depends who we're talking about."

"We're still talking about the manufacturer," I said.

"Ah. A corporation?"

"A private company with one man in charge."

He produced a smile packed with worldly disillusion.

"Such a man can print his own millions."

"How, exactly?" I asked.

"The easiest way," he said, "is to ship the product in two parts." He pulled the plastic gun again into components. "Say you packed all the pieces into a box, like this, omitting only the barrel. A barrel, say, made of special plastic that won't melt or buckle from the heat caused by the friction of the bullet passing through."

He looked at us to see if we appreciated such simple matters, and seemingly reassured, went on. "The manufacturer exports the barrels separately. This, he says, ensures that if either shipment is diverted—which is a euphemism for stolen—in passage, the goods will be useless. Only when both shipments have reached their destination safely can the pistols be assembled. Right?"

"Right," we both said.

"The manufacturer does all the correct paperwork. Each shipment is exported accompanied by customs dockets, each shipment is what it purports to be, everything is legal. The next step depends on how badly the customer wants the guns."

"How do you mean?" Litsi said.

"Suppose," Mohammed answered, enjoying himself, "the customer's need is great and pressing. The manufacturer sends the guns without the barrels. The customer pays. The manufacturer sends the barrels. Good?"

We nodded.

"The manufacturer tells the customer he must pay the price on the invoices to the manufacturing company, but he must also pay a sum into a different bank account—number and country supplied—and when *that* payment is safely in the manufacturer's secret possession, then he will dispatch the barrels."

"Simple," I said.

"Of course. A widespread practice. The sort of thing that goes on the whole world over. Money up front, aboveboard settlement, offshore funds sub rosa."

"Kickbacks," I said.

"Of course. In many countries it is the accepted system. Trade cannot continue without it. A little commission, here and there . . ." He shrugged. "Your manufacturer with an all-plastic reliable cheaply made handgun could pass an adequate profit through his company's books and pocket a fortune for himself out of sight."

He reassembled the gun dexterously and held it out to me.

"Feel it," he said. "An all-plastic gun would be much lighter even than this."

I took the gun, looking at its matt black surface of purposeful shape, the metal rim of the barrel showing at the business end. It certainly was remarkably light to handle, even with metal parts. All-plastic, it could be a plaything for babies.

With an inward shiver I gave it to Litsi. It was the

second time in four days I'd been instructed in the use of handguns, and although I'd handled one before, I wasn't a good shot, nor ever likely to practice. Litsi weighed the gun thoughtfully in his palm and returned it to its owner.

"Are we talking of any manufacturer in particular?" Mohammed asked.

"About one who wants to be granted a license to manufacture and export plastic guns," I said, "but who hasn't been in the arms business before."

He raised his eyebrows. "In France?"

"Yes," Litsi said without surprise, and I realized that Mohammed must have known the inquiry had come to him through French channels, even if it hadn't been he who'd spoken to Litsi on the telephone.

Mohammed pursed his lips under the big mustache. "To get a license your manufacturer would have to be a person of particularly good standing. These licenses, you understand, are never thrown about like confetti. He must certainly have the capability, the factory, that is to say, also the prototype, also probably definite orders, but above all he must have the good name."

"You've been extremely helpful," Litsi said.

Mohammed radiated bonhomie.

"How would the manufacturer set about selling his guns? Would he advertise?" I said.

"Certainly. In firearms and trade magazines the world over. He might also engage an agent, such as myself." He smiled. "I work on commission. I am well known. People who want guns come to me and say, 'What will suit us best? How much is it? How soon can you get it?'" He spread his palms. "I'm a middleman. We are indispensable." He looked at his watch. "Anything else?"

I said on impulse, "If someone wanted a humane killer, could you supply it? A captive bolt?"

"Obsolete," he said promptly. "In England, made by Accles and Shelvoke in Birmingham. Do you mean those? Point 405 caliber, perhaps? One point two-five grain caps?"

"I daresay," I said. "I don't know."

"I don't deal in humane killers. They're too specialized. It wouldn't be worth your while to pay me to find you one. There are many around, all out of date. I would ask older veterinarians, they might be pleased to sell. You'd need a license to own one, of course." He paused. "To be frank, gentlemen, I find it most profitable to deal with customers to whom personal licenses are irrelevant."

"Is there anyone," I asked, "and please don't take this as an insult, because it's not meant that way, but is there anyone to whom you would refuse to sell guns?"

He took no offense. He said, "Only if I thought they couldn't or wouldn't pay. On moral grounds, no. I don't ask what they want them for. If I cared, I'd be in the wrong trade. I sell the hardware, I don't agonize over its use."

Both Litsi and I seemed to have run out of questions. Mohammed put the pistol back into its box, where it sat neatly above its prim little rows of bullets. He replaced the lid on the box and returned the whole to the suitcase.

"Never forget," he said, still smiling, "that attack and defense are as old as the human race. Once upon a time I would have been selling nicely sharpened spearhead flints."

"Mr. Mohammed," I said, "thank you very much."

He nodded affably. Litsi stood up and shook hands again with the diamond ring, as did I, and Mohammed said if we saw his friend loitering in the passage not to worry and not to speak to him, he would return to the room when we had gone.

We paid no attention to the friend waiting by the elevators and rode down without incident to the ground floor. It wasn't until we were in a taxi on the way back to Eaton Square that either of us spoke.

"He was justifying himself," Litsi said.

"Everyone does. It's healthy."

He turned his head. "How do you mean?"

"The alternative is guilty despair. Self-justification may be an illusion, but it keeps you from suicide."

"You could self-justify suicide."

I smiled at him sideways. "So you could."

"Nanterre," he said, "has a powerful urge to sharpen flints."

"Mm. Lighter, cheaper, razorlike flints."

"Bearing the de Brescou cachet."

"I had a powerful vision," I said, "of Roland shaking hands on a deal with Mohammed."

Litsi laughed. "We must save him from the justification."

"How did you get hold of Mohammed?" I asked.

"One of the useful things about being a prince," Litsi said, "is that if one seriously asks, one is seldom refused. Another is that one knows and has met a great many people in useful positions. I simply set a few wheels in motion, much as you did yesterday, incidentally, with Lord Vaughnley." He paused. "Why is a man you defeated so anxious to please you?"

"Well, in defeating him I also saved him. Maynard Allardeck was out to take over his newspaper by fair means and definitely foul, and I gave him the means of stopping him permanently, which was a copy of that film."

"I do see," Litsi said ironically, "that he owes you a favor or two."

"Also," I said, "the boy who gambled half his inheritance away under Maynard's influence was Hugh Vaughnley, Lord Vaughnley's son. By threatening to publish the film, Lord Vaughnley made Maynard give the inheritance back. The inheritance, actually, was shares in the *Towncrier* newspaper."

"A spot of poetic blackmail. Your idea?"

"Well, sort of."

He chuckled. "I suppose I should disapprove. It was surely against the law."

"The law doesn't always deliver justice. The victim mostly loses. Too often the law can only punish, it can't put things right."

"And you think righting the victims' wrongs is more important than anything else?"

"Where it's possible, the highest priority."

"And you'd break the law to do it?"

"It's too late at night for being tied into knots," I said, "and we're back at Eaton Square."

We went upstairs to the sitting room and, the princess and Beatrice having gone to bed, drank a brandy nightcap in relaxation. I liked Litsi more and more as a person, and wished him permanently on the other side of the globe; and looking at him looking at me, I wondered if he were possibly thinking the same thing.

"What are you doing tomorrow?" he said.

"Racing at Bradbury."

"Where's that?"

"Halfway to Devon."

"I don't know where you get the energy." He yawned. "I spent a gentle afternoon walking round Ascot racecourse, and I'm whacked."

Large and polished, he drank his brandy, and in time we unplugged the recording telephone, carried it down to the basement, and replugged it in the hallway there. Then we went up to the ground floor and paused for a moment outside Litsi's door.

"Goodnight," I said,

"Goodnight." He hesitated, and then held out his hand. I shook it. "Such a silly habit," he said with irony, "but what else can one do?" He gave me a sketchy wave and went into his room, and I continued on up to see if I were still to sleep among the bamboo shoots, which it seemed I was.

I dozed on top of the bedclothes for an hour or so and then went down, out, and round the back to get the car to fetch Danielle.

I thought, as I walked quietly into the dark, deserted alley, that it really was a perfect place for an ambush.

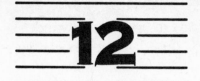

The alley was a cobbled cul-de-sac about twenty feet wide and a hundred yards long, with a wider place at the far end for turning, the backs of tall buildings closing it all in like a canyon. Its sides were lined with garage doors, the wide garages themselves running in under the backs of the buildings, and unlike many other mews where the garages had originally been built as housing for coaches and horses, Falmouth Mews, as it was called, had no residential entrances.

By day the mews was alive and busy, as a firm of motor mechanics occupied several of the garages, doing repairs for the surrounding neighborhood. At night, when they'd gone home, the place was a shadowy lane of big closed doors, lit only from the windows of the buildings above.

The garage where Thomas kept the Rolls was farther than halfway in. Next, beyond, was a garage belonging to the mechanics, which Thomas had persuaded them to rent temporarily to the princess, to accommodate Danielle's car (now recovered from the menders by Thomas). My Mercedes, unhoused, was parked along outside Danielle's garage doors, and other cars, here and there along the mews, were similarly placed. In a two-car family, one typically was in the generous-sized lockup, the second lengthways outside.

Around and behind these second cars there were a myriad of hiding places.

I ought to have brought a torch, I thought. Tomorrow I would buy one. The mews could shelter a host of monsters . . . and Beatrice knew what time I set off each night to Chiswick.

I walked down the center of the alley feeling my heart thud, yet I'd gone down there the night before without a tremor. The power of imagination, I thought wryly: and nothing rustled in the undergrowth, nothing pounced, the tiger wasn't around for the goat.

The car looked exactly as I'd left it, but I checked the wiring under the hood and under the dashboard before switching on the ignition. I checked there was no oil leaking from under the engine, and that all the tires were hard, and I tested the brakes with a sudden stop before turning out into the road.

Satisfied, I drove without trouble to Chiswick, collecting Danielle at two o'clock. She was tired from the long day and talked little, telling me only that they'd spent all evening on a story about snow and ice houses that she thought was a waste of time.

"What snow and ice houses?" I asked, more just to talk to her than from wanting to know.

"Sculptures for a competition. Some of the guys had

been out filming them in an exhibition. Like sandcastles, only made of snow and ice. Some of them were quite pretty and even had lights inside them. The guys said the place they were in was like filming in an igloo without a blanket. All good fun, I guess, but not world news."

She yawned and fell silent, and in a short while we were back in the mews: it was always a quick journey at night, with no traffic.

"You can't keep coming to pick me up," she said, as we walked round into Eaton Square.

"I like to."

"Litsi told me that the man in the hood was Henri Nanterre." She shivered. "I don't know if it makes it better or worse. Anyway, I'm not working Friday nights right now, or Saturdays or Sundays, of course. You can sleep, Friday night."

We let ourselves into the house with the new keys and said goodnight again on her landing. We never had slept in the same bed in that house, so there were no such memories or regrets to deal with, but I fiercely wished as I walked up one more flight that she would come up there with me: yet it had been no use suggesting it, because her goodnight kiss had again been a defense, not a promise, and had landed again any way but squarely.

Give her time. Time was an aching anxiety with no certainty ahead.

Breakfast, warmth and newspapers were to be found each day down in the morning room, whose door was across the hall from Litsi's. I was in there about nine on that Thursday morning, drinking orange juice and checking on the day's runners at Bradbury, when the intercom buzzed, and

Dawson's voice told me there was a call from Mr. Harlow.

I picked up the outside receiver fearfully.

"Wykeham?"

"Oh, Kit. Look, I thought I'd better tell you, but don't alarm the princess. We had a prowler last night."

"Are the horses all right? Kinley?"

"Yes, yes. Nothing much happened. The man with the dog said his dog was restless, as if someone was moving about. He says his dog was very alert and whining softly for a good half hour, and that they patrolled the courtyards twice. They didn't see anyone, though, and after a while the dog relaxed again. So what do you think?"

"I think it's a bloody good job you've got the dog."

"Yes, it's very worrying."

"What time was all this?"

"About midnight. I'd gone to bed, of course, and the guard didn't wake me, as nothing had happened. There's no sign that anyone was here."

"Just keep on with the patrols," I said, "and make sure you don't get the man that slept in the hay barn."

"No. I told them not to send him. They've all been very sharp, since that first night."

We discussed the two horses he was sending to Bradbury, neither of them the princess's. He sometimes sent his slowest horses to Bradbury in the belief that if they didn't win there, they wouldn't win anywhere, but he avoided it most of the time. It was a small country course, with a flat circuit of little more than a mile, easy to ride on if one stuck to the inside.

"Give Melissande a nice ride, now."

"Yes, Wykeham," I said. Melissande had been before my time. "Do you mean Pinkeye?"

"Well, of course." He cleared his throat. "How long are you staying in Eaton Square?"

"I don't know. I'll tell you, though, when I leave."

We disconnected and I put a slice of wholemeal bread in the toaster and thought about prowlers.

Litsi came in and poured himself some coffee. "I thought," he said conversationally, assembling a bowl of muesli and cream, "that I might go to the races today."

"To Bradbury?" I was surprised. "It's not like Ascot. It's the bare bones of the industry. Not much comfort."

"Are you saying you don't want to take me?"

"No. Just warning you."

He sat down at the table and watched me eat toast without butter or marmalade.

"Your diet's disgusting."

"I'm used to it."

He watched me swallow a pill with black coffee. "What are those for?" he asked.

"Vitamins."

He shook his head resignedly and dug into his own hopelessly fattening concoction, and Danielle came in looking fresh and clear-eyed in a baggy white sweater.

"Hi," she said to neither of us in particular. "I wondered if you'd be here. What are you doing today?"

"Going to the races," Litsi said.

"Are you?" She looked at him directly, in surprise. "With Kit?"

"Certainly, with Kit."

"Oh. Then . . . er . . . can I come?"

She looked from one of us to the other, undoubtedly seeing double pleasure.

"In half an hour," I said, smiling.

"Easy."

So all three of us went to Bradbury races, parting in the hall from the princess, who had come down to go through some secretarial work with Mrs. Jenkins and who looked wistfully at our outdoor clothes, and also from Beatrice, who had come down out of general nosiness.

Her sharp round gaze fastened on me. "Are you coming back?" she demanded.

"Yes, he is," the princess said smoothly. "And tomorrow we can all go to see my two runners at Sandown, isn't that nice?"

Beatrice looked not quite sure how the one followed on the other and, in the moment of uncertainty, Litsi, Danielle and I departed.

Bradbury racecourse, we found when we arrived, was undergoing an ambitious upgrading. There were notices everywhere apologizing for the inconvenience of heaps of builders' materials and machines. A whole new grandstand was going up inside scaffolding in the cheaper ring, and most of the top tier of the members' stand was being turned into a glassed-in viewing room with tables, chairs and refreshments. They had made provision up there also for a backward-facing viewing gallery, from which one could see the horses walk round in the parade ring.

There was a small model on a table outside the weighing room, showing what it would all be like when finished, and the racecourse executives were going around with pleased smiles accepting compliments.

Litsi and Danielle went off in search of a drink and a sandwich in the old unrefurbished bar under the emerging dream, and I, sliding into nylon tights, breeches and boots, tried not to think about that too much. I pulled on a thin vest, and my valet neatly tied the white stock around my neck. After that I put on the padded back-guard, which saved one's spine and kidneys from too much damage, and on top of that the first set of colors for the day. Crash helmet, goggles, whip, number cloth, weight cloth, saddle; I checked them all, weighed out, handed the necessary to Dusty to go and saddle up, put on an anorak because of the cold and went out to ride.

I wouldn't have minded, just once, having a day when I could stand on the stands and go racing with Danielle like anyone else. Eat a sandwich, have a drink, place a bet. I saw them smiling and waving to me as I rode onto the track, and I waved back, wanting to be right there beside them on the ground.

The horse I was riding won the race, which would surprise and please Wykeham but not make up for Col's losing the day before.

Besides Wykeham's two runners I'd been booked for three others. I rode one of those without results in the second race and put Pinkeye's red and blue striped colors on for the third, walking out in my warming anorak toward the parade ring to talk to the fussiest and most critical of all Wykeham's owners.

I didn't get as far as the parade ring. There was a cry high up, and a voice calling, "Help," and along with everyone else I twisted my head round to see what was happening.

There was a man hanging by one hand from the new viewing balcony high on the members' stand. A big man in a dark overcoat.

Litsi.

In absolute horror I watched him swing round until he

177

had two hands on the top of the balcony wall, but he was too big and heavy to pull himself up, and below him there was a fifty-foot drop direct to hard tarmac.

I sprinted over there, tore off my anorak and laid it on the ground directly under where Litsi hung.

"Take off your coat," I said to the nearest man. "Lay it on the ground."

"Someone must go up and help him," he said. "Someone will go."

"Take off your coat." I turned to a woman. "Take off your coat. Lay it on the ground. Quick, quick, lay coats on the ground."

She looked at me blindly. She was wearing a full-length expensive fur. She slid out of her coat and threw it on top of my anorak, and said fiercely to the man next to her, "Take off your coat, take off your coat."

I ran from person to person, "Take off your coat, quick, quick . . . Take off your coat."

A whole crowd had collected, staring upward, arrested on their drift back to the stands for the next race.

"Take off your coat," I could hear people saying. "Take off your coat."

Dear God, Litsi, I prayed, just hang on.

There were other people yelling to him, "Hang on, hang on," and one or two foolishly screaming, and it seemed to me there was a great deal of noise, although very many were silent.

A little boy with huge eyes unzipped his tiny blue anorak and pulled off his small patterned jersey and flung them onto the growing, spreading pile, and I heard him running about in the crowd, in his bright cotton T shirt, his high voice calling, "Quick, quick, take off your coats."

It was working. The coats came off in dozens and were thrown, were passed through the crowd, were chucked higgledy-piggledy to form a mattress, until the circle on the ground was wide enough to contain him if he fell, but could be thicker, thicker.

No one had reached Litsi from the balcony side: no strong arms clutching to haul him up.

Coats were flying like leaves. The word had spread to everyone in sight. "Take off your coat, take off your coat, quick . . . quick . . ."

When Litsi fell he looked like another flying overcoat, except that he came down fast, like a plummet. One second he was hanging there, the next he was down. He fell straight to begin with, then his heavy shoulders tipped his balance backward and he landed almost flat on his back.

He bounced heavily on the coats and rolled and slid off them and ended with his head on one coat and his body on the tarmac, sprawling on his side, limp as a rag.

I sprang to kneel beside him and saw immediately that although he was dazed, he was truly alive. Hands stretched to help him up, but he wasn't ready for that, and I said, "Don't move him. Let him move first. You have to be careful."

Everyone who went racing knew about spinal injuries and not moving jockeys until it was safe, and there I was, in my jockey's colors, to remind them. The hands were ready, but they didn't touch.

I looked up at that crowd, all in shirtsleeves, all shivering with cold, all saints. Some were in tears, particularly the woman who'd laid her mink on the line.

"Litsi," I said, looking down and seeing some sort of order return to his eyes. "Litsi, how are you doing?"

"I . . . Did I fall?" He moved a hand, and then his feet, just a little, and the crowd murmured with relief.

"Yes, you fell," I said. "Just stay there for a minute. Everything's fine."

Somebody above was calling down, "Is he all right?" and there, up on the balcony, were the two men who'd apparently gone up to save him.

The crowd shouted, "Yes," and started clapping, and in almost gala mood began collecting their coats from the pile. There must have been almost two hundred of them, I thought, watching. Anoraks, huskies, tweeds, raincoats, furs, suit jackets, sweaters, even a horse rug. It was taking much longer to disentangle the huge heap than it had to collect it.

The little boy with big eyes picked up his blue anorak and zipped it on over his jersey, staring at me. I hugged him. "What's your name?" I said.

"Matthew."

"You're a great guy."

"That's my daddy's coat," he said, "under the man's head."

"Ask him to leave it there just another minute."

Someone had run to fetch the first-aid men, who arrived with a stretcher.

"I'm all right," Litsi said weakly, but he was still winded and disorientated, and made no demur when they made preparations for transporting him.

Danielle was suddenly there beside him, her face white.

"Litsi," she was saying, "oh, God . . ." She looked at me. "I was waiting for him . . . someone said a man fell . . . is he all right?"

"He's going to be," I said. "He'll be fine."

"Oh . . ."

I put my arms round her. "It's all right. Really it is. Nothing seems to be hurting him, he's just had his breath knocked out."

She slowly disengaged herself and walked away beside the stretcher when they lifted it onto a rolling platform, a gurney.

"Are you his wife?" I heard a first-aid man say.

"No . . . a friend."

The little boy's father picked up his coat and shook my hand. The woman picked up her squashed mink, brushed dust off it and gave me a kiss. A Steward came out and said would I now please get on my horse and go down to the start, as the race would already be off late, and I looked at the racecourse clock and saw in amazement that it was barely fifteen minutes since I'd walked out of the weighing room.

All the horses, all the owners and trainers were still in the parade ring, as if time had stopped, but now the jockeys were mounting; death had been averted, life could thankfully go on.

I picked up my anorak. All the coats had been reclaimed, and it lay there alone on the tarmac, with my whip underneath. I looked up at the balcony, so far above, so deserted and unremarkable. Nothing suddenly seemed real, yet the questions hadn't even begun to be asked. Why had he been up there? How had he come to be clinging to life by his fingertips? In what way had he not been careful?

Litsi lay on a bed in the first-aid room until the races were over, but insisted then that he had entirely recovered and was ready to return to London.

He apologized to the racecourse executive for having been so foolish as to go up to the balcony to look at the new, much-vaunted view, and said that it was entirely his own clumsiness that had caused him to stumble over some builders' materials and lose his balance.

When asked for his name, he'd given a shortened version of his surname without the "prince" in front, and he hoped there wouldn't be too much public fuss over his stupidity.

He was sitting in the back of the car, telling us all this, Danielle sitting beside him, as we started toward London.

"How did you stumble?" I asked, glancing at him from time to time in the driving mirror. "Was there a lot of junk up there?"

"Planks and things." He sounded puzzled. "I don't really know how I stumbled. I stood on something that rocked, and I put a hand out to steady myself, and it went out into space, over the wall. It happened so fast . . . I just lost my footing."

"Did anyone push you?" I asked.

"Kit!" Danielle said, horrified, but it had to be considered, and Litsi, it seemed, had already done so.

"I've been lying there all afternoon," he said slowly, "trying to remember exactly how it happened. I didn't see anyone up there at all, I'm certain of that. I stood on something that rocked like a seesaw, and totally lost my balance. I wouldn't say I was pushed."

"Well," I said thoughtfully, "do you mind if we go back there? I should have gone up for a look when I'd finished racing."

"The racecourse people went up," Litsi said. "They came and told me that there was nothing particularly dangerous, but of course I shouldn't have gone."

"We'll go back," I said, and although Danielle protested that she'd be late for work, back we went.

Leaving Danielle and Litsi outside in the car, I walked through the gates and up the grandstand. As with most grandstands, it was a long haul to the top, up not-too-generous stairways, and one could see why, with a stream of people piling up that way to the main tier to watch the race, those going up to rescue Litsi from above had been a fair time on their journey.

The broad viewing steps of the main tier led right down to the ground and were openly accessible, on the side facing the racecourse, but the upper tier could be reached only by the stairways, of which there were two, one at each end.

I went up the stairway at the end nearest the weighing room, the stairway Litsi said he had used to reach the place where he'd overbalanced. Looking up at the back of the grandstand from the ground, that place was near the end of the balcony, on the left.

The stairway led first onto the upper steps of the main tier, and then continued upward, and I climbed to the top landing, where the refreshment room was in process of construction.

The whole area had been glassed in, leaving only the balcony open. The balcony ran along the back of the re-freshment room, which had several glass doors, now closed, to lead eventually to the sandwiches. Inside the glass and without, there were copious piles of builders' materials, planks, drums of paint and ladders.

I went gingerly forward to the cold, open, windy balcony, toward the place where Litsi had overbalanced, and saw what had very likely happened. Planks lay side by side and several deep along all the short passage to the balcony, raising one, as one walked along them, higher than normal in proportion to the chest-high wall. When I was walking on the planks, the wall ahead seemed barely waist-high and Litsi was taller than I by three or four inches.

Whatever had rocked under Litsi's feet was no longer rocking, but several planks by the balcony wall itself were scattered like spillikins, not lying flat as in the passage. I picked my way among them, feeling them move when I pushed, and reached the spot where Litsi had fallen.

With my feet firmly on the floor, I looked over. One could see all the parade-ring area beautifully, with magnificent hills beyond. Very attractive, that balcony, and with one's feet on the floor, very safe.

I went along its whole length intending to go down by the stairway at the other end, nearest the car park, but found I couldn't: the stairs themselves were missing, being in the middle of reconstruction. I walked back to the end where I had come up, renegotiated the planks, and descended to ground level.

"Well?" Litsi asked, when I was back in the car. "What did you think?"

"Those planks looked pretty unsafe."

"Yes," he said ruefully, as I started the car and drove out of the racecourse gates. "I thought, after I'd overbalanced, and managed somehow to catch hold of the wall, that if I just hung on, someone would come and rescue me, but you know, my fingers just gave way. I didn't leave go consciously. When I was falling, I thought I would die . . . and I would have done . . . it's incredible that all those people took off their coats." He paused, "I wish I could thank them," he said.

"I couldn't think where you'd got to," Danielle reflected. "I was waiting for you on the stands, where we'd arranged to meet after I'd been to the ladies' room. I didn't imagine . . ."

"But," said Litsi, "I went up to that balcony because I was supposed to meet you up there, Danielle."

I stopped the car abruptly.

"Say that again," I said.

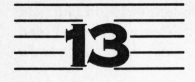

Litsi said it again. "I got this message that Danielle was waiting for me up on the balcony to look at the view."

"I didn't send any such message," Danielle said blankly. "I was waiting where we'd watched the race before, where we'd said we'd meet."

"Who gave you the message?" I asked Litsi.

"Just a man."

"What did he look like?"

"Well . . . an ordinary man. Not very young. He had a *Sporting Life* in his hands, and a sort of form book, with his finger keeping the place, and binoculars."

"What sort of voice?"

"Just . . . ordinary."

I let the brakes off with a sigh and started off toward Chiswick. Litsi had walked straight into a booby trap that had been meant either to frighten him or to kill him, and no one would have set it but Henri Nanterre. I hadn't seen Nanterre at the races, and neither Litsi nor Danielle knew him by sight.

If Nanterre had set the trap, he'd known where Litsi would be that day, and the only way he could have known was via Beatrice. I couldn't believe that she would have known what use would be made of her little tit-bit, and it occurred to me that I didn't want her to know, either. It was important that Beatrice should keep right on telling.

Litsi and Danielle were quiet in the back of the car, no doubt traveling along much the same mental track. They protested, though, when I asked them not to tell Beatrice about the fake message.

"But she's got to know," Danielle said vehemently. "Then she'll see she must *stop* it. She'll see how murderous that man is."

"I don't want her to stop it just yet," I said. "Not until Tuesday."

"Why ever not? Why Tuesday?"

"We'll do what Kit wants," Litsi said. "I'll tell Beatrice just what I told the racecourse people, that I went up to look at the view."

"She's dangerous," Danielle said.

"I don't see how we can catch Nanterre without her," I said. "So be a darling."

I wasn't sure whether it was the actual word that silenced her, but she made no more objections, and we traveled for a while without saying anything significant. Litsi's arms and shoulders were aching from the strain of having hung on to the wall so long, and he shifted uncomfortably from time to time, making small grunts.

I went back to thinking about the man who had delivered the misleading message, and asked Litsi if he was absolutely positive the man had used the word "Danielle."

"Positive," Litsi said without hesitation. "What he said to me first was, 'Do you know someone called Danielle?' When I said I did, he said she wanted me to go up the stairs to the balcony to look at the view. He pointed up there. So I went."

"OK," I said. "Then we'll take a spot of positive action."

Like almost everyone in the racing world, I had a telephone in my car, and I put a call through to the *Towncrier* and asked for the Sports Desk. I wasn't sure whether their racing correspondent, Bunty Ireland, would be in the office at that time, but it seemed he was. He hadn't been at Bradbury: he went mostly to major meetings and on other days wrote his column in the office.

"I want to pay for an advertisement," I told him, "but it has to be on the racing page and in a conspicuous place."

"Are you touting for rides?" he asked sardonically. "A Grand National mount? Have saddle, will travel, that sort of thing?"

"Yeah," I said. "Very funny." Bunty had an elephantine sense of humor but he was kind at heart. "Write this down word for word, and persuade the racing-page editor to print it in nice big noticeable letters."

"Fire away, then."

"Large reward offered to anyone who passed on a message from Danielle at Bradbury races on Thursday afternoon." I dictated it slowly and added the telephone number of the house in Eaton Square.

Bunty's mystification came clearly across the air waves. "You want the personal column for that," he said.

"No. The racing page. Did you get it straight?"

He read it over, word for word.

"Hey," he said, "if you were riding at Bradbury perhaps you can confirm this very odd story we've got about a guy falling from a balcony onto a pile of coats. Is someone having us on, or should we print it?"

"It happened," I said.

"Did you see it?"

"Yes," I said.

"Was the guy hurt?"

"No, not at all. Look, Bunty, get the story from someone else, will you? I'm in my car, and I want to get that ad in the *Sporting Life* and the *Racing Post*, before they go to press. And could you give me their numbers?"

"Sure, hold on."

I put the receiver down temporarily and passed my pen and notebook back to Danielle, and when Bunty returned with the numbers, repeated them aloud for her to write down.

"Hey, Kit," Bunty said, "give me a quote I can use about your chances on Abseil tomorrow."

"You know I can't, Bunty, Wykeham Harlow doesn't like it."

"Yeah, yeah. He's an uncooperative old bugger."

"Don't forget the ad," I said.

He promised to see to it, and I made the calls with the same request to the two sporting papers.

"Tomorrow and Saturday," I said to them. "In big black type on the front page."

"It'll cost you," they said.

"Send me the bill."

Danielle and Litsi listened to these conversations in silence, and when I'd finished, Litsi said doubtfully, "Do you expect any results?"

"You never know. You can't get any results if you don't try."

Danielle said, "Your motto for life."

"Not a bad one," Litsi said.

We dropped Danielle at the studio just on time and returned to Eaton Square. Litsi decided to say nothing at all about his narrow escape, and asked for my advice in the matter of strained muscles.

"A sauna and a massage," I said. "Failing that, a long hot soak and some aspirins. And John Grundy might give you a massage tomorrow morning."

He decided on the home cures and, reaching the house, disappeared into his rooms to deal with his woes in private. I continued up to the bamboo room, still uninvaded territory, where, in the evening routine, I telephoned to Wykeham and picked up my messages.

Wykeham said the owners of Pinkeye were irritated that the race had been delayed, and had complained to him that I'd been offhand with them afterward.

"But Pinkeye won," I said. I'd ridden the whole race automatically, like driving a well-known journey with a preoccupied mind and not remembering a yard of it on arrival. When I'd gone past the winning post I hadn't been able to remember much about the jumps.

"You know what they're like," Wykeham said. "Never satisfied, even when they win."

"Mm," I said. "Is the horse all right?"

All the horses were fine, Wykeham said, and Abseil (pronounced Absail) was jumping out of his skin and should trot up on the morrow.

"Great," I said. "Well, goodnight, Wykeham."

"Goodnight, Paul."

Normality, I thought with a smile, disconnecting, was definitely on its way back.

Dinner was a stilted affair of manufactured conversations, with Roland de Brescou sitting at the head of the table in his wheelchair, looking abstracted.

Beatrice spent some time complaining that Harrods was now impossible (*busloads* of tourists, Casilia) and that Fortnums was too crowded, and that her favorite fur shop had closed and vanished. Beatrice's day of shopping had included a visit to the hairdresser, with a consequent intensification of peach tint. Beatrice's pleasures, I saw, were a way of passing time that had no other purpose: a vista of smothering pointlessness, infinitely depressing. No wonder, I thought, that she complained, with all that void pursuing her.

She looked at me, no doubt feeling my gaze, and said with undisguisable sudden venom, "It's you that's standing in the way of progress. I know it is, don't deny it. Roland admitted it this morning. I'm sure he would have agreed to Henri's plans if it hadn't been for you. He admitted you're against it. You've influenced him. You're evil."

"Beatrice," the princess remonstrated, "he's our guest."

"I don't care," she said passionately, "he shouldn't be. It's he all the time who's standing in my way."

"In *your* way, Beatrice?" Roland asked.

Beatrice hesitated. "In my room," she said finally.

"It's true," I said without aggression, "that I'm against Monsieur de Brescou signing anything against his conscience."

"I'll get rid of you," she said.

"No, Beatrice, really, that's too much," the princess exclaimed. "Kit, please accept my apologies."

"It's all right," I assured her truthfully. "Perfectly all right. I do stand in Mrs. Bunt's way. In the matter of Monsieur acting against his conscience, I always will."

Litsi looked at me speculatively. I had made a very explicit and provocative declaration, and he seemed to be wondering if I was aware of it. I, on the other hand, was glad to have been presented with the opportunity, and I would repeat what I'd said, given the chance.

"You are after Danielle's money," Beatrice said furiously.

"You know she has none."

"After her inheritance from Roland."

The princess and Roland were looking poleaxed. No one, I guessed, had conducted such open warfare before at that polite dinner table.

"On the contrary," I said civilly. "If selling guns would make Monsieur richer, and if I were after Danielle's mythical inheritance, then I would be urging him to sign at once."

She stared at me, temporarily silenced. I kept my face entirely noncommittal, a habit learned from dealing with Maynard Allardeck, and behaved as if we had been having a normal conversation. "In general," I said pleasantly, "I would implacably oppose anyone trying to get their way by threats and harassment. Henri Nanterre has behaved like a thug, and while I'm here I'll try my hardest to ensure he fails in his objective."

Litsi opened his mouth, thought better of it, and said nothing. The speculation however disappeared from his forehead to be replaced by an unspecified anxiety.

"Well," Beatrice said, "well . . ."

I said mildly, as before, "It's really as well to make oneself perfectly clear, isn't it? As you have admirably done, Mrs. Bunt?"

We were eating Dover sole at the time. Beatrice decided there were a good many bones all of a sudden demanding her attention, and Litsi smoothly said that he had been invited to the opening of a new art gallery in Dover Street, on the following Wednesday, and would his Aunt Casilia care to go with him.

"Wednesday?" The princess looked from Litsi to me. "Where's the racing next Wednesday?"

"Folkestone," I said.

The princess accepted Litsi's invitation, because she didn't go to Folkestone normally, and he and she batted a few platitudes across the table to flatten out those Bunt-Fielding ripples. When we moved to the sitting room Litsi again helped make sure I was next to the telephone, but it remained silent all evening. No messages, threats or boasting from Nanterre. It was too much to hope for, I thought, that he had folded his tents and departed.

When Roland, the princess and Beatrice finally went to bed, Litsi, rising to his feet to follow them, said, "You elected yourself as goat, then?"

"I don't intend to get eaten," I said, smiling and standing also.

"Don't go up to any balconies."

"No," I said. "Sleep well."

I did the rounds of the house, but everything seemed safe, and in due time went to the car, to go to fetch Danielle.

The alley seemed just as spooky, and I took even more

precautions with the guts of the car, but again everything appeared safe, and I drove to Chiswick without incident.

Danielle looked pale and tired. "A hectic evening," she said. Her job as bureau coordinator involved deciding how individual news stories should be covered and dispatching camera crews accordingly. I'd been in the studio with her several times and seen her working, seen the mental energy and drive that went into making her the success she'd proved there. I'd seen her decisiveness and her inspirational sparkle, and knew that afterward they could die away fast into weary silence.

The silences between us, though, were no longer companionable spaces of deep accord, but almost embarrassments, as between strangers. We had been passionate weekend lovers through November, December and January, and in her the joy had evaporated from one week to the next.

I drove back to Eaton Square thinking how very much I loved her, how much I longed for her to be as she had been, and when I stopped the car in the mews I said impulsively, before she could get out, "Danielle, please . . . please . . . tell me what's wrong."

It was clumsily said and came straight from desperation, and I was disregarding the princess's advice; and as soon as I'd said it I wished I hadn't because the last thing on earth I wanted to hear her say was that she loved Litsi. I thought I might even be driving her into saying it, and in a panic I said, "Don't answer. It doesn't matter. Don't answer."

She turned her head and looked at me, and then looked away.

"It was wonderful, at the beginning, wasn't it?" she said. "It happened so fast. It was . . . magic."

I couldn't bear to listen. I unlatched the car door to start
to get out.

"Wait," she said, "I must—now I've started."

"No," I said. "Don't."

"About a month ago," she said, all the repressed things
pouring out in a jumble, "when you had that dreadful fall
at Kempton and I saw you lying on a stretcher unconscious
while they unloaded you from the ambulance . . . and it
gave me diarrhea, I was so frightened you would die . . .
and I was overwhelmed by how much danger there is in
your life . . . and how much pain . . . and I seemed to see
myself here in a strange country . . . with a commitment
made for my whole life . . . not just enjoying a delicious
unexpected romance but trapped forever into a life far
from home, full of fear every day . . . and I didn't know it
was so cold and wet here and I was brought up in California . . . and then Litsi came . . . and he knows so much
. . . and it seemed so simple being with him going to safe
things like exhibitions and not hearing my heart thud . . . I
could hear the worry in your voice on the telephone and
see it this week in your face, but I couldn't seem to tell
you . . ." She paused very briefly. "I told Aunt Casilia. I
asked her what to do."

I loosened my throat. "What did she say?" I said.

"She said no one could decide for me. I asked her if she
thought I would get used to the idea of living forever in a
foreign country, like she has, and also of facing the possibility you'd be killed or horrifically injured . . . and don't
say it doesn't happen, there was a jockey killed last week
. . . and I asked her if she thought I was stupid."

She swallowed. "She said that nothing would change
you, that you are as you are, and I was to see you clearly.

She said the question wasn't whether I could face life here with you, but whether I could face life anywhere without you."

She paused again. "I told her how calm I felt with Litsi . . . She said Litsi was a nice man . . . She said in time I would see . . . understand . . . what I wanted most . . . She said time has a way of resolving things in one's mind . . . she said you would be patient, and she's right, you are, you are . . . But I can't go on like this forever, I know it's unfair. I went racing yesterday and today to see if I could go back . . . but I can't. I hardly watch the races. I blank out of my mind what you're doing . . . that you're there. I promised Aunt Casilia I'd go . . . and try . . . but I just talked to Litsi . . ." Her voice faded in silence, tired and unhappy.

"I love you very much," I said slowly. "Do you want me to give up my job?"

"Aunt Casilia said if I asked, and you did, and we married, it would be disastrous. We would be divorced within five years. She was very vehement. She said I must not ask it, it was totally unfair, I would be destroying you because I don't have your courage." She swallowed convulsively, tears filling her eyes.

I looked along the shadowy mews and thought of danger and fear, those old tamed friends. One couldn't teach anyone how to live with them: it had to come from inside. It got easier with practice, like everything else, but also it could vanish overnight. Nerve came and nerve went: there could be an overload of the capacity for endurance.

"Come on," I said, "it's getting cold." I paused. "Thank you for telling me."

"What . . . are you going to do?"

"Go indoors and sleep till morning."

"No . . ." she sobbed on a laugh. "About what I said."

"I'm going to wait," I said, "like Princess Casilia told me to."

"Told you!" Danielle exclaimed. "Did you tell her?"

"No, I didn't. She said it out of the blue in the parade ring at Ascot."

"Oh," Danielle said in a small voice. "It was on Tuesday, while you were in Devon, that I asked her."

We got out of the car and I locked the doors. What Danielle had said had been bad enough, but not as bad as an irrevocable declaration for Litsi. Until she took off the engagement ring she still wore, I would cling to some sort of hope.

We walked back side by side to the square, and said goodnight again briefly on the landing. I went on upstairs and lay on the bed and suffered a good deal, for which there was no aspirin.

When I went in to breakfast, both Litsi and Danielle were already in the morning room, he sitting at the table reading the *Sporting Life,* she leaning over his shoulder to do the same.

"Is it in?" I said.

"Is what in?" Litsi asked, intently reading.

"The advertisement," I said, "for the message-passer."

"Yes . . . it's in," Litsi said. "There's a picture of you in the paper."

I fetched some grapefruit juice, unexcited. There were photographs of me in newspapers quite often: result of the job.

"It says here," Litsi said, "that champion jockey Kit Fielding saved the life of a man at Bradbury by persuading the crowd to take off their coats . . ." He lowered the paper and stared at me. "You didn't say a word about it being your idea."

Danielle too was staring. "Why didn't you tell us?"

"An uprush of modesty," I said, drinking the juice.

Litsi laughed. "I won't thank you, then."

"No, don't."

Danielle said to me, "Do you want some toast?"

"Yes . . . please," I said.

She walked over to the sideboard, cut a slice of wholemeal bread and put it in the toaster. I watched her do it, and Litsi, I found, watched me. I met his eyes and couldn't tell what he was thinking, and wondered how much had been visible in my own face.

"How are the muscles?" I asked.

"Stiff."

I nodded. The toast popped up in the toaster and Danielle put the slice on a plate, brought it over and put it down in front of me.

"Thank you," I said.

"You're welcome." It was lightly said, but not a return to November. I ate the toast while it was still hot, and was grateful for small mercies.

"Are you busy again this afternoon?" Litsi asked.

"Five rides," I said. "Are you coming?"

"Aunt Casilia said we're all going."

"So she did." I reflected a little, remembering the morning conversation in the hall. "It might be a good idea," I said to Danielle, "if you could casually mention in front of Beatrice, but so as to make sure she hears, that you'll only be working on Monday next week."

She looked astonished. "But I'm not. I'm working a normal schedule."

"I want Beatrice to think Monday's your last night for coming home so late."

"Why?" Danielle asked. "I don't mean I won't do it, but why?"

Litsi was watching me steadily. "What else?" he said.

I said conversationally, "There's no harm in laying out a line with a few baited hooks. If the fish doesn't take the opportunity, nothing will have been lost."

"And if he does?"

"Net him."

"What sort of line and hooks?" Danielle asked.

"A time and place," I said, "for removing an immovable object."

She said to Litsi, "Do you know what he means?"

"I'm afraid I do," he said. "He told Beatrice last night that while he was here to prevent it, Roland would never sign a contract for arms. Kit is also the only one of us that Nanterre hasn't directly attacked in any way, although he has twice promised to do it. Kit's directing him to a time and place that we may be able to turn to our advantage. The time, I gather, is early Tuesday morning, when he leaves this house to fetch you from work."

"And the place?" Danielle said, her eyes wide.

Litsi glanced at me. "We all know the perfect place," he said.

After the briefest of pauses, she said flatly, "The alley."

I nodded. "When Thomas drives the princess and Beatrice to the races today, he'll say he's forgotten something essential that he has to fetch from the garage on the way. He's going to drive the Rolls right down the mews to the turning circle, to give Beatrice a full view of it, and on the way back he'll stop by the garage but behind my Mercedes. He's going to say how deserted and dark the alley is at night. He's going to point out that the Mercedes is my car, and he's going to mention that I fetch you in it every night. If Beatrice does her stuff, there's just a chance Nanterre will come. And if he doesn't, as I said, nothing's lost."

"Will you be there," Danielle said, "in the alley?" She didn't wait for an answer. "Silly question," she said.

"I'll hire a chauffeur-driven car to go to Chiswick to bring you back," I said.

"Couldn't Thomas?"

"Thomas," I said, "says he wouldn't miss the show for anything. He and Sammy will both be there. I'm not walking into that alley on my own."

"I won't be able to work," Danielle said. "I don't think I'll go."

"Indeed you must," Litsi said. "Everything must look normal."

"But what if he comes?" she said. "What if you catch him, what then?"

"I'll make him an offer he can't resist," I said, and although they both wanted to know what it was, I thought I wouldn't tell them just yet.

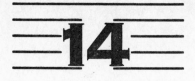

We all went to Sandown races, except of course for Roland, still in the care of Sammy.

The recording telephone was in Mrs. Jenkins' office, with instructions to everybody that if anyone telephoned about any messages from Danielle, every word was to be recorded, and the caller must be asked for a number or an address for us to get back to him.

"He may ask about a reward," I said to the wispy-waif secretary, and also to Dawson and to Sammy. "If he does, assure him he'll get one." And they all nodded and asked no questions.

Litsi, Danielle and I delayed leaving the house until after Thomas had driven away with the princess and Beatrice, who was complaining that she didn't like going to the races twice in one week. Thomas, closing her into the back seat, gave me a large wink before settling himself behind the wheel, and I thought how trusting all the princess's staff were, doing things whose purpose they didn't wholly understand, content only to be told that it was ultimately for the princess's sake.

There was no sign of the Rolls when we walked round to the mews, and I alarmed Litsi and Danielle greatly by checking my car again for traps. I borrowed the sliding mirror-on-wheels that the mechanics used for quick inspections of cars' undersides, but found no explosive sticky strangers, yet all the same I wouldn't let the other two get into the car before I'd started it, driven it a few yards, and braked fiercely to a halt.

"Do you do this every time you go out?" Litsi asked thoughtfully, as they eventually took their seats.

"Every time, just now."

"Why don't you park somewhere else?" Danielle asked reasonably.

"I did think of it," I said. "But it takes less time to check than find parking places."

"Apart from which," Litsi said, "you want Nanterre to know where you keep your car, if he doesn't know already."

"Mm."

"I wish this wasn't happening," Danielle said.

When we reached the racecourse they again went off to lunch and I to work. Litsi might have been lucky enough to dodge the publicity, but too many papers had spelled my name dead right, and so many strangers shook my hand that I found the whole afternoon embarrassing.

The one who was predictably upset by the general climate of approval was Maynard Allardeck, who seemed to be dogging my footsteps, presumably hoping to catch me in some infringement of the rules.

Although not one of the Stewards officially acting at that meeting, he was standing in the parade ring before every race, watching everything I did, and each time I returned I found him on the weighing-room steps, his eyes hostile and intent.

He was looking noble as usual, a pillar of society, a gentleman who wouldn't know an asset if it stripped in front of him. When I went out for the third of my rides, on the princess's runner Abseil, she at once remarked on Maynard's presence at a distance of no more than a few yards.

"Mr. Allardeck," she said, when I joined her, Litsi, Danielle and Beatrice in the parade ring, "is staring at you."

"Yes, I know."

"Who is Mr. Allardeck?" Beatrice demanded.

"Kit's sister's husband's father," Danielle answered succinctly, which left her aunt not much better informed.

"It's unnerving," Litsi said.

I nodded. "I think it's supposed to be. He's been doing it all afternoon."

"You don't, however, appear to be unnerved."

"Not so far." I turned to the princess. "I always meant to ask you what he said after Cascade won last week."

The princess made a small gesture of distress at the thought of her horse's fate, but said, "He insisted you'd flogged the horse unmercifully. Those were his words. If he'd been able to find a mark on Cascade . . ." She shrugged. "He wanted me to confirm you'd been excessively cruel."

"Thank you for not doing it."

She nodded, knowing I meant it.

"I'll be gentle on Abseil," I said.

"Not too gentle." She smiled. "I do like to win."

"He's still staring," Danielle said. "If looks could kill, you'd be in your grave."

The princess decided on a frontal approach, and as if spotting Maynard for the first time raised both gloved hands in greeting and said, "Ah, Mr. Allardeck, such a splendid day, isn't it?" walking three or four paces toward him to make talking easier.

He removed his hat and bowed to her, and said rather hoarsely for him that yes, it was. The princess said how nice it was to see the sun again after so much cloudy weather, and Maynard agreed. It was cold, of course, the princess said, but one had to expect it at this time of the year. Yes, Maynard said.

The princess glanced across to us all and said to Maynard, "I do enjoy Sandown, don't you? And my horses all seem to jump well here always, which is most pleasing."

This on-the-face-of-it-innocent remark produced in Maynard an intenser-than-ever stare in my direction—a look of black and dangerous poison.

"Why," Litsi said in my ear, puzzled, "did that make him so angry?"

"I can't tell you here," I said.

"Later, then."

"Perhaps."

The signal was given for jockeys to mount, and with a sweet smile the princess wished Maynard good fortune for the afternoon and came to say, before I went off to where Abseil waited, "Come back safely."

"Yes, Princess," I said.

Her eyes flicked momentarily in the direction of Danielle, and I suddenly understood her inner thought: come back safe because your young woman will be lost forever if you don't.

"Do your best," the princess said quietly, as if negating her first instruction, and I nodded and cantered Abseil to the start thinking that certainly I could ride round conscious chiefly of safety, and certainly to some extent I'd been doing it all week, but if I intended to do it forever I might as well retire at once. Caution and winning were incompatible. A too-careful jockey would lose his reputation, his owners, his career . . . and in my case anyway, his self-respect. The stark choice between Danielle and my job, unresolved all night, had sat on my shoulder already that afternoon through two undemanding hurdle races, and I had, in fact, been acutely aware of her being there on the stands in a way I hadn't been when I hadn't known of her turmoil of fears.

Abseil, a gray eight-year-old steeplechaser, was a fluid, agile jumper with reasonable speed and questionable stamina. Together we'd won a few races, but had more often finished second, third or fourth, because he could produce no acceleration in a crisis. His one advantage was his boldness over fences: if I restrained him in that we could trail in last.

Sandown racecourse, right-handed, undulating, with seven fences close together down the far side, was a track where good jumpers could excel. I particularly liked riding there, and it was a good place for Abseil, except that the uphill finish could find him out. To win there, he had to be flying in the lead coming round the last long bend, and jump the last three fences at his fastest speed. Then, if he faded on the hill, one might just hang on in front as far as the post.

Abseil himself was unmistakably keen to race, sending me signals of vigor and impatience. "Jumping out of his skin," Wykeham had said; and this one would be wound up tight because he wouldn't be running at the Cheltenham Festival, he wasn't quite in the top class.

The start of the two-mile, five-furlong 'chases was midway down the far side, with one's back to the water jump. There were eight runners that day, a pleasant-sized field, and Abseil was second favorite. We set off in a bunch at no great pace, because no one wanted to make the running, and I had no trouble at all being careful over the first three fences, also round the long bottom bend, over the three fences that would be the last three next time round, and uphill past the stands.

It was when we turned right-handed at the top of the hill to go out on the second circuit that the decision was immediately there, staring me in the face. To go at racing pace over the next fence with its downhill landing, graveyard of many a hope, or to check, rein back, jump it carefully, lose maybe four lengths . . .

Abseil wanted to go. I kicked him. We flew the fence, passing two horses in midair, landing on the downhill slope with precision and skimming speed, going round the bend into the back straight in second place.

The seven fences along there were so designed that if one met the first right, one met them all right, like traffic lights. The trick was to judge one's distance a good way back from the first, to make any adjustments early, so that when one's mount reached the fence he was in the right place for jumping without shortening or lengthening his stride. It was a skill learned young by all successful jockeys, becoming second nature. Abseil took a hint, shortened one stride, galloped happily on, and soared over the first of the seven fences with perfection.

The decision had been made almost unconsciously. I

couldn't do anything else. What I was, what I could do, lay there in front of me, and even for Danielle I couldn't deny it.

Abseil took the lead from the favorite at the second of the seven fences, and I sent him mental messages—"Go on there, go for it, pull the stops out, this is the way it is, and you're going to get your chance, I am as I am and I can't help it, this is living . . . get on and fly."

He flew the open ditch and then the water jump. He sailed over the last three fences on the far side. He was in front by a good thirty yards all the way round the last bend.

Three more fences.

He had his ears pricked, enjoying himself. Caution had long lost the battle, in his mind as in mine. He went over the first of them at full racing pace, and over the second, and over the last of all with me almost lying on his neck to keep up with him, weight forward, head near his head.

He tired very fast on the hill, as I'd feared he would. I had to keep him balanced, but I could feel him begin to flounder and waver and tell me he'd gone far enough.

"Come on, hang on to it, we've almost done it, just keep on, keep going, you old bugger, we're not losing it now, we're so near, so get on . . ."

I could hear the crowd yelling, which one usually couldn't. I could hear another horse coming behind me, hooves thudding. I could see him in my peripheral vision, the jockey's arms swinging high in the air as he scented Abseil flagging . . . and the winning post came just in time for me that time, not three strides too late.

Abseil was proud of himself, as he deserved to be. I patted his neck hugely and told him he was OK, he'd done a good job of work, he was a truly great fellow, and he trotted back toward the unsaddling enclosure with his ears still pricked and his fetlocks springy.

The princess was flushed and pleased in the way she always was after close races.

I slid to the ground, smiled at her, and began to unbuckle the girths.

"Is that," she said, without censure, "what you call being gentle?"

"I'd call it compulsion," I said.

Abseil was practically bowing to the crowd, knowing the applause had been his. I patted his neck again, thanking him. He tossed his gray head, turning it to look at me with both eyes, blowing down his nostrils, nodding again.

"They talk to you," the princess said.

"Some of them."

I looped the girths round my saddle, and turned to go in to weigh in, and found Maynard Allardeck standing directly in my path, much as Henri Nanterre had done at Newbury. Maynard's hatred came across loud and clear.

I stopped. I never liked speaking to him, because anything I said gave him offense. One of us was going to have to give way, and it was going to be me, because in any sort of confrontation between a Steward and a jockey, the jockey would lose.

"Why, Mr. Allardeck," said the princess, stepping to my side, "are you congratulating me? Wasn't that a delightful win?"

Maynard took off his hat and manfully said he was delighted she'd been lucky, especially as her jockey had come to the front far too soon and nearly thrown away the race on the run-in.

"Oh, but Mr. Allardeck," I heard her saying sweetly as I

sidestepped Maynard politely and headed for the weighing-room door, "if he hadn't opened up such a lead he couldn't have hung on to win."

She wasn't only a great lady, I thought gratefully, sitting on the scales, she actually understood what had been going on in a race, which many owners didn't.

Maynard troubled me, though, because it had looked very much as if he were trying to force me into jostling him, and I was going to have to be extremely careful pretty well forever to avoid physical contact. The film I'd made of him would destroy his credibility where it mattered, but it was an ultimate defense, not to be lightly used, as it shielded Bobby and Holly from any destructive consequences of Maynard's obsession, not just myself. If I used it, Maynard's life would be in tatters, but his full fury would be unleashed. He would have nothing more to lose, and we would all be in real peril.

Meanwhile, as always, there were more races to ride. I went twice more from start to finish without caution and, the gods being kind, also without hitting the turf. Maynard continued glaring and I continued being carefully civil, and somehow or other persevered unscathed to teatime.

I changed into street clothes and went up to the princess's box, and found Lord Vaughnley there with her and Litsi and Danielle: no sign of Beatrice.

"My dear chap," Lord Vaughnley said, his large bland face full of kindness, "I came to congratulate Princess Casilia. Well done, well done, my dear fellow, a nice tactical race."

"Thank you," I said mildly.

"And yesterday, too. That was splendid, absolutely first class."

"I didn't have any runners yesterday," the princess said smiling.

"No, no, not a winner. Saving that fellow's life, don't you know, at Bradbury races."

"What fellow?" the princess asked.

"Some damn fool who went where he shouldn't and fell off a balcony. Didn't Kit tell you? No," he considered, "I suppose he wouldn't. Anyway, everyone has been talking about it all afternoon and it was in most of the papers."

"I didn't see the papers this morning," the princess said.

Lord Vaughnley obligingly gave her a full secondhand account of the proceedings that was accurate in essence. Litsi and Danielle looked studiously out of the windows and I wished I could eat the cream cakes, and eventually Lord Vaughnley ran out of superlatives.

"By the way," he said to me, picking up a large brown envelope that lay on the tea table, "this is for you. All we could find. Hope it will be of some help." He held the envelope toward me.

"Thank you very much," I said, taking it.

"Right," said Lord Vaughnley, beaming. "Thank you so much, dear Princess Casilia, for my tea. And again, congratulations." He went away in clouds of benevolence, leaving the princess wide-eyed.

"You were at Bradbury," the princess said to Danielle and Litsi. "Did you see all this?"

"No," Danielle said, "we didn't. We read about it this morning in the *Sporting Life*."

"Why didn't you tell me?"

"Kit didn't want a fuss."

The princess looked at me.

I said, shrugging, "That's true, I didn't. And I'd be

awfully grateful, Princess, if you didn't tell Mrs. Bunt."

She had no chance to ask me why not, as Beatrice reappeared as if on cue, coming into the box with a smug expression, which visibly deepened when she saw I was there. Watching me all the time she ate a cream cake with gusto, as if positively enjoying my hunger. I could more easily put up with that, I thought wryly, than with most other tribulations of that day.

The princess told Beatrice it was time to leave, the last race being long over, and shepherded her off to the Rolls. There was no chance of Litsi going with them, even if he wanted to, as Danielle clung firmly to his arm all the way to the car park. She didn't want to be alone with me after her explanations in the night, and I saw, as I suppose I'd known all day, that she couldn't have come at all without his support. Racing was again at Sandown the next day, and I began to think it would be less of a strain for everybody if she stayed away.

When we reached the car Litsi sat in the front at Danielle's insistence, with herself in the rear, and before starting the car I opened the large brown envelope Lord Vaughnley had brought.

Inside there was a small clipping from a newspaper, a larger piece from a color magazine, a black-and-white eight-by-ten photograph, and a compliments slip from Lord Vaughnley, asking me to return the pieces to the *Towncrier*, which now only had photocopies.

"What is it?" Litsi said.

I passed him the black-and-white photograph, which was of a prize-giving ceremony after a race, a group of people giving and receiving a trophy. Danielle looked over Litsi's shoulder and asked, "Who are those people?"

"The man receiving the pot is Henri Nanterre."

They both exclaimed, peering closer.

"The man at his side is the French racehorse trainer Villon, and at a guess, the racecourse is Longchamp. Look at the back, there might be some information."

Litsi turned the photograph over. "It just says 'After the Prix de la Cité, Villon, Nanterre, Duval.'"

"Duval is the jockey," I said.

"So that's what Nanterre looks like," Litsi said thoughtfully. "Once seen, easily remembered." He passed the photograph back to Danielle. "What other goodies do you have?"

"This piece is from an English magazine and seems to be a Derby preview from last year. Villon apparently had a runner, and the article says 'fresh from his triumph at Longchamp.' Nanterre's mentioned as one of his owners."

The newspaper clipping, also from an English paper, was no more helpful. Prudhomme, owned by French industrialist H. Nanterre, trained by Villon, had come to run at Newmarket and dropped dead of a heart attack on pulling up: end of story.

"Who took the photograph?" I asked, twisting round to see Danielle. "Does it say?"

"Copyright *Towncrier*," she said, reading the back.

I shrugged. "They must have gone over for some big race or other. The Arc, I daresay."

I took the photograph back and put all the bits into the envelope.

"He has a very strong face," Danielle said, meaning Nanterre.

"And a very strong voice."

"And we're no further forward," Litsi said.

I started the car and drove us to London, where we found that nothing of any interest had happened at all, with the result that Sammy was getting bored.

"Just by being here," I said, "you earn your bread."

"No one knows I'm here, man."

"They sure do," I said dryly. "Everything that happens in this house reaches the ears of the man you're guarding its owner against, so don't go to sleep."

"I'd never," he said, aggrieved.

"Good." I showed him the *Towncrier*'s photograph. "That man, there," I said, pointing. "If ever you see him, that's when you take care. He carries a gun, which may or may not have bullets in it, and he's full of all sorts of tricks."

He looked at the photograph long and thoughtfully. "I'll know him," he said.

I took Lord Vaughnley's offerings up to the bamboo room, telephoned Wykeham, picked up my messages, dealt with them: the usual routine. When I went down to the sitting room for a drink before dinner, Litsi, Danielle and the princess were discussing French Impressionist painters exhibiting in Paris around 1880.

Cézanne . . . Pissarro . . . Renoir . . . Degas . . . at least I'd heard of them. I went across to the drinks tray and picked up the scotch.

"Berthe Morisot was one of the best," Litsi said to the room in general. "Don't you think?"

"What did he paint?" I asked, opening the bottle.

"He was a she," Litsi said.

I grunted slightly and poured a trickle of whiskey. "She, then, what did she paint?"

"Young women, babies, studies in light."

I sat in an armchair and drank the scotch, looking at Litsi. At least he didn't patronize me, I thought.

"They're not all easy to see," he said. "Many are in private collections, some are in Paris, several are in the National Gallery of Art in Washington."

I was unlikely, he must have known, to chase them up.

"Delightful pictures," the princess said. "Luminous."

"And there was Mary Cassatt," Danielle said. "She was brilliant too." She turned to me. "She was American, but she was a student of Degas in Paris."

I would go with her to galleries, I thought, if that would please her. "One of these days," I said casually, "you can educate me."

She turned her head away almost as if she would cry, which hadn't in the least been my intention; and perhaps it was as well that Beatrice arrived for her "bloody."

Beatrice was suffering a severe sense-of-humor failure over Sammy, who had, it appeared, said, "Sorry, me old darlin', not used to slow traffic," while again cannoning into her on the stairs.

She saw the laugh on my face, which gravely displeased her, and Litsi smothered his in his drink. The princess, with twitching lips, assured her sister-in-law that she would ask Sammy to be more careful and Beatrice said it was all my fault for having brought him into the house. It entirely lightened and enlivened the evening, which passed more easily than some of the others: but there was still no one telephoning in response to the advertisements, and there was again no sound from Nanterre.

Early next morning, well before seven, Dawson woke me again with the intercom, saying there was a call for me from Wykeham Harlow.

I picked up the receiver, sleep forgotten.

"Wykeham?" I said.

"K–K–Kit." He was stuttering dreadfully. "C–c–come down here. C–come at once."

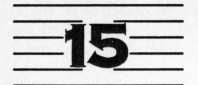

He put the receiver down immediately, without telling me what had happened, and when I instantly rang back there was no reply. With appalling foreboding I flung on some clothes, sprinted round to the car, did very cursory checks on it, and drove fast through the almost empty streets toward Sussex.

Wykeham had sounded near disintegration, shock and age trembling ominously in his voice. By the time I reached him, they had been joined by anger, which filled and shook him with impotent fire.

He was standing in the parking space with Robin Curtiss, the vet, when I drove in.

"What's happened?" I said, getting out of the car.

Robin made a helpless gesture with his hands and Wykeham said with fury, "C—come and look."

I followed him into the courtyard next to the one that

216

had held Cascade and Cotopaxi. Wykeham, shaky on his knees but straight-backed with emotion, went across to one of the closed doors and put his hand flat on it.

"In there," he said.

The box door was closed but not bolted. Not bolted, because the horse inside wasn't going to escape.

I pulled the doors open, the upper and the lower, and saw the body lying on the peat.

Bright chestnut, three white socks, white blaze.

It was Col.

Speechlessly I turned to Wykeham and Robin, feeling all of Wykeham's rage and a lot of private despair. Nanterre was too quick on his feet, and it wouldn't take much more for Roland de Brescou to crumble.

"It's the same as before," Robin said. "The bolt." He bent down, lifted the chestnut forelock, showed me the mark on the white blaze. "There's a lot of oil in the wound . . . the gun's been oiled since last time." He let go of the forelock and straightened. "The horse is stone cold. It was done early, I should say before midnight."

Col . . . gallant at Ascot, getting ready for Cheltenham, for the Gold Cup.

"Where was the patrol?" I said, at last finding my voice.

"He was here," Wykeham said. "In the stable, I mean, not in the courtyard."

"He's gone, I suppose."

"No, I told him to wait for you. He's in the kitchen."

"Col," I said, "is the only one . . . isn't he?"

Robin nodded. "Something to be thankful for."

Not much, I thought. Cotopaxi and Col had been two of the princess's three best horses, and it could be no coincidence that they'd been targeted.

"Kinley," I said to Wykeham. "You did check Kinley, didn't you?"

"Yes, straightaway. He's in the corner box still, in the next courtyard."

"The insurers aren't going to like this," Robin said, looking down at the dead horse. "With the first two, it might have been just bad luck that they were two good ones, but three . . ." He shrugged. "Not my problem, of course."

"How did he know where to find them?" I said, as much to myself as to Robin and Wykeham. "Is this Col's usual box?"

"Yes," Wykeham said. "I suppose now I'll have to change them all around, but it does disrupt the stable . . ."

"Abseil," I said, "is he all right?"

"Who?"

"Yesterday's winner."

Wykeham's doubts cleared. "Oh, yes, he's all right."

Abseil was as easy to recognize as the others, I thought. Not chestnut, not nearly black like Cascade, but gray, with a black mane and tail.

"Where is he?" I asked.

"In the last courtyard, near the house."

Although I was down at Wykeham's fairly often, it was always to do the schooling, for which we would drive up to the Downs, where I would ride relays of the horses over jumps, teaching them. I almost never rode the horses in or out of the yard, and although I knew where some of the horses lived, like Cotopaxi, I wasn't sure of them all.

I put a hand down to touch Col's foreleg, and felt its rigidity, its chill. The foreleg that had saved us from disaster at Ascot, that had borne all his weight.

"I'll have to tell the princess," Wykeham said unhappily. "Unless you would, Kit?"

"Yes, I'll tell her," I said. "At Sandown."

He nodded vaguely. "What are we running?" he said.

"Helikon for the princess, and three others."

"Dusty has the list, of course."

"Yeah," I said.

Wykeham took a long look again at the dead splendor on the peat.

"I'd kill the shit who did that," he said, "with his own damned bolt."

Robin sighed and closed the stable doors, saying he would arrange for the carcass to be collected, if Wykeham liked.

Wykeham silently nodded, and we all walked out of the courtyard and made our way to Wykeham's house, where Robin went off to telephone in the office. The dog-handler was still in the kitchen, restive but chastened, with his dog, a black Doberman, lying on the floor and yawning at his feet.

"Tell Kit Fielding what you told me," Wykeham said.

The dog-handler, in a navy-blue battle-dress uniform, was middle-aged and running to fat. His voice was defensively belligerent and his intelligence middling, and I wished I'd had the speedy Sammy here in his place. I sat at the table across from him and asked how he'd missed the visitor who had shot Col.

"I couldn't help it, could I?" he said. "Not with those bombs going off."

"What bombs?" I glanced at Wykeham, who'd clearly heard about the bombs before. "What bombs, for God's sake?"

The dog-handler had a mustache, which he groomed

frequently with a thumb and forefinger, working outward from the nose.

"Well, how was I to know they wasn't proper bombs?" he said. "They made enough noise."

"Just start," I said, "at the beginning. Start with when you came on duty. And, er . . . have you been here any other nights?"

"Yes," he said. "Monday to Friday, five nights."

"Right," I said. "Describe last night."

"I come on duty sevenish, when the head-lad's finished the feeding. I make a base here in the kitchen and do a recce every half hour. Standard procedure."

"How long do the recces take?"

"Fifteen minutes, maybe more. It's bitter cold these nights."

"And you go into all the courtyards?"

"Never miss a one," he said piously.

"And where else?"

"Look in the hay barn, tack room, feed shed, round the back where the tractor is, and the harrow, muck-heap, the lot."

"Go on, then," I said, "how many recces had you done when the bombs went off?"

He worked it out on his fingers. "Nine, say. The head-lad had been in for a quick look round last thing, like he does, and everything was quiet. So I comes back here for a bit of a warm, and goes out again half eleven, I should say. I start on the rounds, and there's this almighty bang and crashing round the back. So I went off there with Ranger . . ." He looked down at his dog. "Well, I would, wouldn't I? Stands to reason."

"Yes," I said. "Where exactly, round the back?"

"I couldn't see at first because there isn't much light round there, and there was this strong smell of burning, got right down your throat, and then another one went off not ten feet away. Nearly burst my eardrums."

"Where were the bombs?" I said again.

"The first one was round the back of the muck-heap. I found what was left of it with my torch, after."

"But you don't use your torch all the time?"

"You don't need to in the courtyards. Most of them have lights in."

"Mm. OK. Where was the second one?"

"Under the harrow."

Wykeham, like many trainers, used the harrow occasionally for raking his paddocks, keeping them in good shape.

"Did it blow up the harrow?" I said, frowning.

"No, see, they weren't that sort of bomb."

"What other sort is there?"

"It went off through the harrow with a huge shower of sparks. Golden sparks, all over. Little burning sparks. Some of them fell on me . . . They were fireworks. I found the empty boxes. They said 'bomb' on them, where they weren't burned."

"Where are they now?" I asked.

"Where they went off. I didn't touch them, except to kick them over to read what was on the side."

"So what was your dog doing all this time?"

The dog-handler looked disillusioned. "I had him on the leash. I always do, of course. He didn't like the bangs or the sparks or the smell. He's supposed to be trained to ignore gunshots, but he didn't like the fireworks. He was barking fit to bust, and trying to run off."

"He was trying to run in a different direction, but you stopped him?"

"That's right."

"Maybe he was trying to run after the man who shot the horse."

The dog-handler's mouth opened and snapped shut. He smoothed his mustache several times and grew noticeably more aggressive. "Ranger was barking at the bombs," he said.

I nodded. It was too late for it to matter.

"And I suppose," I said, "that you didn't hear any other bangs in the distance . . . you didn't hear the shot?"

"No, I didn't. My ears were ringing and Ranger was kicking up a racket."

"So what did you do next?"

"Nothing," he said. "I thought it was some of those lads who work here. Proper little monkeys. So I just went on with the patrols, regular like. There wasn't anything wrong . . . it didn't look like it, that's to say."

I turned to Wykeham, who had been gloomily listening. "Didn't *you* hear the fireworks?" I asked.

"No, I was asleep." He hesitated, then added, "I can't seem to sleep at all these days without sleeping pills. We'd had four quiet nights and I'd been awake most of those, so . . . last night I took a pill."

I sighed. If Wykeham had been awake, he would anyway have gone toward the commotion and nothing would have been different.

I said to the dog-handler, "You were here on Wednesday, when you had the prowler?"

"Yes, I was. Ranger was whining but I couldn't find anyone."

Nanterre, I thought, had come to the stable on Wednesday night, intending to kill, and had been thwarted by the dog's presence: and he'd come back two nights later with his diversions.

He must have been at Ascot, I supposed, and learned what Col looked like, but I hadn't seen him, as I hadn't seen him at Bradbury either: but among large crowds on racecourses, especially while I was busy, that wasn't extraordinary.

I looked down at Ranger, wondering about his responses.

"When people arrive here," I asked, "like I did a short while ago, how does Ranger behave?"

"He gets up and goes to the door and whines a bit. He's a quiet dog, mostly. Doesn't bark. That's why I knew it was the bombs he was barking at."

"Well, er, during your spells in the kitchen, what would you be doing?"

"Making a cuppa. Eating. Relieving myself. Reading. Watching the telly." He smoothed his mustache, not liking me or my questions. "I don't doze off, if that's what you mean."

It was what I meant, and obviously what he'd done, at some point or another. During four long quiet cold nights I supposed it was understandable, if not excusable.

"Over the weekend," I said to Wykeham, "we'll have double and treble patrols. Constant."

He nodded. "Have to."

"Have you told the police yet?"

"Not yet. Soon, though." He looked with disgust at the dog-handler. "They'll want to hear what you've said."

The dog-handler however stood up, announced it was an

hour after he should have left and if the police wanted him they could reach him through his firm. He, he said, was going to bed.

Wykeham morosely watched him go and said, "What the hell is going on, Kit? The princess knows who killed them all, and so do you. So tell me."

It wasn't fair, I thought, for him not to know, so I told him the outline: a man was trying to extract a signature from Roland de Brescou by attacking his family wherever he could.

"But that's . . . terrorism." Wykeham used the word at arm's length, as if its very existence affronted him.

"In a small way," I said.

"Small?" he exclaimed. "Do you call three dead great horses small?"

I didn't. It made me sick and angry to think of them. It was small on a world scale of terrorism, but rooted in the same wicked conviction that the path to attaining one's end lay in slaughtering the innocent.

I stirred. "Show me where all the princess's horses are," I suggested to Wykeham, and together we went out again into the cold air and made the rounds of the courtyards.

Cascade's and Cotopaxi's boxes were still empty, and no others of the princess's horses had been in the first courtyard. In the second had been only Col. In the one beyond that, Hillsborough and Bernina, with Kinley in the deep corner box there.

About a third of the stable's inmates were out at exercise on the Downs, and while we were leaving Kinley's yard, they came clattering back, filling the whole place with noise and movement, the lads dismounting and leading their horses into the boxes. Wykeham and I sorted our way round as the lads brushed down their charges, tidied the bedding, filled the buckets, brought hay to the racks, propped their saddles outside the boxes, bolted the doors and went off to their breakfasts.

I saw all the old friends in their quarters; among them North Face, Dhaulagiri, Icicle and Icefall, and young Helikon, the four-year-old hurdler going to Sandown that afternoon. Wykeham got half of their names right, waiting for me to prompt him on the others. He unerringly knew their careers, though, and their personalities; they were real to him in a way that needed no name tags. His secretary was adept at sorting out what he intended when he wrote down his lists of entries to races.

In the last courtyard we came to Abseil and opened the top half of his door. Abseil came toward the opening daylight and put his head out inquiringly. I rubbed his gray nose and upper lip with my hand and put my head next to his and breathed out gently like a reversed sniff into his nostril. He rubbed his nose a couple of times against my cheek and then lifted his head away, the greeting done. Wykeham paid no attention. Wykeham talked to horses that way himself, when they were that sort of horse. With some, one would never do it, one could get one's nose bitten off.

Wykeham gave Abseil a carrot from a deep pocket, and closed him back into his twilight.

Wykeham slapped his hand on the next box along. "That's Kinley's box usually. It's empty now I don't like keeping him in that corner box, it's dark and boring for him."

"It won't be for much longer, I hope," I said, and suggested going round to see the "bombs."

Wykeham had seen them earlier, and pointed them out to me, and as expected they were the bottom parts of cardboard containers, each four inches square in shape, the top parts burned away. They were both the same, with gaudy red and yellow pictured flames still visible on the singed surfaces, and the words "golden bomb" in jazzy letters on the one under the harrow.

"We'd better leave them there for the police," I said.

Wykeham agreed, but he said fireworks would convince the police even more that it was the work of boys.

We went back into the house, where Wykeham telephoned the police and received a promise of attention, and I got through to Dawson, asking him to tell the princess I was down at Wykeham's and would go to Sandown from there.

Wykeham and I had breakfast and drove up to the Downs in his big-wheeled pickup to see the second lot exercise, and under the wide cold windy sky he surprised me by saying apropos of nothing special that he was thinking of taking another assistant. He'd had assistants in the past, I'd heard, who'd never lasted long, but there hadn't been one there in my time.

"Are you?" I said. "I thought you couldn't stand assistants."

"They never knew anything," he said. "But I'm getting old. It'll have to be someone the princess likes. Someone you get on with, too. So if you think of anyone, let me know. I don't know who's around so much these days."

"All right," I said, but with misgivings. Wykeham, for all his odd mental quirks, was irreplaceable. "You're not going to retire, are you?"

"No, I'm not. Never. I wouldn't mind dying up here, watching my horses." He laughed suddenly, in his eyes a flash of the vigor that had been there always not so long ago, when he'd been a titan. "I've had a great life, you know. One of the best."

"Stick around," I said.

He nodded. "Maybe next year," he said, "we'll win the Grand National."

Wykeham's four runners at Sandown were in the first three races and the fifth, and I didn't see the princess until she came down to the parade ring for Helikon's race, which was the third on the card.

Beatrice was with her, and also Litsi, and also Danielle, who after the faintest of greetings was busy blanking me out, it seemed, by looking carefully at the circling horses. The fact that she was there, that she was still trying, was something, I supposed.

"Good morning," the princess said, when I bowed to her. "Dawson said Wykeham telephoned early . . . again." There was a shade of apprehension in her face, which abruptly deepened at what she read in my own.

She walked a little away from her family, and I followed.

"*Again?*" she said, not wanting to believe it. "Which ones?"

"One," I said. "Col."

She absorbed the shock with a long blink.

"The same way . . . as before?" she said.

"Yes. With the bolt."

"My poor horse."

"I'm so sorry."

"I will not tell my husband," she said. "Please tell none of them, Kit."

227

"It will be in the newspapers tomorrow or on Monday," I said, "probably worse than before."

"Oh . . ." The prospect affected her almost as much as Col's death. "I will not add to the pressure on my husband," she said fiercely. "He cannot sign this wretched contract. He will die, you know, if he does. He will not survive the disgrace in his own mind. He will wish to die . . . as all these years, although his condition is such a trial to him, he has wished to live." She made a small gesture with her gloved hand. "He is . . . very dear to me, Kit."

I heard in my memory my grandmother saying, "I love the old bugger, Kit," of my pugnacious grandfather, an equal declaration of passion for a man not obviously lovable.

That the princess should have made it was astonishing, but not as impossible as before the advent of Nanterre. A great deal, I saw, had changed between us in the last eight days.

To save his honor, to save his life, to save their life together . . . My God, I thought, what a burden. She needed Superman, not me.

"Don't tell him about Col," she said again.

"No, I won't."

Her gaze rested on Beatrice.

"I won't tell other people," I said. "But it may not stay a secret on the racecourse. Dusty and the lads who came with Wykeham's horses all know, and they'll tell other lads. It'll spread, I'm afraid."

She nodded slightly, unhappily, and switched her attention from Beatrice to Helikon, who happened to be passing. She watched him for several seconds, turning her head after him as he went.

"What do you think of him?" she asked, her defense mechanism switching on smoothly. "What shall I expect?"

"He's still a bit hot-headed," I said, "but if I can settle him he should run well."

"But not another Kinley?" she suggested.

"Not so far."

"Do your best."

I said as usual that I would, and we rejoined the others as if all we'd been talking about was her hurdler.

"Have you noticed who's still staring?" Danielle said, and I answered that indeed I had, those eyes followed me everywhere.

"Doesn't it get on your nerves?" Danielle asked.

"What nerves?" Litsi said.

"Are you talking about Mr. Allardeck?" Beatrice demanded. "I can't think why you don't like him. He looks perfectly darling."

The perfectly darling man was projecting his implacable thoughts my way from a distance that signaled unmistakable invasion of psychological territory, and I thought uneasily again about the state of mind that was compelling him to do it. The evil eye, I thought: and no shield from it that I could see.

The time came to mount, and hot-headed Helikon and I went out onto the track. He was nervous as well as impetuous; not a joy to ride. I tried to get him to relax on the way to the start, but as usual it was like trying to relax a coil of barbed wire. The princess had bought him as a yearling and had great hopes for him, but although he jumped well enough, neither Wykeham nor I had been able to straighten out his kinks.

There were twenty or more runners, and Helikon and I

set off near the front because if he were bumped in the pack he'd be frightened into stopping; yet I also had to keep a tight hold, as he could take charge and decamp.

He went through the routine of head-tossing against the restraint, but I had him anchored and running fairly well, and by the third flight of hurdles I thought the worst was over, we could now settle a little and design a passable race.

It wasn't his day. At the fourth flight the horse nearest ahead put his foot through the obstacle and went down with a crash, slithering along the ground on his side. Helikon fell over him, going down fast, pitching me off: and I didn't actually see the subsequent course of events all that clearly, though it was a pile-up worthy of a fog on a highway. Five horses, I found afterward, hit the deck at that jump. One of them seemed to land smack on top of me; not frightfully good for one's health.

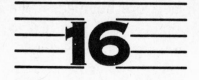

I lay on the grass, assessing things.

I was conscious and felt like a squashed beetle, but I hadn't broken my legs, which I always feared most.

One of the other jockeys from the melee squatted beside me and asked if I was all right, but I couldn't answer him on account of having no breath.

"He's winded," my colleague said to someone behind me, and I thought, "Just like Litsi at Bradbury, heigh ho." My colleague unbuckled my helmet and pushed it off, for which I couldn't thank him.

Breath came back, as it does. By the time the ambulance arrived along with a doctor in a car, I'd come to the welcome conclusion that nothing was broken at all and that it was time to stand up and get on with things. Standing, I felt hammered and sore in several places, but one had to accept that, and I reckoned I'd been lucky to get out of that sort of crash so lightly.

One of the other jockeys hadn't been so fortunate and was flat out, white and silent, with the first-aid men kneeling anxiously beside him. He woke up slightly during the ambulance ride back to the stands and began groaning intermittently, which alarmed his attendants, but at least showed signs of life.

When we reached the first-aid room and the ambulance's rear doors were opened, I climbed out first, and found the other jockey's wife waiting there, pregnant and pretty, screwed up with anxiety.

"Is Joe all right?" she said to me, and then saw him coming out on the stretcher, very far from all right. I saw the deep shock in her face, the quick pallor, the dry mouth . . . the agony.

That was what had happened to Danielle, I thought. That was much what she'd seen, and that was what she'd felt.

I put my arm round Joe's wife and held her close, and told her Joe would be fine, he would be fine, and neither of us knew if he would.

Joe was carried into the first-aid room, the door closing behind him, but presently the doctor came out with kindness and told Joe's wife they would be sending him to the hospital as soon as an outside ambulance could be brought.

"You can come in and sit with him, if you like," he said to her, and to me added, "You'd better come in too, hadn't you?"

I went in and he checked me over, and said, "What aren't you telling me?"

"Nothing."

"I know you," he said. "And everywhere I touch you, you stifle a wince."

"Ouch, then," I said.

"Where is ouch?"

"Ankle, mostly."

He pulled my boot off and I said "ouch" quite loudly but, as I'd believed, there were no cracked bits. He said to get some strapping and some rest, and added that I could ride on Monday, if I could walk and if I were mad enough.

He went back to tending Joe, and one of the nurses answered a knock on the door, coming back to tell me that I was wanted outside. I put my boot on again, ran my fingers through my hair and went out, to find Litsi and Danielle there, waiting.

Litsi had his arm round Danielle's shoulders, and Danielle looked as if this were the last place on earth she wanted to be.

I was aware of my disheveled state, of the limp I couldn't help, of the grass stains and the tear in my breeches down my left thigh.

Litsi took it all in, and I smiled at him slightly.

"The nitty gritty," I said.

"So I see." He looked thoughtful. "Aunt Casilia sent us to see how you were."

It had taken a great deal of courage, I thought, for Danielle to be there, to face what might have happened again as it had happened in January. I said to Litsi, but with my eyes on Danielle, "Please tell her I'm all right, I'll be riding on Monday."

"How can you ride?" Danielle said intensely.

"Sit in the saddle, put the feet in the stirrups, pick up the reins."

"Don't be damn stupid. How can you joke . . . and don't answer that. I know both the answers. Easily or with difficulty, whichever is funnier."

She suddenly couldn't help laughing, but it was partly

hysterical, and it was against Litsi's big shoulder she smothered her face.

"I'll come up to the box," I said to him, and he nodded, but before they could leave, the first-aid-room door opened and Joe's wife came out.

"Kit," she said with relief, seeing me still there. "I've got to go to the ladies' . . . my stomach's all churning up . . . they say I can go to the hospital with Joe but if they come for him while I'm not here they may take him without me . . . Will you wait here and tell them? Don't let him go without me."

"I'll see to it," I said.

She said "thanks" faintly and half ran in the direction of relief, and Danielle, her eyes stretched wide, said, "But that's . . . just like me. Is her husband hurt . . . badly?"

"It's too soon to tell, I think."

"How can she stand it?"

"I don't know," I said. "I really don't know. It's much simpler from Joe's side . . . and mine."

"I'll go and see if she needs help," Danielle said abruptly, and, leaving Litsi's shelter, set off after Joe's wife.

"Seriously," Litsi said, watching her go, "how can you joke?"

"Seriously? Seriously not about Joe, nor about his wife, but about myself, why not?"

"But . . . is it worth it?"

I said, "If you could paint as you'd like to, would you put up with a bit of discomfort?"

He smiled, his eyebrows rising. "Yes, I would."

"Much the same thing," I said. "Fulfillment."

We stood in a backwater of the racecourse, with the

stands and bustle out in the mainstream, gradually moving toward the next race. Dusty arrived at a rush, his eyes searching, suspicious.

"I've wrenched my ankle," I said. "You'll have to get Jamie for the fifth race, I know he's free. But I'm cleared for Monday. Is Helikon all right?"

He nodded briskly a couple of times and departed, wasting no words.

Litsi said, "It's a wonder you're not worse. It looked atrocious. Aunt Casilia was watching through binoculars, and she was very concerned until she saw you stand up. She said then that you accepted the risks and one had to expect these things from time to time."

"She's right," I said.

He, in the sober suiting of civilization, looked at the marks of the earth on the princess's colors, looked at my torn green-stained breeches, and at the leg I was putting no weight on.

"How do you face it, over and over again?" he said. He saw my lips twitch and added, "Easily or with difficulty, whichever is funnier."

I laughed. "I never expect it, for a start. It's always an unpleasant surprise."

"And now that it's happened, how do you deal with it?"

"Think about something else," I said. "Take a lot of aspirins and concentrate on getting back as soon as possible. I don't like other jockeys loose on my horses, like now. I want to be on them. When I've taught them and know them, they're mine."

"And you like winning."

"Yes, I like winning."

The hospital ambulance arrived only moments before

Danielle and Joe's wife returned, and Litsi, Danielle and I stood with Joe's wife while Joe was transferred. He was still half conscious, still groaning, looking gray. The ambulance men helped his wife into the interior in his wake, and we had a final view of her face, young and frightened, looking back at us, before they closed the doors and drove slowly away.

Litsi and Danielle looked at me, and I looked at them; and there was nothing to say, really.

Litsi put his arm again round Danielle's shoulders, and they turned and walked away; and I hobbled off and showered and changed my clothes after just another fall, in just a day in a working life.

When I went out of the weighing room to go to the princess's box, Maynard Allardeck stepped into my way. He was looking, as always, splendidly tailored, the total English gentleman from Lock's hat to hand-sewn shoes. He wore a silk striped tie and pigskin gloves, and his eyes were as near madness as I'd ever seen them.

I stopped, my spirits sinking.

Outside the weighing room, where we stood, there was a covered veranda with three wide steps leading down to the area used for unsaddling the first four in every race. There was a tarmac path across the grass there, giving access to the rest of the paddock.

The horses from the fifth race had been unsaddled and led away, and there was a scatter of people about, but not a crowd.

Maynard stood between me and the steps, and to avoid him I would have to edge sideways and round him.

"*Fielding*," he said with intensity; and he wasn't simply addressing me by name, he was using the word as a curse, in the way the Allardecks had used it for vengeful generations. He was cursing my ancestry and my existence, the feudal spite like bile in his mouth, the irrational side of his hatred for me well in command.

He overtopped me by about four inches and outweighed me by fifty pounds, but he was twenty years older and unfit. Without the complication of a sprained ankle I could have dodged him easily, but as it was, when I took a step sideways, so did he.

"Mr. Allardeck," I said neutrally. "Princess Casilia's expecting me."

He gave no sign of hearing, but when I took another sideways step he didn't move. Nor did he move when I went past him, but two steps further on, at the top of the steps, I received a violent shove between the shoulders.

Unbalanced, I fell stumbling down the three steps, landing in a sprawl on the tarmac path. I rolled, half expecting Maynard to jump down on me, but he was standing on the top step, staring, and as I watched, he turned away, took three paces and attached himself to a small group of similar-looking men.

A trainer I sometimes rode for, who happened to be near, put a hand under my elbow and helped me to my feet.

"He pushed you," he said incredulously. "I saw it. I can't believe it. That man stepped right behind you and pushed."

I stood on one leg and brushed off some of the debris from the path. "Thanks," I said.

"But he pushed you! Aren't you going to complain?"

"Who to?"

"But Kit . . ." He slowly took stock of the situation. "That's Maynard Allardeck."

"Yeah."

"But he can't go around attacking you. And you've hurt your leg."

"He didn't do that," I said. "That's from a fall in the third race."

"That was some mess." He looked at me doubtfully. "If you want to complain, I'll say what I saw."

I thanked him again and said I wouldn't bother, which he still found inexplicable. I glanced briefly at Maynard, who by then had his back to me as if unaware of my presence, and with perturbation set off again toward the princess's box.

The push itself had been a relatively small matter, but as Maynard was basically murderous, it had to be taken as a substitute killing, a relief explosion, a jet of steam to stop the top blowing off the volcano.

The film, I thought uneasily, would keep that volcano in check; and I supposed I could put up with the jets of steam if I thought of them as safety valves reducing his boiling pressure. I didn't want him uncontrollably erupting. I'd rather fall down more steps; but I would also be more careful where I walked.

The princess was out on the balcony when I reached her box, huddled into her furs, and alone.

I went out there to join her, and found her gazing blind-eyed over the racecourse, her thoughts obviously unwelcome.

"Princess," I said.

She turned her head, her eyes focusing on my face.

"Don't give up," I said.

"No." She stretched her neck and her backbone as if to disclaim any thought of it. "Is Helikon all right?" she asked.

"Dusty said so."

"Good." She sighed. "Have you any idea what's running next week? It's all a blank in my mind."

It was a fair blank in mine also. "Icefall goes on Thursday at Lingfield."

"How did Helikon fall?" she asked, and I told her that it wasn't her horse's fault, he'd been brought down.

"He was going well at the time," I said. "He's growing up and getting easier to settle. I'll school him next week one morning to get his confidence back."

She showed a glimmer of pleasure in an otherwise un-pleasurable day. She didn't ask directly after my state of health, because she never did: she considered the results of falls to lie within the domain of my personal privacy into which she wouldn't intrude. It was an attitude stemming from her own habit of reticence, and far from minding it, I valued it. It was fussing I couldn't stand.

We went inside for some tea, joining Danielle, Litsi and Beatrice, and presently Lord Vaughnley appeared on one of his more or less regular visits to the princess's box.

His faint air of anxiety vanished when he saw me drinking there, and after a few minutes he managed to cut me off from the pack and steer me into a corner.

I thanked him for his packet of yesterday.

"What? Oh, yes, my dear chap, you're welcome. But that's not what I wanted to say to you, not at all. I'm afraid there's been a bit of a leak . . . it's all very awkward."

"What sort of leak?" I asked, puzzled.

"About the film you made of Maynard Allardeck."

I felt my spine shiver. I desperately needed that film to remain secret.

"I'm afraid," Lord Vaughnley said, "that Allardeck

knows you sent a copy of it to the Honours people in Downing Street. He knows he will never again be considered for a knighthood, because of your sending it." He smiled half anxiously but couldn't resist the journalistic summary: "Never Sir Maynard, never Lord Allardeck, thanks to Kit Fielding."

"How in hell's teeth did he find out?" I demanded.

"I don't know," Lord Vaughnley said uncomfortably. "Not from me, my dear fellow, I assure you. I've never told anyone. But sometimes there are whispers of these things. Someone in the civil service, don't you know."

I looked at him in dismay. "How long has he known?" I said.

"I think since sometime last week." He shook his head unhappily. "I heard about it this morning in a committee meeting of the charity of which Allardeck and I are both directors. He's chairman, of course. The civil service charity, you remember."

I remembered. It was through good works for the sick and needy dependents of civil servants that Maynard had tried hardest to climb to his knighthood.

"No one in the charity has seen the film, have they?" I asked urgently.

"No, no, my dear fellow. They've simply heard it exists. One of them apparently asked Allardeck if he knew anything about it."

Oh, God, I thought; how leaks could trickle through cracks.

"I thought you'd better know," Lord Vaughnley said. "And don't forget I've as strong an interest in that film as you have. If it's shown all over the place, we'll have lost our lever."

"Maynard will have lost his saintly reputation."

"He might operate without it."

"The only copies," I said, "are the ones I gave to you and to the Honours people, and the three I have in the bank. Unless you or the Honours people show them . . . I can't believe they will," I said explosively. "They were all so hush-hush."

"I thought I should warn you."

"I'm glad you did."

It explained so much, I thought, about Maynard's recent behavior. Considering how he must be seething with fury, just pushing me down the steps showed amazing restraint.

But then I did still have the film, and so far it hadn't been shown to a wider audience, and Maynard really wouldn't want it shown, however much he had lost through it already.

Lord Vaughnley apologized to the princess for monopolizing her jockey, and asked if I was still interested in more information regarding Nanterre.

"Yes, please," I said, and he nodded and said it was still flickering through computers, somewhere.

"Trouble?" Litsi asked at my elbow, when Lord Vaughnley had gone.

"Allardeck trouble, not Nanterre." I smiled lopsidedly. "The Fieldings have had Allardeck trouble for centuries. Nanterre's much more pressing."

We watched the last race, on my part without concentration, and in due course returned to the cars, Litsi and Danielle, deserting the Rolls, saying they were coming with me.

On the walk from the box to the car park, I stopped a few times to take the weight off my foot. No one made a remark, but when we arrived at my car Danielle said positively, "I'm driving. You can tell me the way."

"You don't need a left foot with automatic transmission," I pointed out.

"I'm driving," she said fiercely. "I've driven your car before." She had, on a similar occasion.

I sat in the passenger seat without more demur, and asked her to stop at a chemist's shop a short distance along the road.

"What do you need?" she said brusquely, pulling up. "I'll get it."

"Some strapping, and mineral water."

"Aspirin?"

"There's some here in the glove compartment."

She went with quick movements into the shop and returned with a paper bag, which she dumped on my lap.

"I'll tell you the scenario," she said to Litsi with a sort of suppressed violence as she restarted the car and set off toward London. "He'll strap his own ankle and sit with it surrounded by icepacks to reduce the swelling. He'll have hoof-shaped bruises that'll be black by tomorrow, and he'll ache all over. He won't want you to notice he can't put that foot on the ground without pain shooting up his leg. If you ask him how he feels he'll say 'with every nerve ending.' He doesn't like sympathy. Injuries embarrass him and he'll do his best to ignore them."

Litsi said, when she paused, "You must know him very well."

It silenced Danielle. She was driving with the same throttled anger, and took a while to relax.

I swallowed some aspirins with the mineral water and thought about what she'd said. And Litsi was right, I reflected: she did truly know me. She unfortunately sounded as if she wished she didn't.

"Kit, you never did tell me," Litsi said after a while, "why it annoyed Maynard Allardeck so much when the princess said her horses always jumped well at Sandown. Why on earth should that anger anyone?"

"Modesty forbids me to tell you," I said, smiling.

"Well, have a try."

"She was paying me a compliment that Maynard didn't want to hear."

"Do you mean it's because of your skill that her horses jump well?"

"Experience," I said. "Something like that."

"He's obsessed," Litsi said.

He was dangerous, I thought: and there was such a thing as contract killing, by persons unknown, which I didn't like the thought of very much. To remove the mind from scary concepts, I asked Danielle if she'd managed to tell Beatrice that Monday was her last evening stint.

Danielle, after a lengthy pause, said that no, she hadn't.

"I wish you would," I said, alarmed. "You said you would."

"I can't tell her . . . What if Nanterre turns up and shoots you?"

"He won't," I said. "But if we don't catch him . . ." I paused. "The princess told me today that if Roland signs the arms contract to save us all, he will literally die of shame. He wouldn't want to go on living. She's extremely worried that he'll give in. She loves him. She wants him alive. So we've got to stop Nanterre; and stop him soon."

Danielle didn't answer for two or three miles, and it was Litsi eventually who broke the silence.

"I'll tell Beatrice," he said firmly.

"No," Danielle protested.

"Last night," I said, "Nanterre killed another of the princess's horses. The princess doesn't want Roland to know. Or Beatrice, who would tell him."

They both exclaimed in distress.

"No wonder she's been so sad," Litsi said. "It wasn't just Helikon falling."

"Which horse?" Danielle asked.

"Col," I said. "The one I rode at Ascot."

"That didn't quite win?" Litsi asked.

"Yes," Danielle said, "her Gold Cup horse." She swallowed. "If Litsi tells Beatrice Monday's my last day, I won't deny it."

We spent another slightly claustrophobic evening in the house. Roland came down to dinner, and conversation was a trifle stilted owing to everyone having to remember what was not known and shouldn't be said.

Litsi managed to tell Beatrice positively but naturally that the last time I would be fetching Danielle at night would be Monday, as Danielle would no longer be working in the evenings, a piece of news that surprised the princess greatly.

Beatrice took in the information satisfactorily, with her eyes sliding my way, and one could almost see the cogs clicking as she added the hour to the place.

I wondered if she understood the nature of what I hoped she was going to arrange. She seemed to have no doubts or compunction about laying an ambush that would remove me from her path; but of course she didn't know about the attack on Litsi or about Col's death, which we couldn't tell her because either she would instantly apply breaking-point pressure to her brother by informing him, or she would suffer renewed pangs of remorse and not set up the ambush at all.

Beatrice was a real wild card, I thought, who could win us or lose us the game.

Nanterre again didn't telephone; and there had been no one all day asking about a Bradbury reward.

The advertisements had been prominent in the racing papers for two days, and noticeable in the *Towncrier*, but the message-bearer either hadn't seen them or hadn't thought answering worthwhile.

Well, I thought in disappointment, going a little painfully to bed, it had seemed a good idea at the time, as Eve no doubt told Adam after the apple.

Dawson buzzed through on the intercom before seven on Sunday morning. Phone call, he said.

Not again, I thought: Christ, not again.

I picked up the receiver with the most fearful foreboding, trying hard not to shake.

"Look here," a voice said, "this message from Danielle. I don't want any trouble, but is this reward business straight up?"

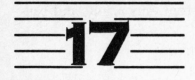

17

"**Y**es," I said, dry-mouthed, "it is."

"How much then?"

I took a deep breath, hardly believing, my heart thumping.

"Quite a lot," I said. "It depends how much you can tell me. I'd like to come and see you."

"Don't know about that," he said grudgingly.

"The reward would be bigger," I said. "And I'd bring it with me." Breathing was easier. My hands had stopped trembling.

"I don't want any trouble," he said.

"There won't be any. You tell me where you'll meet me, and I'll come."

"What's your name?" he demanded.

I hesitated fractionally. "Christmas," I said.

"Well, Mr. Christmas, I'm not meeting you for less than

a hundred quid." He was belligerent, suspicious and cautious, all in one.

"All right," I said slowly. "I agree."

"Up front, on the table," he said.

"Yes, all right."

"And if I tell you what you want to hear, you'll double it."

"If you tell me the truth, yes."

"Huh," he said sourly. "Right then. You're in London, aren't you? That's a London number."

"Yes."

"I'll meet you in Bradbury," he said. "In the town, not the racecourse. You get to Bradbury by twelve o'clock, I'll meet you in the pub there. The King's Head, halfway along the High Street."

"I'll be there," I said. "How will I know you?"

He thought, breathing heavily. "I'll take the *Sporting Life* with your ad in it."

"And . . . er . . . what's your name?" I asked.

He had the answer to that question all ready. "John Smith," he said promptly. "I'll see you, then, Mr. Christmas. OK?"

"OK," I said.

He disconnected and I lay back on the pillows feeling more apprehensive than delighted. The fish, I thought, hadn't sounded securely on the hook. He'd nibbled at the bait, but was full of reservations. I just hoped to hell he'd turn up where and when he'd said, and that he'd be the right man if he did.

His accent had been country English, not broad, just the normal local speech of Berkshire that I heard every day in Lambourn. He hadn't seemed overbright or cunning, and the amount he'd asked for, I thought, revealed a good deal about his income and his needs.

Large reward . . . When I hadn't objected to one hundred, he'd doubled it to two. But to him, two hundred equated large.

He was a gambler: Litsi had described him as having a sporting paper, a form book and binoculars. What was now certain was that he gambled small, a punter to whom a hundred was a substantial win. I supposed I should be glad he didn't think of a hundred as a basic stake: a large reward to someone like that might have been a thousand.

Thankfully I set about the business of getting up, which on the mornings after a crunch was always slow and twingy. The icepacks from bedtime had long melted, but the puffball my ankle had swollen to on the previous afternoon had definitely contracted. I took the strapping off, inspected the blackening bruising, and wrapped it up again snugly; and I could still get my shoe on, which was lucky.

In trousers, shirt and sweater I went down by elevator to the basement and nicked more ice cubes from the fridge, fastening them into plastic bags and wedging them down inside my sock. Dawson appeared in his dressing gown to see what was going on in his kitchen and merely raised his eyebrows much as he had the evening before, when I'd pinched every ice cube in the house.

"Did I do right," he asked, watching, "putting that phone call through to you?"

"You certainly did."

"He said it was to do with the advertisement: he said he was in a hurry as he was using a public telephone."

"Was he?" I pushed the trouser leg down over the loaded

sock, feeling the chill strike deep through the strapping.

"Yes," Dawson said. "I could hear the pips. Don't you give yourself frostbite, doing that?"

"Never have, yet."

Breakfast, he said a shade resignedly, would be ready in the morning room in half an hour, and I thanked him and spent the interval waking up Litsi, who said bleary-eyed that he was unaccustomed to life before ten on Sunday mornings.

"We've had a tug on the line," I explained, and told him about John Smith.

"Are you sure it isn't Nanterre setting a trap?" Litsi said, waking up thoroughly. "Don't forget, Nanterre could have seen that advertisement too. He could be reeling *you* in, not the other way round. I suppose you did think of that?"

"Yes, I did. But I think John Smith is genuine. If he'd been a trap he would've been different, more positive."

He frowned. "I'll come with you," he said.

I shook my head. "I'd like your company but Sammy has the day off because we're all here, and if we both go . . ."

"All right," he said. "But don't go onto balconies. How's your ankle? Or am I not supposed to ask?"

"Halfway to normal," I said. "Danielle exaggerates."

"Not so much." He rubbed a hand through his hair. "Have you enough cash for John Smith?"

"Yes, in my house. I'll go there on the way. I'll be back this afternoon, sometime."

"All being well," he said dryly.

I drove to Lambourn after a particularly thorough inspection of the car. It was still possible that John Smith was a trap, though on balance I didn't believe it. Nanterre couldn't have found an actor to convey the subtleties in John Smith's attitudes, nor could he himself possibly have imitated the voice. John Smith might be someone trying to snatch the reward without any goods to deliver; he might be a fraud, I thought, but not a deadly danger.

My house felt cold and empty. I opened all the letters that had accumulated there since Monday, took the ones that mattered, and dumped the junk into the dustbin along with several unread newspapers. I leafed through the present Sunday's papers and found two or three mentions, both as general news stories and as special paragraphs on the sports pages about Col being shot. All the stories recalled Cascade and Cotopaxi, but raised no great questions of *why*, and said *who* was still a complete mystery. I hadn't seen Beatrice reading any English newspaper since she'd arrived, and just hoped to hell she wouldn't start that morning.

I collected a few things to take with me: clean clothes, the cash, some writing paper, a pocket-sized tape recorder, spare cassettes and a few photographs sorted from a disorganized drawerful.

I also loaded into the car the video-recorder I'd used to make parts of the film indicting Maynard, and some spare tapes and batteries for that, but more on an "in case" basis than with any clear plans for their use: and I picked up from the kitchen, where I kept it, a small gadget I'd bought in New York that started cars from a distance. It worked by radio, transmitting to a receiver in the car that then switched on the ignition and activated the starter-motor. I liked gadgets, and that one was most useful in freezing weather, since one could start one's car from indoors and warm up the engine before plunging out into snowstorms oneself.

I checked my answering machine for messages and dealt with those, repacked my sock with new ice cubes and finally set off again to Bradbury, arriving in the small country town with ten minutes in hand.

The King's Head, I found, was a square smallish brick building, relatively modern and dedicated to beer. No old-world charm, no warming pans, oak beams, red lampshades, pewter mugs. The Bradbury Arms, across the road, looked plentifully supplied with everything.

I parked in the street and went into the King's Head public bar, finding a darts board, several benches, low tables, sisal matting and an understocked bar.

No customers.

I tried the saloon bar, genteelly furnished with glass-topped tables and moderately comfortable wooden arm-chairs, in one of which I sat while I waited.

A man appeared behind the bar there and asked what I'd like.

"Half of mild," I said.

He pulled it, and I paid.

I laid on the glass-topped table in front of me the large brown envelope that contained Lord Vaughnley's file photograph of Nanterre. The envelope currently bulged also with the tape recorder, four more photographs, two bundles of banknotes in small separate envelopes and some plain writing paper. All that I needed for John Smith was ready, but there was no sign of John Smith.

A few local people well known to the innkeeper came into the bar, ordering "the usual" and eyeing me, the stranger. None of them carried a newspaper. None of them, I noticed with surprise, was a woman.

I could hear the thud . . . thud . . . thud of someone playing darts in the public bar, so I picked up my envelope and my beer and walked back there to look.

There were three customers by that time; two playing darts and one sitting on the edge of a bench looking at his watch.

Beside him on the bench lay Saturday's *Sporting Life*, the bold-printed advertisement uppermost.

With a great sigh of relief I went over and sat down on the bench, leaving the newspaper between him and me.

"Mr. Smith?" I said.

He jumped nervously, even though he'd watched me walk across to join him.

He was perhaps in his fifties, wore a zip-fronted fawn jacket and had an air of habitual defeat. His hair, still black, was brushed in careful lines across a balding scalp, and the tip of his nose pointed straight downward, as if someone had punched it that way long ago.

"My name's Christmas," I said.

He looked at me carefully and frowned. "I know you, don't I?"

"Maybe," I said. "I brought your money. Would you like a drink?"

"I'll get it," he said. He stood up with alacrity to go over to the bar, and from that distance studied me doubtfully. I put a hand into the big envelope, switched on the tape recorder, and drew out the first of the packets of money, laying it on the table beside my glass.

He came back at length with a pint and drank a third of it thirstily.

"Why are you limping?" he said, putting the glass down watchfully.

"Twisted my ankle."

"You're that jockey," he said. "Kit Fielding."

I could feel alarm vibrating in him at the identification and pushed the money toward him, to anchor him, to prevent flight.

"A hundred," I said, "up front."

"It wasn't my fault," he said in a rush, half aggressively, on the defensive.

"No, I know that. Take the money."

He stretched out a big-knuckled hand, picked up the booty, checked it, and slotted it into an internal pocket.

"Tell me what happened," I said.

He wasn't ready, however. The unease, cause and effect, had to be dealt with first.

"Look, I don't want this going any further," he said nervously. "I've been in two minds . . . I saw this advertisement Friday . . . but, look, see, by right I shouldn't have been at the races. I'm telling you I was there, but I don't want it going no further."

"Mm," I said noncommittally.

"But, see, I could do with some untaxed dosh, who couldn't? So I thought, maybe if it was worth two hundred to you, I'd tell you."

"The rest's in here," I said, pointing to the brown envelope. "Just tell me what happened."

"Look, I was supposed to be at work. I made out I'd got flu. I wouldn't get fired if the bosses found out, just a dressing down, but I don't want the wife knowing, see what I mean? She thought I was at work. I went home my regular time. She'd bellyache something chronic if she knew. She's dead set against gambling, see what I mean?"

"And you," I said, "like your little flutter."

"Nothing wrong in that, is there?" he demanded.

"No," I said.

"The wife doesn't know I'm here," he said. "This isn't my local. I told her I had to come into Bradbury for a part for my motor. I'm draining the sump and I need a new filter. I'll have to keep quiet about meeting you, see? I had to ring you up this morning while I was out with the dog. So, see what I mean, I don't want this getting about."

I thought without guilt of my sharp-eared little recorder, but reflected that Mr. Smith's gusher would dry in a microsecond if he found it was there. He seemed, however, not the sort of man who would ever suspect its existence.

"I'm sure it won't get about, Mr. Smith," I said.

He jumped again slightly at the name.

"See, the name's not Smith, I expect you guessed. But well, if you don't know, I'm that much safer, see what I mean?"

"Yes," I said.

He drank most of the beer and wiped his mouth with a handkerchief: white with brown lines and checks round the edge. The two men playing darts finished their game and went out to the saloon bar, leaving us alone in our spartan surroundings.

"I'd been looking at the horses in the paddock," he said, "and I was going off toward the bookies when this character came up to me and offered me a fiver to deliver a message."

"A fiver," I said.

"Yeah . . . well, see what I mean, I said, 'Ten, and you're on.'" He sniffed. "He wasn't best pleased. He gave me a right filthy look, but in the end he coughed up. Ten smackers. It meant I'd be betting free on that race, see what I mean?"

"Yes," I said.

"So he says, this character, that all I'd got to do was walk over to a man he would point out, and tell him that Danielle wanted him to go up to the balcony to see the view."

"He said that precisely?"

"He made me repeat this twice. Then he gave me two fivers, pointed at a big man in a dark overcoat, very distinguished-looking, and when I turned round, he'd gone. Anyway, he paid me to pass on the message, so I did. I didn't think anything of it, see what I mean? I mean, there didn't seem any harm in it. I knew the balcony wasn't open, but if he wanted to go up there, so what, see what I mean?"

"I can see that," I said.

"I passed on the message, and the distinguished-looking gent thanked me, and I went on out to the bookies and put two fivers on Applejack."

Mr. Smith was a loser, I thought. I'd beaten Applejack into second place, on Pinkeye.

"You're not drinking," he observed, eyeing my still-full glass.

Beer was fattening. "You can have it," I said, "if you like."

He took the glass without ado and started on the contents.

"Look," he said. "You'd better tell me. Was it the man I gave the message to, who fell off the balcony?" His eyes were worried, almost pleading for any answer but the one he feared.

"I'm afraid so," I said.

"I thought it would be. I didn't see him fall, I was out front with the bookies, see what I mean? But later on, here and there, I heard people talking about coats and such. I didn't know what they were on about, though, until the next day, when it was all in the paper." He shook his head. "I couldn't say anything, though, could I, on account of being at the races when I'd said I wasn't."

"Difficult," I agreed.

"It wasn't my fault he fell off the balcony," he said aggrievedly. "So I thought, what was the point of telling anyone about the message. I'd keep my mouth shut. Maybe this Danielle pushed him, I thought. Maybe he was her husband and her lover got me to send him up there, so she could push him off. See what I mean?"

I stifled a smile and saw what he meant.

"I didn't want to be mixed up with the police, see? I mean, he wasn't killed, thanks to you, so no harm done, was there?"

"No," I said. "And he wasn't pushed. He overbalanced on some loose planks the builders had left there. He told me about it, explaining how he'd fallen."

"Oh." Mr. Anonymous Smith seemed both relieved and disappointed that he hadn't been involved in an attempted crime of passion. "I see."

"But," I said, "he was curious about the message. He thought he'd like to know who asked you to give it to him, so we decided to put that advertisement in the paper."

"Do you know him then?" he said, perplexed.

"I do now," I said.

"Ah." He nodded.

"The man who gave you the message," I said, casually, "do you remember what he looked like?"

I tried not to hold my breath. Mr. Smith, however, sensed that this was a crucial question and looked meaningfully at the envelope, his mind on the second installment.

"The second hundred's yours," I said, "if you can describe him."

"He wasn't English," he said, taking the plunge. "Strong sort of character, hard voice, big nose."

"Do you remember him clearly?" I asked, relaxing greatly inside. "Would you know him again?"

"I've been thinking about him since Thursday," he said simply. "I reckon I would."

Without making a big thing of it I pulled the five photographs out of the envelope: all eight-by-ten-black-and-white glossy pictures of people receiving trophies after races. In four of the groups the winning jockey was Fielding, but I'd had my back to the camera in two of them: the pictures were as fair a test as I'd been able to devise at short notice.

"Would you look at these photographs," I said, "and see if he's there?"

He brought out a pair of glasses and sat them on the flattened nose: an ineffectual man, not unhappy.

He took the photographs, and looked at them carefully, one by one. I'd put Nanterre's picture in fourth place of the five; and he glanced at it and passed on. He looked at the fifth and put them all down on the table, and I hoped he wouldn't guess at the extent of my disappointment.

"Well," he said judiciously, "yes, he's there."

I watched him breathlessly and waited. If he could truly recognize Nanterre, I would play any game he had in mind.

"Look," he said, as if scared by his own boldness. "You're Kit Fielding, right? You're not short of a bob or two. And that man who fell, he looked pretty well heeled. See what I mean? Make it two fifty, and I'll tell you which one he is."

I breathed deeply and pretended to be considering it with reluctance.

"All right," I said eventually. "Two fifty."

He flicked through the photographs and pointed unerringly to Nanterre.

"Him," he said.

"You've got your two fifty," I said. I gave him the second of the small envelopes. "There's a hundred in there." I fished out my wallet and sorted out fifty more. "Thanks," I said.

He nodded and put the money away carefully, as before.

"Mr. Smith," I said easily. "What would you do for another hundred?"

He stared at me through the glasses. "What do you mean?" Hopefully, on the whole.

I said, "If I write a sentence on a sheet of paper, will you sign your name to it? The name John Smith will do very well."

"What sentence?" he said, looking worried again.

"I'll write it," I said. "Then see if you will sign."

"For a hundred?"

"That's right."

I pulled a sheet of plain writing paper from the envelope, unclipped my pen and wrote,

At Bradbury races [I put the date] I gave a man a message to the effect that Danielle wanted him to go up to the viewing balcony. I identify the man who gave me that message as the man I have indicated in the photograph.

I handed it to Mr. Smith. He read it. He was unsure of the consequences of signing, but he was thinking of a hundred pounds.

"Sign it John Smith?" he said.

"Yes. With a flourish, like a proper signature."

I handed him my pen. With almost no further hesitation he did as I'd asked.

"Great," I said, taking the page and slipping it, with the photographs, back into the envelope. I took out my wallet again and gave him another hundred pounds, and saw him looking almost hungrily at the money he could see I still had.

"There's another hundred and fifty in there," I said, showing him. "It would round you up to five hundred altogether."

He liked the game increasingly. He said, "For that, what would you want?"

"To save me following you home," I said pleasantly, "I'd like you to write your real name and address down for me, on a separate sheet of paper."

I produced a clean sheet from the envelope. "You still have my pen," I reminded him. "Be a good fellow and write."

He looked as if I'd punched him in the brain.

"I came in on the bus," he said faintly.

"I can follow buses," I said.

He looked sick.

"I won't tell your wife you were at the races," I said.

"Not if you'll write down your name so I won't have to follow you."

"For a hundred and fifty?" he said weakly.

"Yes."

He wrote a name and address in capital letters:

A. V. HODGES,

44, CARLETON AVENUE,

WIDDERLAWN, NR. BRADBURY.

"What does the A. V. stand for?" I asked.

"Arnold Vincent," he said without guile.

"OK," I said. "Here's the rest of your money." I counted it out for him. "Don't lose it all at once."

He looked startled and then shamefacedly raised a laugh. "I can't go racing often, see what I mean? My wife knows how much money I've got."

"She doesn't now," I said cheerfully. "Thank you very much, Mr. Smith."

18

I had plenty of time and thought I might as well make sure. I dawdled invisibly around while John Smith bought his oil filter at a garage and caught his bus, and I followed the bus unobtrusively to Widderlawn.

John Smith descended and walked to Carleton Avenue where at number 44, a well-tended council semi-detached, he let himself in with a latchkey.

Satisfied on all counts, I drove back to London and found Litsi coming out of the library as I entered the hall.

"I saw you coming," he said lazily. The library windows looked out to the street. "I'm delighted you're back." He had been watching for me, I thought.

"It wasn't a trap," I said.

"So I see."

I smiled suddenly and he said, "A purring cat, if ever I saw one."

I nodded toward the library. "Let's go in there, and I'll tell you."

I carried the bag with clothes and the big envelope into the long paneled room with its grille-fronted bookshelves, its Persian rugs, its net and red velvet curtains. A nobly proportioned room, it was chiefly used for entertaining callers not intimate enough to be invited upstairs, and to me had the lifeless air of expensive waiting rooms.

Litsi looked down at my feet. "Are you *squelching?*" he asked disbelievingly.

"Mm." I put down the bag and the envelope and peeled off my left shoe, into which one of the icepacks had leaked.

To his discriminating horror I pulled the one intact bag out of my sock and emptied the contents onto a convenient potted plant. The second bag, having emptied itself, followed the first into the wastepaper basket. I pulled off my drenched sock, left it folded on top of my bag, and replaced my wet shoe.

"I suppose," Litsi said, "all that started out as mobile refrigeration."

"Quite right."

"I'd have kept a sprain warm," he said thoughtfully.

"Cold is quicker."

I took the envelope over to where a pair of armchairs stood, one on each side of a table with a lamp on it: switched on the lamp, sat in a chair. Litsi, following, took the other armchair. The library itself was perpetually dark, needing lights almost always, the gray afternoon on that day giving up the contest in the folds of cream net at the street end of the room.

"Mr. Smith," I said, "can speak for himself."

I put the small recorder on the table, rewound the cassette, and started it going. Litsi, the distinguished-looking gent, listened with wry fascination to the way he'd been set up, and toward the end his eyebrows started climbing, a sign with him that meant a degree of not understanding.

I showed him the paper John Smith had signed, and while he watched drew a circle with my pen round the head of Nanterre in the photograph.

"Mr. Smith did live where he wrote," I said. "I did follow him home, to make sure."

"But," Litsi said surprised, "if you followed him anyway, why did you give him the last hundred and fifty?"

"Oh . . . mm . . . it saved me having to discover his name from the neighbors." Litsi looked skeptical. "Well," I said, "he deserved it."

"What are you going to do with these things?" he asked, waving a hand.

"With a bit of luck," I said, "this." And I told him.

Grateful for the elevator, I went up three floors to the bamboo room to stow away my gear, to shower and change, to put on dry strapping and decide on no more ice.

The palatial room was beginning to feel like home, I thought. Beatrice seemed to have given up plans for active invasion, though leaving me in no doubt about the strength of her feelings; and as my affection for the room grew, so did my understanding of her pique.

She wasn't in the sitting room when I went down for the evening; only Danielle and the princess, with Litsi pouring their drinks.

I bowed slightly to the princess, as it was the first time I'd seen her that day, and kissed Danielle on the cheek.

"Where have you been?" she asked neutrally.

"Fishing."

"Did you catch anything?"

"Sharkbait," I said.

She looked me swiftly, laughingly, in the eyes, the old loving Danielle there and gone in a flash. I took the glass into which Litsi had poured a scant ounce of scotch and tried to stifle regret.

Beatrice walked into the room with round dazed eyes and stood vaguely in the center as if not sure what to do next. Litsi began to mix her drink the way she liked it: he'd have made a good king but an even better barman, I thought, liking him. Beatrice went across to the sofa where the princess was sitting and took the place beside her as if her knees had given way.

"There we are, Beatrice," Litsi said with good humor, setting the red drink down on the low table in front of her. "Dash of Worcestershire, twist of lemon."

Beatrice looked at the drink unseeingly.

"Casilia," she said, as if the words were hurting her throat. "I have been such a fool."

"My dear Beatrice . . ." the princess said.

Beatrice without warning started to cry, not silently but with "Ohs" of distress that were close to groans.

The princess looked uncomfortable, and it was Litsi who came to Beatrice's aid with a large white handkerchief and comforting noises.

"Tell us what's troubling you," he said, "and surely we can help you."

Beatrice wailed "Oh" again with her open mouth twisted into an agonized circle and pressed Litsi's handkerchief hard to her eyes.

"Do try to pull yourself together, Beatrice, dear," the princess said with a touch of astringency. "We can't help you until we know what's the matter."

Beatrice's faintly theatrical paroxysm abated, leaving a real distress showing. The overbid for sympathy might have misfired, but the need for it existed.

"I can't help it," she said, drying her eyes and blotting her mascara carefully, laying the folded edge of handkerchief flat over her lower eyelid and blinking her top lashes onto it, leaving tiny black streaks. No one in extremis, I thought, wiped their eyes so methodically.

"I've been such a fool," she said.

"In what way, dear?" asked the princess, giving the unmistakable impression that she already thought her sister-in-law a fool in most ways most of the time.

"I . . . I've been talking to Henri Nanterre," Beatrice said.

"When?" Litsi asked swiftly.

"Just now. Upstairs, in my room."

Both he and I looked at the recording telephone, which had remained silent. Neither Litsi nor I had lifted a receiver at the right time after all.

"You telephoned him?" Litsi said.

"Yes, of course." Beatrice began to recover such wits as she had. "Well, I mean . . ."

"What did he say," Litsi asked, not pursuing it, "that has so upset you?"

"I . . . I . . . He was so charming when he came to see me in Palm Beach, but I've been wrong, terribly wrong."

"What did he say just now?" Litsi asked again.

"He said"—she looked at him a shade wildly—"that he'd thought Roland would crack when you were nearly killed. He asked me why he hadn't. But I . . . I didn't know you'd been nearly killed. I said I hadn't heard anything about it, and I was sure Roland and Casilia hadn't, and he was furiously angry, *shouting* . . ." She shook her head. "I had to hold the telephone away from my ear . . . he was hurting me."

The princess was looking astounded and distressed.

"Litsi! What happened? You never said . . ."

"Henri boasted," Beatrice said miserably, "that he organized an accident for Litsi that would have brilliantly succeeded, except that this . . . this . . ." She didn't know what to call me, and contented herself in pointing. "*He* saved Litsi's life." Beatrice gulped. "I never thought . . . never ever . . . that he would do anything so *frightful*. That he would really *harm* anyone. And he said . . . he said . . . he thought Roland and Casilia wouldn't have wanted any more horses killed, and how had she reacted about her horse called Col? And when I told him I didn't know anything about it, he flew into a *rage*. He asked if Roland knew and I said I didn't know. He was shouting down the telephone . . . he was totally *furious*. He said he'd never thought that they would hold out so long. He said it was all taking too long and he would step up the pressure."

Beatrice's shock was deep.

"He said the jockey was always in his way, blocking him, bringing in guards and recording telephones; so he would get rid of the jockey first. Then after that, Danielle would lose her beauty—and then no one would stop Roland signing. He said," she added, her eyes round and dry again, "I was to tell Roland what he'd threatened. I was to say he had telephoned here and I'd happened to answer."

The princess, aghast but straight-backed, said, "I won't let you tell Roland anything, Beatrice."

"Henri put the telephone down," Beatrice said, "and I sat there thinking he didn't mean it, he couldn't possibly spoil Danielle's face. She's my niece as well as Roland's. I wouldn't want that, not for all the money in the world. I tried to make myself believe it was just a threat, but he did chase after her that evening, and he did kill the horses; he boasted of it . . . and I didn't want to believe he had tried to kill Litsi . . . to kill! . . . it wasn't possible . . . but he sounded so vicious . . . I wouldn't have believed he could be like that." She turned imploringly to the princess. "I may have been foolish, but I'm not *wicked*, Casilia."

I listened to the outpouring with profound disturbance. I didn't want her late-flowering remorse tangling the carefully laid lines. I would much have preferred her purposefulness to remain strong and intact.

"Did you ring him back?" I asked.

Beatrice didn't like talking to me, and didn't answer until Litsi asked her the same question.

"I did," she said passionately, asking for absolution, "but he'd already gone."

"Already?" Litsi asked.

Beatrice said in a much smaller voice, "He'd said I couldn't reach him again at that number. He wasn't there half the time in any event. I mean . . ."

"How many times have you talked to him?" Litsi asked mildly. "And at what time of day?"

Beatrice hesitated but answered, "Today and yesterday, at about six, and Thursday morning, and . . ." She tried to remember. "It must have been Wednesday evening at six, and Monday twice, after I'd found out . . ." Her voice trailed away, the admission, half out, suddenly alarming her.

"Found out what?" Litsi asked without censure.

She said unhappily, "The make and color of Danielle's car. He wanted to know. I had no idea," she suddenly wailed, "that he meant to attack her. I couldn't believe it, when he said on the telephone . . . when he told Litsi . . . saying that young women shouldn't drive alone at night. Danielle," she said beseechingly, turning to her, "I'd never cause harm to you, ever."

"But on Thursday you told him Danielle and I were going to Bradbury races," Litsi commented.

"Yes, but he *asked* me to tell him things like that," Beatrice said fiercely. "He wanted to know the least little thing, every time. He asked what was happening . . . he said as it was important to me for him to succeed, I should help him with details, any details, however tiny."

I said, in Litsi's unprovoking manner, "To what extent was it important to you, Mrs. Bunt?"

She was provoked all the same: glared at me and didn't answer.

Litsi rephrased the question, "Did Henri promise you perhaps a nice present if he succeeded?"

Beatrice looked uncertainly at the princess, whose gaze was on the hands on her lap, whose face was severe. No blandishments on earth would have induced her to spy comprehensively for her host's, her brother's, enemy, and she was trying hard, I imagined, not to show open disgust.

To Litsi, Beatrice said, self-excusingly, "I have the de Brescou trust fund, of course, but it's expensive to keep one's *position* in Palm Beach. My soirees, you know, just for fifty dear friends . . . nothing large . . . and my servants, just a married couple . . . are barely *enough*, and Henri said . . Henri promised . . ." She paused doubtfully.

"A million dollars?" Litsi suggested.

"No, no," she protested, "not so much. He said when the pistols were in production and when he'd made his first good arms deal, which would be in under a year, he thought, he would send a gift of two hundred and fifty thousand, and a hundred thousand each year afterward for three years. Not so very much, but it would have made a useful difference to me, you see."

A soiree for a hundred, I thought sardonically. A small rise in status among the comfortably rich. More than half a million dollars overall. One could see the difference with clarity.

"I didn't see any wrong in trying to persuade Roland," she said. "When I came over here I was certain I could do it, and have Henri's lovely money to spend afterward."

"Did he give you a written contract?" I asked.

"No, of course not," she said, forgetting she was speaking to me, "but he promised. He's a *gentleman*."

Even she, once she'd said it, could see that although Nanterre was many things, from an aristocrat to an entrepreneur, a gentleman he was not.

"He promised," she reiterated.

Beatrice seemed to be feeling better about things, as if full confession excused the sin.

I was anxious to know how much information she'd passed on before the dawn of realization and the consequent change of heart: a lot of good plans had gone down the drain if she hadn't relayed what we'd wanted.

"Mrs. Bunt," I said diffidently, "if Henri Nanterre told

you he was going to get rid of the jockey, did he say how? Or perhaps when? Or where?"

"No, he didn't," she said promptly, looking at me with disfavor.

"But did you perhaps tell him where I'd be going, and when, in the way you told him about Danielle and Litsi?"

She simply stared at me.

Litsi, understanding what I wanted to know, said, "Beatrice, if you've told Nanterre where Kit might be vulnerable, you must tell us now, seriously you must."

She looked at him defensively. "It's because of him," she meant me, "that Roland hasn't agreed to Henri's plans. Roland told me so. So did *he*." She jerked her head in my direction. "He said it straight out at dinner . . . you heard him . . . that while he was here Roland wouldn't sign. He has so much power. You all do what he says. If he hadn't been here, Henri said, it would all have been settled on the very first day, even before I got here. Everything's *his* fault. It was *he* who drove Henri to do all those awful things. It's because of *him* that I probably won't get my money. So when Henri asked me if I could find out when and where the jockey would be alone . . . well . . . I said I would. I was glad to!"

"Aunt Beatrice!" Danielle exclaimed. "How could you?"

"He has my room," Beatrice said explosively. "*My room.*"

There was a small intense silence. Then I said mildly, "If you'd tell us what you told Henri Nanterre, then I wouldn't go there, wherever."

"You must tell us," the princess said vehemently. "If any harm comes to Kit because of you, Beatrice, you will never be received again either in this house or in the chateau."

Beatrice looked stunned by this direst of threats.

"Moreover," Litsi said in a tone loaded with strength, "you are not my sister, my sister-in-law or my aunt. I have no family feeling for you. You gave information that might have led to my death. If you've done the same regarding Kit, which it appears you have, and Nanterre succeeds in killing him, you'll be guilty of conspiracy to murder, and I shall inform the police to that effect."

Beatrice crumbled totally inside. It was all far more than she'd meant to involve herself in, and Litsi's threat sounded like the heavy tread of an unthinkable future of penal reckoning.

Beatrice said to Litsi with a touch of sullenness, "I told Henri where he keeps his car, while he's here. This evening I told Henri that he'll be fetching Danielle for the last time tomorrow, that he goes round to his car at one-thirty in the morning. Henri said that was excellent. But then he talked about you at Bradbury . . . and the horses dying . . and he started shouting, and I realized . . . how he'd used me." Her face crumpled as if she would cry again, but perhaps sensing a universal lack of sympathy, she smothered the impulse and looked from one to the other of us, searching for pity.

Litsi was looking quietly triumphant, much as I was feeling myself. The princess however was shocked and wide-eyed.

"That dark mews!" she said, horrified. "Kit, don't go down there."

"No," I assured her. "I'll park somewhere else." She relaxed, clearly satisfied by the simple solution, and Danielle looked at me broodingly, knowing I wouldn't.

I winked at her.

She almost laughed. "How can you?" she said. "How can you joke? Don't say it, don't say it . . . easily."

The princess and Beatrice looked mystified but paid not much attention.

"Are you absolutely certain," I said to Beatrice, "that you can't get in touch with Nanterre again?"

"Yes, I am," she said uncertainly, and looked nervously at Litsi. "But . . . but . . ."

"But what, Beatrice?"

"He's going to telephone here this evening. He wanted me to tell Roland about your accident and about Col being shot, and then he would find out if Roland was ready to sign . . . and if not . . ." She squirmed. "I couldn't let him hurt Danielle. I couldn't!"

Her eyes seemed to focus on her untouched drink. She stretched out a scarlet-nailed much-beringed hand and gave a good imitation of one fresh from the desert. The princess, hardly able to look at her sister-in-law, headed for the door, motioning with her hand for me to go with her.

I followed. She went into the dining room where dinner was laid and asked me to close the door, which I did.

She said, with intense worry, "Nothing has changed, has it, because of what Beatrice has told us?"

"No," I said, with a thankfulness she didn't hear.

"We can't go on and on. We can't risk Danielle's face. You can't risk that." The dilemma was dreadful, as Nanterre had meant.

"No," I said. "I can't risk that. But give me until Tuesday. Don't let Monsieur know of the threats until then. We have a plan. We have a lever, but we need a stronger one. We'll get rid of Nanterre," I promised, "if you'll give us that time."

"You and Litsi?"

"Yes."

"Litsi was the man who fell from the balcony," she said, wanting confirmation.

I nodded, and told her of the decoy message but not about finding the messenger.

"Dear heaven. Surely we must tell the police."

"Wait until Tuesday," I begged. "We will then, if we have to."

She agreed easily enough because police inquiries could lead to publicity; and I hoped for Arnold Vincent Hodges's sake that we wouldn't have to drop him into hot water with his wife.

I asked the princess if I could have ten minutes' private conversation with her husband that evening, and without more ado she whisked us both up in the elevator and arranged it on the spot, saying it was a convenient time as he would not be coming down to dinner.

She saw me in and left us, and I took the red leather armchair as indicated by Roland.

"How can I help you?" he said civilly, his head supported by the high-backed wheelchair. "More guards? I have met Sammy," he smiled faintly. "He's amusing."

"No, monsieur, not more guards. I wondered if I could go to see your lawyer, Gerald Greening, early tomorrow morning. Would you mind if I made an appointment?"

"Is this to do with Henri Nanterre?"

"Yes, monsieur."

"Could you say why you want Gerald?"

I explained. He said wearily that he saw no prospect of success, but that I needn't go to Gerald's office, Gerald would come to the house. The world, I saw in amusement, was divided between those who went to lawyers' offices and those to whom lawyers came.

Roland said that if I would look up Gerald's home number and get through to it, he would speak to Gerald himself, if he were in, and in a short time the appointment was made.

"He will come here on his way to his office," Roland said, handing me the receiver to replace. "Eight-thirty. Give him breakfast."

"Yes, monsieur."

He nodded a fraction. "Goodnight, Kit."

I went down to dinner, which took place in more silence than ever, and later, as he'd threatened, Nanterre telephoned.

When I heard his voice, I pressed the record button, but again not that for conference.

"I'll talk to anyone but you," he said.

"Then no one."

He shouted, "I want to talk to Casilia."

"No."

"I will talk to Roland."

"No."

"To Beatrice."

"No."

"You'll regret it," he yelled, and crashed down the receiver.

Litsi and I entertained Gerald Greening in the morning room, where he ate copiously of kippers followed by eggs and bacon, all furnished by Dawson, forewarned.

"Mm, mm," Greening grunted as we explained what we wanted. "Mm, no problem at all. Would you pass me the butter?"

He was rounded and jovial, patting his stomach. "Is there any toast?"

From his briefcase he produced a large pad of white paper upon which he made notes. "Yes, yes," he said busily, writing away. "I get the gist, absolutely. You want your intentions cast into foolproof legal language, is that right?"

We said it was.

"And you want this typed up properly this morning and furnished with seals?"

Yes please, we said. Two copies.

"No problem." He gave me his coffee cup absentmindedly to take to the sideboard for a hot refill. "I can bring them back here by"—he consulted his watch—"say twelve noon. That all right?"

We said it would do.

He pursed his lips. "Can't manage it any faster. Have to draft it properly, get it typed without mistakes, all that sort of thing, checked, drive over from the City."

We understood.

"Marmalade?"

We passed it.

"Anything else?"

"Yes," Litsi said, fetching from a side table the buff French form that had been in the notary's briefcase, "some advise on this."

Gerald Greening said in surprise, "Surely the Frenchmen took that away with them when Monsieur de Brescou refused to sign?"

"This is a duplicate blank copy, not filled in," Litsi said. "We think the one Henri Nanterre wanted signed would have represented the first page of a whole bunch of documents. Kit and I want this unused copy to form page one of our own bunch of documents." He passed it to Greening. "As you see, it's a general form of contract, with spaces for details, and in French, of course. It must be binding, or Henri Nanterre wouldn't have used it. I propose to write in French in the spaces provided, so that this and the accompanying document together constitute a binding contract under French law. I'd be grateful," he said in his most princely tone, "if you would advise me as to wording."

"In French?" Greening said apprehensively.

"In English . . . I'll translate."

They worked on it together until each was satisfied and Greening had embarked on round four of toast. I envied him not his bulk nor his appetite, but his freedom from restraint, and swallowed my characterless vitamins wishing they at least smelled of breakfast.

He left after the fifth slice, bearing away his notes and promising immediate action; and true to his word, he reappeared in his chauffeur-driven car at ten minutes to twelve. Litsi and I were both by then in the library watching the street, and we opened the front door to the bulky solicitor and took him into the office used by the elfin Mrs. Jenkins.

There we stapled to the front page of one of Greening's imposing-looking documents the original French form, and a photocopy of it to the other, each with the new wording typed in neatly, leaving large spaces for signing.

From there we rode up in the elevator to Roland de Brescou's private sitting room, where he and the princess and Danielle were all waiting.

Gerald Greening with vaguely theatrical flourishes presented the documents to each of them in turn, and to Litsi, asking them each to sign their names four times, once on each of the French forms; once at the end of each document.

Each document was sewn through with pink tape down the left-hand margin, as with wills, and each space for a signature at the end was provided with a round red seal.

Greening made everyone say aloud archaic words about signing, sealing and delivering, made them put a finger on each seal and witnessed each signature himself with precision. He required that I also witness each signature, which I did.

"I don't know how much of all this is strictly necessary," he said happily, "but Mr. Fielding wanted these documents unbreakable by any possible quibble of law, as he put it, so we have two witnesses, seals, declarations, everything. I do hope you all understand exactly what you've been signing as unless you should burn them or otherwise destroy them, these documents are irrevocable."

Everyone nodded, Roland de Brescou with sadness.

"That's splendid," Greening said expansively, and began looking around him and at his watch expectantly.

"And now, Gerald, some sherry?" the princess suggested with quiet amusement.

"Princess Casilia, what a splendid idea!" he said with imitation surprise. "A glass would be lovely."

I excused myself from the party on the grounds that I was riding in the two-thirty at Windsor and should have left fifteen minutes ago.

Litsi picked up the signed documents, returned them to the large envelope Gerald Greening had brought them in, and handed me the completed package.

"Don't forget to telephone," he said.

"No."

He hesitated. "Good luck," he said.

They all thought he meant with the races, which was perfectly proper.

The princess had no runners as she almost never went to Windsor races, having no box there. Beatrice was spending the day in the beauty parlor, renovating her self-esteem. Litsi was covering for Sammy, who was supposed to be resting. I hadn't expected Danielle to come with me on her own, but she followed me onto the landing from Roland's room and said, "If I come with you, can you get me to work by six-thirty?"

"With an hour to spare."

"Shall I come?"

"Yes," I said.

She nodded and went off past the princess's rooms to her own to fetch a coat, and we walked round to the mews in a reasonable replica of the old companionship. She watched me check the car and without comment waited some distance away while I started the engine and stamped on the brakes, and we talked about Gerald Greening on the way to Windsor, and about Beatrice at Palm Beach, and about her news bureau: safe subjects, but I was glad just to have her there at all.

She was wearing the fur-lined swinging green-gray showerproof jacket I'd given her for Christmas, also black trousers, a white high-necked sweater and a wide floral chintz headband holding back her cloud of dark hair. The consensus among other jockeys that she was a "knockout" had never found me disagreeing.

I drove fast to Windsor and we hurried from car park to weighing room, finding Dusty hovering about there looking pointedly at the clock.

"What about your ankle?" he said suspiciously. "You're still limping."

"Not when I'm riding," I said.

Dusty gave me a look as good as his name and scurried away, and Danielle said she would go buy a sandwich and coffee.

"Will you be all right by yourself?"

"Of course, or I wouldn't have come."

She'd made friends over the past months with the wife of a Lambourn trainer I often rode for, and with the wives of one or two of the other jockeys, but I knew the afternoons were lonely when she went racing without her aunt.

"I'm not riding in the fourth; we can watch that together," I said.

"Yes. Go in and change. You're late."

I'd taken the packet of documents into the racecourse rather than leave them in the car, and in the changing room gave them into the safekeeping of my valet. My valet's safekeeping would have shamed the vaults of the Bank of England and consisted of stowing things (like one's wallet) in the capacious front pocket of a black vinyl apron. The apron, I guessed, had evolved for that purpose: there were no lockers in the changing rooms, and one hung one's clothes on a peg.

It wasn't a demanding day from the riding point of view. I won the first of my races (the second on the card) by twenty lengths, which Dusty said was too far, and lost the next by the same distance, again to his disapproval. The next was the fourth race, which I spent on the stands with Danielle, having seen her also briefly on walks from the weighing room to parade ring. I told her the news of Joe, the jockey injured at Sandown, who was conscious and on the mend, and she said she'd had coffee with Betsy, the Lambourn trainer's wife. Everything was fine, she said, just fine.

It was the third day of March, blustery and cold, and the Cheltenham National Hunt Festival was all of a sudden as near as next week.

"Betsy says it's a shame about the Gold Cup," Danielle said. "She says you won't have a ride in it, now Col's dead."

"Not unless some poor bugger breaks his collarbone."

"Kit!"

"That's how it goes."

She looked as if she didn't need to be reminded, and I was sorry I had. I went out to the fifth race wondering if that day was some sort of test: if she were finding out for herself with finality whether or not she could permanently face what life with me entailed. I shivered slightly in the wind and thought the danger of losing her the worst one of all.

I finished third in the race, and when I returned to the unsaddling enclosure Danielle was standing there waiting, looking strained and pale and visibly trembling.

"What is it?" I said sharply, sliding down from the horse. "What's the matter?"

"He's here," she said with shock. "Henri Nanterre. I'm sure . . . it's him."

"Look," I said, "I've got to weigh in, just sit on the scales. I'll come straight back out. You just stand right outside the weighing-room door . . . don't move from there."

"No."

She went where I pointed, and I unsaddled the horse and made vaguely hopeful remarks to the mildly pleased owners. I passed the scales, gave my saddle, whip and helmet to my valet and went out to Danielle, who had stopped actually trembling but still looked upset.

"Where did you see him?" I asked.

"On the stands, during the race. He seemed to be edging toward me, coming up from below, coming sideways, saying 'excuse me' to people and looking at me now and then as if checking where I was."

"You're sure it was him?"

"He was just like the photograph. Like you've described him. I didn't realize to begin with . . . then I recognized him. I was"—she swallowed—"terrified. He sort of snaked round people, sliding like an eel."

"That's him," I said grimly.

"I slid away from him," Danielle said. "It was like panic. I couldn't move fast . . . so many people, all watching the race and annoyed with me. When I got off the stands the race was over . . . and I ran. What am I going to do? You're riding in the next race."

"Well, what you're going to do is dead boring, but you'll be safe." I smiled apologetically. "Go into the Ladies' and stay there. Find a chair there and wait. Tell the attendant you're sick, faint, tired, anything. Stay there until after the race, and I'll come and fetch you. Half an hour, not much more. I'll send someone in with a message . . . and don't come out for any message except mine. We'll need a password . . ."

"Christmas Day," she said.

"OK. Don't come out without the password, not even if you get a message saying I'm on my way to hospital, or something like that. I'll give my valet the password and tell him to fetch you if I can't . . . but I will," I said, seeing the extra fright in her expression. "I'll ride bloody carefully. Try not to let Nanterre see you going in there, but if he does . . ."

"Don't come out," she said. "Don't worry, I won't."

"Danielle . . ."

"Yes?"

"I do love you," I said.

She blinked, ducked her head, and went away fast. I thought Nanterre would have known I would be at Windsor races, he had only to look in the newspaper, and that I and anyone in the princess's family was vulnerable everywhere, not just in dark alleys.

I followed Danielle, keeping her in sight until her back-view vanished into the one place Nanterre couldn't follow, and then hurried back to change colors and weigh out. I didn't see the Frenchman anywhere, which didn't mean he hadn't seen me. The highly public nature of my work on racecourses, however, I thought, might be acting in our favor: Nanterre couldn't easily attack me at the races because everywhere I went, people were watching. In parade rings, on horses, on the stands . . . wherever a jockey went in breeches and colors, heads turned to look. Anonymity took over at the racecourse exits.

I rode that last race at Windsor with extreme concentration, particularly as it was a steeplechase for novice jumpers, always an unpredictable event. My mount was trained not by Wykeham but by Betsy's husband, the Lambourn trainer, and it would be fair to say he got a good schooling run rather than a flat-out scramble.

Betsy's husband was satisfied with fourth place because the horse had jumped well, and I said, "Next time, he'll win," as one does, to please him and the owners.

I weighed in for fourth place, changed fast, collected my valuables from the valet and wrote a short note for Danielle.

"Christmas Day has dawned. Time to go.'

It was Betsy, in the end, who took the note into the Ladies', coming out smiling with Danielle a minute later.

I sighed with relief: Danielle also, it seemed. Betsy shook her head over our childish games, and Danielle and I went out to the rapidly emptying car park.

"Did you see Nanterre?" Danielle asked.

"No. Nowhere."

"I'm sure it was him."

"Yes, so am I."

My car stood almost alone at the end of a line, its neighbors having departed. I stopped well before we reached it and brought the car-starter out of my pocket.

"But that," Danielle said in surprise, "is your toy for freezes."

"Mm," I said, and pressed its switch.

There was no explosion. The engine started sweetly, purring to life. We went on toward the car and I did the other checks anyway, but finding nothing wrong.

"What if it had blown up?" Danielle said.

"Better the car than us."

"Do you think he *would?*"

"I really don't know. I don't mind taking precautions that turn out to be unnecessary. It's 'if only' that would be embarrassing."

I drove out onto the highway and at the first intersection went off it and round and started back in the opposite direction.

"More avoidance of 'if only'?" Danielle said with irony.

"Do you want acid squirted in your face?"

"Not especially."

"Well, we don't know what sort of transport Nanterre's got. And one car can sit inconspicuously behind you for hours on a motorway. I'd not like him to jump us in those small streets at Chiswick."

When we reached the next intersection I reversed the process and Danielle studied the traffic out of the rear window.

"Nothing came all the way round after us," she said.
"Good."
"So can we relax?"
"The man who's coming to fetch you tonight is called
Swallow," I said. "When the car comes for you, get those
big men on the studio reception desk to ask him his name.
If he doesn't say Swallow, check up with the car-hire firm."
I slid my wallet out. "Their card's in there, in the front."
She took the card and passed the wallet back.
"What haven't you thought of?"
"I wish I knew."
Even with the wrong-direction detour, it was a short
journey from Windsor to Chiswick, and we arrived in the
streets leading to the studio a good hour before six-thirty.
"Do you want to go in early?" I asked.
"No . . . Park the car where we can sit and look at the
river."
I found a spot where we could see brown water sliding
slowly upstream, covering the mud-flats as the tide came
in. There were seagulls flying against the wind, raucously
calling, and a coxed four feathering their oars with curved
fanatical backs.
"I have . . . er . . . something to tell you," Danielle said
nervously.
"No," I said with pain.
"You don't know what it is."
"Today was a test," I said.
Danielle said slowly, "I forget sometimes that you can
read minds."
"I can't. Not often. You know that."
"You just did."
"There are better days than today," I said hopelessly.

"And worse."

I nodded.

"Don't look so sad," she said. "I can't bear it."

"I'll give it up if you'll marry me," I said.

"Do you mean that?"

"Yes."

She didn't seem overjoyed. I'd lost, it seemed, on all counts.

"I . . . er . . ." she said faintly. "If you don't give it up, I'll marry you."

I thought I hadn't heard right.

"*What* did you say?" I demanded.

"I said . . ." She stopped. "Do you want to marry me or don't you?"

"That's a bloody silly question."

I leaned toward her and she to me, and we kissed like a homecoming.

I suggested transferring to the rear seat, which we did, but not for gymnastic lovemaking, partly because of daylight and frequent passersby, partly because of the unsatisfactoriness of the available space. We sat with our arms round each other, which after the past weeks I found unbelievable and boringly said so several times over.

"I didn't mean to do this," she said. "When I came back from the Lake District, I was going to find a way of saying it was all over, a mistake."

"What changed your mind?"

"I don't know .   lots of things. Being with you so much . . . missing you yesterday. Odd things. Seeing how Litsi respects you . . . Betsy saying I was lucky . . . and Joe's wife . .   She threw up, you know. Everything up. Everything down. She was sweating and cold . . . and pregnant . . . I asked her how she managed to live with the fear. She said if it was fear and Joe against no fear, no Joe, the choice was easy."

I held her close. I could feel her heart beating.

"Today I was wandering about, looking at things," she said. "Wondering if I wanted a life of racecourses and winter and perpetual anxiety. Watching you go out on those horses, with you not knowing . . . and not caring . . . if it's going to be your last half hour ever . . . and doing that five or six hundred times every year. I looked at the other jockeys on their way out to the parade ring, and they're all like you, perfectly calm, as if they're going to an office."

"Much better than an office."

"Yes, for you." She kissed me. "You can thank Aunt Casilia for shaming me into going racing again . . . but most of all, Joe's wife. I thought today clearly of what life would be like without you: no fear, no Kit . . . like she said . . . I guess I'll take the fear."

"And throw up."

"Everything up, everything down. She said it was like that for all of the wives, sometime or other. And a few husbands, I guess."

It was odd, I thought, how life could totally change from one minute to the next. The fog of wretchedness of the past month had vanished like ruptured cobwebs. I felt light-headedly, miraculously happy, more even than in the beginning. Perhaps one truly had to have lost and regained, to know that sort of joy.

"You won't change your mind, will you?" I said.

"No, I won't," she answered, and spent a fair time doing her best, in the restricted circumstances, to show me she meant it.

I saw her eventually into the studio and drove back

toward Eaton Square on euphoric autopilot, returning to earth in time to park carefully and methodically in the usual place in the mews.

I switched off the engine and sat looking vaguely at my hands, sat there for a while thinking of what might lie ahead. Then with a mental shiver I telephoned to the house, and got Litsi immediately, as if he'd been waiting.

"I'm in the alley," I said.

We didn't know how he would come, or when, or even *if*.

We'd shown him an opportunity and loaded him with a motive. Given him a time and place when he could remove an immovable obstruction: but whether he would accept the circuitous invitation, heaven alone knew.

Henri Nanterre . . . his very name sounded threatening.

I thought about his being at Windsor and making his way through the crowds on the stands, moving upward and sideways, approaching Danielle. I thought that until that afternoon he might not have reliably known what she looked like. He'd seen her in the dark the previous Monday, when he'd opened her tire valves and chased her, but it had been her car he had identified her by, not her face.

He'd probably have seen her with Litsi at Bradbury, but

maybe not from close to. He'd have known she was the young woman with Litsi because Beatrice had told him they were going together with me.

Nanterre might not have known that Danielle had gone to Windsor at all until he'd seen her with me several times in the paddock and on the stands during the fourth race. He couldn't have gone to Windsor with any advance plans, but what he'd meant to do if he'd reached Danielle was anyone's nightmare.

I was sitting with these thoughts not in my own car but on a foam cushion on the floor inside the garage where Danielle was keeping her little Ford. One of the garage doors was open about a hand's span, enough for me to see the Mercedes and a good deal of the mews, looking up toward the road entrance. A few people were coming home from work, opening their garages, shunting the cars in, closing and locking. A few were reversing the process, going out for the evening. The mechanics had long gone, all their garages silent. Several cars, like the Mercedes, were parked in the open, close to the sides, leaving a scant passage free in the center.

Dusk had turned to night, and local bustle died into the restless distant roar of London's traffic. I sat quietly with a few pre-positioned necessities to hand, like Perrier, smoked salmon and an apple, and rehearsed in my mind all sorts of eventualities, none of which happened.

Every half hour or so, I rose to my feet, stretched my spine, paced round Danielle's car, and sat down again. Nothing of much interest occurred in the mews, and the hands of my watch traveled like slugs; eight o'clock, nine o'clock, ten.

I thought of Danielle, and of what she'd said when I left her.

"For Aunt Casilia's sake I must hope that the rattlesnake turns up in the mews, but if you get yourself killed, I'll never forgive you."

"A thought for eternity," I said.

"You just make sure eternity is spent right here on earth, with me."

"Yes, ma'am," I said, and kissed her.

The rattlesnake, I thought, yawning as eleven o'clock passed, was taking his time. I normally went round to the mews at one-thirty so as to be at Chiswick before two, and I thought that if Nanterre was planning a direct physical attack of any sort he would be there well before that time, seeking a shadow to hide in. He hadn't been there before seven, because I'd searched every cranny before settling in the garage, and there were no entrances other than the way in from the street. If he'd sneaked in somehow since then without my seeing him, we were maybe in trouble.

At eleven-fifteen, I stretched my legs round Danielle's car and sat down again.

At eleven-seventeen, unaware, he came to the lure.

I'd been hoping against hope, longing for him to come, wanting to expect it . . . and yet, when he did, my skin crawled with animal fear as if the tiger were indeed stalking the goat.

He walked openly down the center of the mews as if he owned a car there, moving with his distinctive eel-like lope, fluid and smooth, not a march.

He was turning his head from side to side, looking at the silent parked cars, and even in the dim light filtering down from the high windows of the surrounding buildings, the shape of nose and jaw were unmistakable.

He came closer and closer; and he wasn't looking for a hiding place, I saw, but for my car.

For one appalling moment he looked straight at the partly opened door of the garage where I sat, but I was immobile in dark clothes in dark shadow, and I started breathing again when he appeared to see nothing to alarm him or frighten him away.

Nanterre was there, I thought exultantly; right there in front of my eyes, and all our planning had come to pass. Whatever should happen, I reckoned that that was a triumph.

Nanterre looked back the way he'd come, but nothing stirred behind him.

He came close to my car. He stopped beside it, about the length of a Rolls-Royce away, and he coolly fiddled about and opened the passenger's seat door with some sort of key as if he'd spent a lifetime thieving.

Well bloody well, I thought, and heard him unlatch the hood with the release knob inside the car. He raised the hood, propped it open with its strut, and leaned over the engine with a lighted torch as if working on a fault: anyone coming into the mews at that point would have paid no attention.

After a while, he switched off the torch and closed the hood gently, latching it by direct downward pressure of both palms, not by a more normal brisk slam. Finally he shut the open passenger door quietly; and as he turned away to leave, I saw he was smiling.

I wondered whether what he'd left by my engine was plastic, like his guns.

He'd walked several paces along the mews before I stood, slid out through the door and started after him, not wanting him to hear me too soon.

I waited until he was nearing a particular small white car parked on one side, and then I ran swiftly up behind him, quiet in rubber soles on the cobbles, and shone a torch of my own on the back of his neck.

"Henri Nanterre," I said.

He was struck for a long moment into slow motion, unable to move from shock. Then he was fumbling, tearing at the front of a bloused gabardine jacket, trying to free the pistol holstered beneath.

"Sammy," I yelled, and Sammy shot like a screaming cannonball out of the small white car, my voice and his whooping cries filling the quiet place with nerve-breaking noise.

Nanterre, his face rigid, pulled the pistol free. He swung it toward me, taking aim . . . and Sammy, true to his boast, kicked it straight out of his hand.

Nanterre ran, leaving the gun clattering to the ground.

Sammy and I ran after him, and from another, larger, parked car, both Thomas and Litsi, shouting manfully and shining bright torches, emerged to stand in his way.

Thomas and Litsi stopped him and Sammy and I caught hold of him, Sammy tying Nanterre's left wrist to Thomas's right with nylon cord and an intriguingly nice line in knots.

Not the most elegant of captures, I thought, but effective all the same; and for all the noise we'd made, no one came with curious questions to the fracas, no one in London would be so foolish. Dark alleys were dark alleys, and with noise, even worse.

We made Nanterre walk back toward the Mercedes. Thomas half dragging him, Sammy stepping behind him and kicking him encouragingly on the calves of the legs.

When we reached the pistol, Sammy picked it up, weighed it with surprise in his hand, and briefly whistled.

"Bullets?" I asked.

He slid out the clip and nodded. "Seven," he said. "Bright little darlin's."

He slapped the gun together again, looked around him, and dodged off sideways to hide it under a nearby car, knowing I didn't want to use it myself.

Nanterre was beginning to recover his usual browbeating manner and to bluster that what we were doing was against the law. He didn't specify which law, nor was he right. Citizens' arrests were perfectly legal.

Not knowing what to expect, we'd had to make the best plans we could to meet anything that might happen. I'd hired the small white car and the larger dark one, both with tinted windows, and Thomas and I had parked them that morning in spaces that we knew from mews-observation weren't going to obstruct anyone else: the larger car in the space nearest to the way in from the road, the white car halfway between there and the Mercedes.

Litsi, Thomas and Sammy had entered the cars after I'd searched the whole place and telephoned reassuringly again to Litsi, and they'd been prepared to wait until one-thirty and hope.

No one had known what Nanterre would do if he came to the mews. We'd decided that if he came in past Litsi and Thomas and hid himself before he reached the white car, Litsi and Thomas would set up a racket and shine torches to summon Sammy and me to their aid. And we'd reckoned that if he came in past Sammy, I would see him, and everyone would wait for my cue, which they had.

We'd all acknowledged that Nanterre, if he came to the area, might decide to sit in his car out in the street, waiting for me to walk round from the square, and that if he did that, or if he didn't come at all, we'd spent a long while preparing for a big anticlimax.

There had been the danger that even if he came, we could lose him, that he'd slip through our grasp and escape: and there had been the worse danger that we would panic him into shooting, and that one or more of us could be hurt. Yet when that moment had come, when he'd freed his gun and pointed it my way, the peril, long faced, had gone by so fast that it seemed suddenly nothing, not worth the consideration.

We had meant, if we captured Nanterre, to take him into the garage where I'd waited for him to come, but I did a fast rethink on the way down the alley, and stopped by my car.

The others paused inquiringly.

"Thomas," I said, "untie your wrist and attach Mr. Nanterre to the rear-view mirror beside the front passenger door."

Thomas, unquestioning, took a loop of cord off one of his fingers and pulled it, and all the knots round his wrist fell apart: Sammy's talents seemed endless. Thomas tied much more secure knots round the sturdy mirror assembly and Nanterre told us very loudly and continuously that we were making punishable mistakes.

"Shut up," I said equally loudly, without much effect.

"Let's gag him," Thomas said cheerfully. He produced a used handkerchief from his trousers pocket, at the sight of which Nanterre blessedly stopped talking.

"Gag him if someone comes into the mews," I said, and Thomas nodded.

"Was there enough light," 1 asked Litsi, Sammy and Thomas, "for you to see Mr. Nanterre lift up the bonnet of my car?"

They all said that they'd seen.

Nanterre's mouth fell soundlessly open, and for the first

time he seemed to realize he was in serious trouble.

"Mr. Nanterre," I said conversationally to the others, "is an amateur who has left his fingerprints all over my paint-work. It might be a good idea at this point to bring in the police."

The others looked impassive because they knew I didn't want to, but Nanterre suddenly tugged frantically at Sammy's securely tied knots.

"There's an alternative," I said.

Nanterre, still struggling under Sammy's interested gaze, said, "What alternative?" furiously.

"Tell us why you came here tonight, and what you put in my car."

"*Tell you . . .*"

"Yes. Tell us."

He was a stupid man, essentially. He said violently, "Beatrice must have warned you. That cow. She got fright-ened and told you." He glared at me with concentration. "All that stood between me and my *millions* was Roland's signature and you . . . you . . . everywhere, in my way."

"So you decided on a little bomb, and pouf, no obstruc-tions?"

"You made me," he shouted. "You drove me . . . If you were dead, he would sign."

I let a moment go by, then I said, "We talked to the man who gave your message to Prince Litsi at Bradbury. He picked you out from a photograph. We have his signed statement."

Nanterre said viciously, "I saw your advertisement. If Prince Litsi had died, no one would have known of the message."

"Did you mean him to die?"

"Live, die, I didn't care. To frighten him, yes. To get Roland de Brescou to sign." He tried ineffectually still to unravel his bonds. "Let me go."

I went instead into the garage where I'd waited and came out again with the big envelope of signed documents.

"Stop struggling," I said to Nanterre, "and listen carefully."

He paid little attention.

"Listen," I said, "or I fetch the police."

He said sullenly then that he was listening.

"The price of your freedom," I said, "is that you put your signature to these contracts."

"What are they?" he said furiously, looking at their impressive appearance. "What contracts?"

"They change the name of the de Brescou et Nanterre construction company to the Gascony construction company, and they constitute an agreement between the two equal owners to turn the private company into a public company, and for each owner to put his entire holding up for public sale."

He was angrily and bitterly astounded.

"The company is *mine* . . . I manage it . . . I will *never* agree!"

"You'll have to," I said prosaically.

I produced the small tape recorder from the pocket of my jacket, pressed the rewind button slightly, and started it playing.

Nanterre's voice came out clearly, "Live, die, I didn't care. To frighten him, yes. To get de Brescou to sign."

I switched off. Nanterre, incredibly, was silent, remembering, perhaps, the other incriminating things he had said.

"We have the evidence of the messenger at Bradbury," I said. "We have your voice on this tape. We have your bomb, I suspect, in my car. You'll sign the contract, you know."

"There's no bomb in your car," he said furiously.

"Perhaps a firework?" I said.

He looked at me blankly.

"Someone's coming into the mews," Thomas said urgently, producing the handkerchief. "What do we do?" A car had driven in, coming home to its garage.

"If you yell," I said to Nanterre with menace, "the police will be here in five minutes and you'll regret it. They're not kind to people who plant bombs in cars."

The incoming car drove toward us and stopped just before reaching Sammy's white hiding place. The people got out, opened their garage, drove in, closed the doors, and looked our way dubiously.

"Goodnight," I called out, full of cheer.

"Goodnight," they replied, reassured, and walked away to the street.

"Right," I said, relaxing, "time to sign."

"I will not sell the company. *I will not.*"

I said patiently, "You have no alternative except going to prison for attempting to murder both Prince Litsi and myself."

He still refused to face facts: and perhaps he felt as outraged at being coerced to sign against his will as Roland had done.

I brought the car-starting gadget out of my pocket and explained what it was.

Nanterre at last began to shake, and Litsi, Sammy and Thomas backed away from the car in freshly awakened genuine alarm, as if really realizing for the first time what was in there, under the bonnet.

"It'll be lonely for you," I said to Nanterre. "We'll walk to the end of the mews, leaving you here. Prince Litsi and the other two will go away. When they're safely back in the house in Eaton Square, I'll press the switch that starts my engine."

Litsi, Sammy and Thomas had already retreated a good way along the mews.

"You'll die by your own bomb," I said, and put into my voice and manner every shred of force and conviction I could summon. "Goodbye," I said.

I turned away. Walked several steps. Wondered if he would be too scared to call my bluff; wondered if anyone would have the nerve to risk it.

"Come back," he yelled. There was real fear in the rising voice. Real deadly fear.

Without any pity, I stopped and turned.

"Come back . . ."

I went back. There was sweat in great drops on his forehead, running down. He was struggling frantically still with the knots, but also trembling too much to succeed.

"I want to make guns," he said feverishly. "I'd make millions. I'd have *power*. The de Brescous are rich, the Nanterres never were. I want to be rich by world standards, to have power. I'll give you a million pounds . . . more . . . if . . . you get Roland to sign . . . to make guns."

"No," I said flatly, and turned away again, showing him the starter.

"All right, all right . . ." He gave in completely, finally almost sobbing. "Put that thing down . . . put it down."

I called up the mews, "Litsi."

The other three stopped and came slowly back.

"Mr. Nanterre will sign," I said.

"Put that thing down," Nanterre said again faintly, all the bullying megatones gone. "Put it down."

I put the starter back in my pocket, which still frightened him.

"It can't go off by itself, can it?" Litsi asked, not with nervousness, but out of caution.

I shook my head. "The switch needs firm pressure."

I showed Nanterre the contracts more closely and saw the flicker of fury in his eyes when he saw the first page of each was the same sort of form he'd demanded that Roland should sign.

"We need your signature four times," I said. "On each front page, and on each attached document. When you sign the attached documents, put your forefinger on the red seal beside your name. The three of us who are not in any way involved in the de Brescou et Nanterre business will sign under your name as witnesses."

I put my pen into his shaking right hand and rested the first of the documents on top of my car.

Nanterre signed the French form. I turned to the last page of the longer contract and pointed to the space allotted to him. He signed again, and he put his finger on the seal.

With enormous internal relief, I produced the second set for a repeat performance. In silence, with sweat dripping off his cheeks, he signed appropriately again.

I put my name under his in all four places, followed each time by Thomas and Sammy.

"That's fine," I said, when all were completed. "Monsieur de Brescou's lawyers will put the contracts into operation at once. One of these two contracts will be sent to you or your lawyers in France."

I put the documents back into their envelope and handed it to Litsi, who put it inside his coat, hugging it to his chest.

"Let me go," Nanterre said, almost whispering.

"We'll untie you from the mirror so that you can remove what you put in my car," I said. "After that, you can go."

He shuddered, but it seemed not very difficult for him, in the end, to unfix the tampered-with wiring and remove what looked like, in size and shape, a bag of sugar. It was the detonator sticking out of it that he treated with delicate respect, unclipping and separating, and stowing the pieces away in several pockets. "Now let me go," he said, wiping sweat away from his face with the backs of his hands.

I said, "Remember, we'll always have the Bradbury messenger's affidavit and the tape recording of your voice. And we all heard what you said. Stay away from the de Brescous, cause no more trouble."

He gave me a sick, furious and defeated glare. Sammy didn't try to undo his handiwork but cut the nylon cord off Nanterre's wrist with a pair of scissors.

"Start the car," Litsi said, "to show him you weren't fooling."

"Come away from it," I said.

We walked twenty paces up the mews, Nanterre among us, and I took out the starter and pressed the switch.

The engine fired safely, strong, smooth and powerful.

I looked directly at Nanterre, at the convinced droop of his mouth, at the unwilling acceptance that his campaign was lost. He gave us all a last comprehensive, unashamed, unrepentant stare, and with Thomas and Sammy stepping aside to let him pass, he walked away along the mews, that nose, that jaw, still strong, but the shoulders sagging.

We watched him in silence until he reached the end of the mews and turned into the street, not looking back.

Then Sammy let out a poltergeist "Youweee" yell of uncomplicated victory, and went with jumping feet to fetch the pistol from where he'd hidden it.

He presented it to me with a flourish, laying it flat onto my hands.

"Spoils of war," he said, grinning.

Litsi and I drank brandy in the sitting room to celebrate, having thanked Thomas and Sammy copiously for their support; and we telephoned to Danielle to tell her we weren't lying in puddles of blood.

"Thank goodness," she said. "I haven't been able to think what I'm doing."

"I suppose what we did was thoroughly immoral," Litsi commented, after I'd put down the receiver.

"Absolutely," I agreed equably. "We did exactly what Nanterre intended to do: extorted a signature under threat."

"We took the law into our own hands, I suppose."

"Justice," I said, "in our own hands."

"And like you said," he said, smiling, "there's a difference."

"He's free, unpunished and rich," I said, "and in a way

that's not justice. But he didn't, and can't, destroy Roland. It was a fair enough bargain."

I waited up for Danielle after Litsi had gone yawning downstairs, and went to meet her when I heard her come in. She walked straight into my arms, smiling.

"I didn't think you'd go to bed without me," she said.

"As seldom as possible for the rest of my life."

We went quietly up to the bamboo room and, mindful of Beatrice next door, quietly to bed and quietly to love. Intensity, I thought, drowning in sensations, hadn't any direct link to noise and could be exquisite in whispers; and if we were more inhibited than earlier in what we said, the silent rediscovery of each other grew into an increased dimension of passion.

We slept, embracing, and woke again before morning, hungry again after deep satisfaction.

"You love me more," she said, murmuring in my ear.

"I loved you always."

"Not like this."

We slept again, languorously, and before seven she showered in my bathroom, put on yesterday's clothes and went decorously down to her own room. Aunt Casilia, she said with composure, would expect her niece to make a pretense at least of having slept in her own bed.

"Would she mind that you didn't?"

"Pretty much the reverse, I would think."

Litsi and I were already drinking coffee in the morning room when Danielle reappeared, dressed by then in fresh blues and greens. She fetched juice and cereal and made me some toast, and Litsi watched us both with speculation and finally enlightenment.

"Congratulations," he said to me dryly.

"The wedding," Danielle said collectedly, "will take place."

"So I gathered," he said.

He and I, a while later, went up to see Roland de Brescou, to give him and the princess the completed contracts.

"I was sure," Roland said weakly, "that Nanterre wouldn't agree to dissolve the company. Without it, he can't possibly make guns, can he?"

"If ever he does," I said, "your name won't be linked with it."

Gascony, the name we'd given to the new public company, was the ancient name of the province in France where the Chateau de Brescou stood. Roland had been both pleased and saddened by the choice.

"How did you persuade him, Kit?" the princess asked, looking disbelievingly at the Nanterre signatures.

"Um, tied him in knots."

She gave me a brief glance. "Then I'd better not ask."

"He's unhurt and unmarked."

"And the police?" Roland asked.

"No police," I said. "We had to promise no police to get him to sign."

"A bargain's a bargain." Litsi nodded. "We have to let him go free."

The princess and her husband understood all about keeping one's word, and when I left Roland's room she followed me down to the sitting room, leaving Litsi behind.

"No thanks are enough. How *can* we thank you?" she asked with frustration.

"You don't need to. And . . . um . . . Danielle and I will marry in June."

"I'm very pleased indeed," she said with evident pleasure, and kissed me warmly on one cheek and then the other. I thought of the times I'd wanted to hug her; and one day perhaps I would do it, though not on a racecourse.

"I'm so sorry about your horses," I said.

"Yes . . . When you next talk to Wykeham, ask him to start looking about for replacements. We can't expect another Cotopaxi, but next year, perhaps, a runner anyway in the Grand National. And don't forget, next week at Cheltenham, we still have Kinley."

"The Triumph Hurdle," I said.

I went to Folkestone races by train later that morning with a light heart but without Danielle, who had an appointment with the dentist.

I rode four races and won two, and felt fit, well, bursting with health and for the first time in weeks, carefree. It was a tremendous feeling, while it lasted.

Bunty Ireland, the *Towncrier*'s racing correspondent, gave me a large envelope from Lord Vaughnley: "Hot off the computers," Bunty said. The envelope again felt as if it contained very little, but I thanked him for it, and reflecting that I thankfully didn't need the contents anymore, I took it unopened with me back to London.

Dinner that evening was practically festive, although Danielle wasn't there, having driven herself to work in her Ford.

"I thought yesterday was her last night for working," Beatrice said, unsuspiciously.

"They changed the schedules again," I explained.

"Oh, how irritating."

Beatrice had decided to return to Palm Beach the next day. Her darling dogs would be missing her, she said. The princess had apparently told her that Nanterre's case was lost, which had subdued her querulousness amazingly.

I'd grown used to her ways: to her pale-orange hair and round eyes, her knuckleduster rings and her Florida clothes. Life would be quite dull without the old bag; and moreover, once she had gone, I would soon have to leave also. How long, I wondered, would Litsi be staying . . .

Roland came down to dinner and offered champagne, raising his half-full glass to Litsi and to me in a toast. Beatrice scowled a little but blossomed like a sunflower when Roland said that perhaps, with all the extra capital generated by the sale of the business, he might consider increasing her trust fund. Too forgiving, I thought, yet without her we would very likely not have prevailed.

Roland, the princess and Beatrice retired fairly early, leaving Litsi and me passing the time in the sitting room. Quite late I remembered Lord Vaughnley's envelope, which I'd put down on a side table on my return.

Litsi incuriously watched me open it and draw out the contents: one glossy black-and-white photograph, as before, and one short clipping from a newspaper column. Also a brief compliments slip from the *Towncrier:* "Regret nothing more re Nanterre."

The picture showed Nanterre in evening dress surrounded by other people similarly clad, on the deck of a yacht. I handed it to Litsi and read the accompanying clipping.

"Arms dealer Ahmed Fuad's fiftieth birthday bash, held on his yacht *Felissima* in Monte Carlo harbor on Friday evening drew guests from as far as California, Peru and Darwin, Australia. With no expense spared, Fuad fed caviar and foie gras to jet-setting friends from his hobby worlds of backgammon, night clubs and horseracing."

Litsi passed back the photograph and I gave him the clipping.

"That's what Nanterre wanted," I said. "To be the host on a yacht in the Mediterranean, dressed in a white dinner jacket, dispensing rich goodies, enjoying the adulation and the flattery. That's what he wanted . . . those multi-millions, and that power."

I turned the photograph over, reading the flimsy information strip stuck to the back: a list of names, and the date.

"That's odd," I said blankly.

"What is?"

"That party was held last Friday night."

"What of it? Nanterre must have jetted out there and back, like the others."

"On Friday night, Col was shot."

Litsi stared at me.

"Nanterre couldn't have done it," I said. "He was in Monte Carlo."

"But he said he did. He boasted of it to Beatrice."

I frowned. "Yes, he did."

"He must have got someone else to do it," Litsi said.

I shook my head. "He did everything himself. Threatened the princess, chased Danielle, set the trap for you, came to put the bomb in my car. He didn't trust any of that to anyone else. He knows about horses, he wanted to see his own filly shot. He would have shot Col . . . but he didn't."

"He confessed to all the horses," Litsi insisted.

"Yes, but suppose he read about them in the papers . . . read that their deaths were mysterious and no one knew who had killed them . . . He wanted ways to frighten

Roland and the princess. Suppose he *said* he'd killed them, when he hadn't?"

"But in that case," Litsi said blankly, "who did? Who would want to kill her best horses, if not Nanterre?"

I rose slowly to my feet, feeling almost faint.

"What's the matter?" Litsi said, alarmed. "You've gone as white as snow."

"He killed," I said with a mouth stickily dry, "the horse I might have won the Grand National on. The horse on which I might have won the Gold Cup."

"Kit . . ." Litsi said.

"There's only one person," I said with difficulty, "who hates me enough to do that. Who couldn't bear to see me win those races . . . who would take away the prizes I hold dearest, because I took away his prize."

I felt breathless and dizzy.

"Sit down," Litsi said, alarmed.

"Kinley," I said.

I went jerkily to the telephone and got through to Wykeham.

"I was just going to bed," he complained.

"Did you stop the dog patrols?" I demanded.

"Yes, of course. You told me this morning there was no more need for them."

"I think I was wrong. I can't risk that I was wrong. I'm coming down to your stables now, tonight, and we'll get the dog patrols back again, stronger than ever, for tomorrow and every day until Cheltenham, and probably beyond."

"I don't understand," he said.

"Have you taken your sleeping pill?" I asked.

"No, not yet."

"Don't do it until I get down to you, will you? And where's Kinley tonight?"

"Back in his own box, of course. You said the danger was past."

"We'll move him back into the corner box when I get down to you."

"Kit, no, not in the middle of the night."

"You want to keep him safe," I said; and there was no arguing with that.

We disconnected and Litsi said slowly, "Do you mean Maynard Allardeck?"

"Yes, I do. He found out, about two weeks ago, that he'll never get a knighthood because I sent the film I made of him to the Honours department. He's wanted that knighthood since he was a child, when he told my grandfather that one day the Fieldings would have to bow down to him, because he'd be a lord. He knows horses better than Nanterre. He was brought up in his father's racing stable and was his assistant trainer for years. He saw Cascade and Cotopaxi at Newbury, and they were distinctive horses . . . and Col at Ascot . . . unmistakable."

I went to the door.

"I'll telephone in the morning," I said.

"I'll come with you," he said.

I shook my head. "You'd be up all night."

"Get going," he said. "You saved my family's honor. Let me pay some of their debt."

I was grateful, indeed, for the company. We went round again to the dark mews where Litsi said, if I had the car-starter in my pocket, we might as well be sure: but Nanterre and his bombs hadn't returned, and the Mercedes fired obligingly from a fifty-yard distance.

I drove toward Sussex, telephoning to Danielle on the way to tell her where and why we were going. She had no trouble believing anything bad of Maynard Allardeck, saying he'd looked perfectly crazy at Ascot and Sandown, glaring at me continuously in the way he had.

"*Curdling* with hate," she said. "You could feel it like shock waves."

"We'll be back for breakfast," I said, smiling. "Sleep well." And I could hear her laughing as she disconnected.

I told Litsi on the way about the firework bombs that had been used to decoy the dog-handler away from Col's courtyard, and said, "You know, in the alley, when Nanterre said he hadn't put a bomb in my car, I asked him if it was a firework. He looked totally blank. I didn't think much of it then, but now I realize he simply didn't know what I was talking about. He didn't know about the fireworks at Wykeham's because they didn't get into the papers."

Litsi made a "Huh" sort of noise of appreciation and assent, and we came companionably in time into Wykeham's village.

"What are you going to do here?" Litsi said.

I shrugged. "Walk round the stables." I explained about the many little courtyards. "It's not an easy place to patrol."

"You do seriously think Allardeck will risk trying to kill another of Aunt Casilia's horses?"

"Yes. Kinley, particularly, her brilliant hurdler. I don't seriously suppose he'll try tonight rather than tomorrow or thereafter, but I'm not taking chances." I paused. "However am I going to apologize to Princess Casilia . . . to repay . . ."

"What do you mean?"

"Cascade and Cotopaxi and Col died because of the Fielding and Allardeck feud. Because of me."

"She won't think of it that way."

"It's the truth." I turned into Wykeham's driveway. "I won't let Kinley die."

I stopped the car in the parking space, and we stepped out into the silence of midnight under a clear sky sparkling with diamondlike stars. The heights and depths of the universe: enough to humble the sweaty strivings of earth.

I took a deep breath of its peace . . . and heard in the quiet distance the dull unmistakable thudding explosion of a bolt.

Dear God, I thought, *we're too late.*

I ran. I knew where. To the last courtyard, the one nearest to Wykeham's house. Ran with the furies at my heels, my heart sick, my mind a jumble of rage and fear and dreadful regrets.

I could have driven faster . . . I could have started sooner . . . I could have opened Lord Vaughnley's envelope hours before . . . Kinley was dead, and I'd killed him.

I ran into the courtyard, and for all my speed, events on the other side of it moved faster.

As I watched, as I ran, I saw Wykeham struggle to his feet from where he'd been lying on the path outside the doors of the boxes.

Two of the box doors were open, the boxes in shadow, lit only by the light outside in the courtyard. In one box, I could see a horse lying on its side, its legs still jerking in convulsive death throes. Into the other went Wykeham.

While I was still yards away, I saw him pick up something that had been lying inside the box on the brick windowsill. I saw his back going deeper into the box, his feet silent on the peat.

I ran.

I saw another man in the box, taller, grabbing a horse by its head-collar.

I saw Wykeham put the thing he held against the second man's head. I saw the tiny flash, heard the awful bang . . .

When I reached the door there was a dead man on the peat, a live horse tossing his head and snorting in fright, a smell of burning powder and Wykeham standing, looking down, with the humane killer in his hands.

The live horse was Kinley . . . but I felt no relief.

"Wykeham!" I said.

He turned his head, looked at me vaguely.

"He shot my horses," he said.

"Yes."

"I killed him. I said I would . . . and I have."

I looked down at the dead man, at the beautiful suit and the hand-sewn shoes.

He was lying half on his face, and he had a nylon stocking pulled over his head as a mask, with a hole in it behind his right ear.

Litsi ran into the courtyard calling breathlessly, asking what had happened. I turned toward him in the box doorway, obstructing his view of what was inside.

"Litsi," I said, "go and telephone the police. Use the telephone in the car. Press O and you'll get the operator. Ask for the police. Tell them a man has been killed here in an accident."

"A *man!*" he exclaimed. "Not a horse?"

"Both, but tell them a man."

"Yes," he said unhappily. "Right."

He went back the way he'd come and I turned toward Wykeham, who was wide-eyed now, and beginning to tremble.

"It wasn't an accident," he said, with pride somewhere in the carriage of his head, in the tone of his voice. "I killed him."

"Wykeham," I said urgently, "listen. Are you listening?"

"Yes."

"Where do you want to spend your last years, in prison or out on the Downs with your horses?"

He stared.

"Are you listening?"

"Yes."

"There'll be an inquest," I said. "And this was an *accident*. Are you listening?"

He nodded.

"You came out to see if all was well in the yard before you went to bed."

"Yes, I did."

"You'd had three horses killed in the last ten days. The police haven't been able to discover who did it. You knew I was coming down to help patrol the yards tonight, but you were naturally worried."

"Yes."

"You came into this courtyard, and you saw and heard someone shoot one of your horses."

"Yes, I did."

"Is it Abseil?" I longed for him to say no, but he said "Yes."

Abseil . . . racing at breakneck speed over the last three fences at Sandown, clinging to victory right to the post.

I said, "You ran across to try to stop the intruder doing

any more damage. You tried to pull the humane killer out of his hands."

"Yes."

"He was younger and stronger and taller than you. He knocked you down with the humane killer. You fell on the path, momentarily stunned."

"How do you know?" Wykeham asked, bewildered.

"The marks of the end of the barrel are all down your cheek. It's been bleeding. Don't touch it," I said, as he began to raise a hand to feel. "He knocked you down and went into the second box to kill a second horse."

"Yes, to kill Kinley."

"Listen . . . He had the humane killer in his hand."

Wykeham began to shake his head, and then stopped.

I said, "The man was going to shoot your horse. You grabbed at the gun to stop him. You were trying to take it away from him . . . he was trying to pull it back from your grasp. He was succeeding with a jerk, but you still had your hands on the gun, and in the struggle, when he jerked the gun toward him, the thick end of the barrel hit his head, and the jerk also caused your grasp somehow to pull the trigger."

He stared.

"You did *not* mean to kill him; are you listening, Wykeham? You meant to stop him shooting your horse."

"K–Kit . . ." he said, finally stuttering.

"What are you going to tell the police?"

"I . . . t–tried to s–stop him shooting . . ." He swallowed. "He j–jerked the gun . . . against his head . . . It w–went off."

He was still holding the gun by its rough wooden butt.

"Throw it down on the peat," I said.

He did so, and we both looked at it: a heavy, ugly, clumsy instrument of death.

On the windowsill there were several small bright golden caps full of gunpowder. One cocked the gun, fed in the cap, pulled the trigger: the gunpowder exploded and shot out the bolt.

Litsi came back, saying the police would be coming, and it was he who switched the light on, revealing every detail of the scene.

I bent down and took a closer look at Maynard's head. There was oil on the nylon stocking where the bolt had gone through, and I remembered Robin Curtiss saying the bolt had been oiled before Col . . . Robin would remember. There would be no doubt that Maynard had killed all four horses.

"Do you know who it is?" I said to Wykeham, straightening up.

He half knew, half couldn't believe it.

"Allardeck?" he said, unconvinced.

"Allardeck."

Wykeham bent down to pull off the stocking mask.

"Don't do that," I said sharply. "Don't touch it. Anyone can see he came here trying not to be recognized . . . to kill horses. No one out for an evening stroll goes around in a nylon mask carrying a humane killer."

"Did he kill Kinley?" Litsi asked anxiously.

"No, this is Kinley. He killed Abseil."

Litsi looked stricken. "Poor Aunt Casilia. She said how brilliantly you'd won on Abseil. Why kill that one, who couldn't possibly win the Grand National?" He looked down at Maynard, understanding. "Allardeck couldn't bear you being brilliant, not on anything."

The feud was dead, I thought. Finally over. The long obsession had died with Maynard, and he had been dead before he hit the peat, like Cascade and Cotopaxi, Abseil and Col.

A fitting end, I thought.

Litsi said he had told the police he would meet them in the parking place to show them where to come, and presently he went off there.

Wykeham spent a long while looking at Kinley, who was now standing quietly, no longer disturbed, and then less time looking at Maynard.

"I'm glad I killed him," he said fiercely.

"Yes, I know."

"Mind you win the Triumph Hurdle."

I thought of the schooling sessions I'd done with that horse, teaching him distances up on the Downs with Wykeham watching, shaping the glorious natural talent into accomplished experience.

I would do my best, I said.

He smiled. "Thank you, Kit," he said. "Thank you for everything."

The police came with Litsi: two of them, highly official, taking notes, talking of summoning medical officers and photographers.

They took Wykeham through what had happened.

"I came out . . . found the intruder . . . he shot my horse." Wykeham's voice shook. "I fought with him . . . he knocked me down . . . he was going to shoot this horse also . . . I got to my feet . . "

He paused.

"Yes, sir?" the policemen said, not unsympathetically.

They saw, standing before them on the peat inside the

box, standing beside a dead intruder with the intruder's deadly weapon shining with menace in the light, they saw an old thin man with disheveled white hair, with the dark freckles of age on his ancient forehead, with the pistol marks of dried blood on his cheek.

They saw, as the coroner would see, and the lawyers, and the press, the shaking deteriorating exterior, not the titan who still lived inside.

Wykeham looked at Kinley; at the future, at the horse that could fly on the Downs, tail streaming, jumping like an angel to his destiny.

He looked at the policemen, and his eyes seemed full of sky.

"It was an accident," he said.